The kid from Angel Meadow

Also by Malcolm Lynch

The streets of Ancoats (1985)
They fly forgotten (1987)

Malcolm Lynch

The kid from Angel Meadow

Constable · London

First published in Great Britain 1989
by Constable and Company Limited
10 Orange Street London WC2H 7EG
Copyright © 1989 Malcolm Lynch
Photoset in Linotron Ehrhardt 11pt and
printed in Great Britain by
St Edmundsbury Press Limited
Bury St Edmunds, Suffolk

British Library CIP data
Lynch, Malcolm
The kid from Angel Meadow
I. Title
823'.914 [F]

ISBN 0 09 469290 4

The lyrics of 'All I Do the Whole Night Through', on pages 35 and 36, are copyright © 1934 by MGM Corporation, New York; © copyright assigned 1934 to Robbins Music Corporation, New York; and are reproduced by permission of Columbia Pictures Publications and International Music Publications.

The lyrics of 'Nellie Dean' on page 57 are copyright © 1905 M. Witmark & Sons, USA, and are reproduced by permission of B. Feldman & Co. Ltd, London WC2H 0EA.

Dedication

Once upon a time, Granada Television's *Coronation Street* was literally the greatest show on earth. As well as consistently topping the television ratings in Britain, it was shown all over the world, even appearing with Chinese subtitles. The actress greatly responsible for the show's enormous success was Patricia Phoenix, who played the roustabout Elsie Tanner.

Shortly before she was taken to hospital with a fatal illness, she wrote me a letter bubbling with life, and full of enthusiasm for the future. She had just named her latest filly 'Annie Noonan' after her mother. She was indeed proud of her Irishness.

I had suggested she should write a novel about her childhood in the tough Manchester slums, and she replied, 'You're absolutely right about the novel – I have been chewing that one over for a couple of years.'

Not many months later I watched her Requiem on television. It was at the Church of The Holy Name, and her coffin was placed only a few yards from a statue which had always inspired her – that of Joan of Arc.

I thus humbly submit this story of a young Irish girl brought up in Ancoats, who is dedicated to becoming an actress. It is pure fiction, but it might be the kind of book Pat would have written. If nothing else, I offer it as a tribute.

M. L.
1989

The patchy-arsed boys and stitched-bloused girls ran like a pack of hungry dogs into the entry at the back of Angel Meadow. One boy put his hand to his mouth and made a bugle noise like a bugler-boy leading troops into battle. The grown-ups walked quickly in opposite directions, for kids' business was not the affair of adults.

Angel Meadow, the black, crowded huddle of two-up two-down houses built during the Crimean War to stable cotton mill workers, became still and blind: only an occasional eye peeped from the dirty netting and browning newspapers which were pinned to the bedroom windows for curtains. The eyes of old houses didn't want to see the violence of kids.

The lads had got hold of Kitty Noonan. One lad held his warted hand over her mouth so that she couldn't scream.

Mick Dowd brought a white clay pipe from his pocket and held it up for all to see.

'This here's a bloody clay pipe!' he said.

'It bloody is and all!' giggled a few of the lads.

'And I'm going to give this tart a good hiding because of it,' he went on. 'Because she's been mooching in the bins of the clay-pipe works and selling what they'd chucked out for ha'penny each on Sat'day nights outside the Land O' Cakes. And that's what my uncle Al Capone would call a racket, and the only rackets in this part of Ancoats belong to me and my gang. Savvy?'

All the kids watching, the boys and the girls, nodded that they savvied.

'So she's going to get a bloody lesson she'll not bloody forget in a hurry. Right, let the dog see the rabbit!' He nodded to the lads holding the little girl, and they pushed her into the circle and towards Mick. He straightway slammed his clenched fist into her face.

The few eyes peeping from the netted windows disappeared,

for the violence had started. The children looked fascinated. Some of the girls chewed their fingers, others folded their arms and smiled as in a trance.

Mick opened the palms of his hands and clouted her left, right, left right across the face. The smacks echoed in the narrow entry. Kitty collapsed in a splodge of cat muck, and Mick kicked her.

'Get up on yer bloody feet!'

Brendan handed him a cigarette which the lads had been passing around. 'Here, Mick, burn her on the forehead like an Ash Wednesday sin.'

Mick took the cigarette, puffed at it, then flicked it into the crowd like it was a firework. He swung round and smashed Brendan on the nose with his fist. Blood spurted.

'That's for being bloody cruel. This tart is my best tart, and I'm just teaching her a lesson, which she'll thank me for some day. She appreciates it. And them what sticks their noses in, gets them broken. Savvy?'

'Hey! It's Killer Kennedy! Here's bobby!' screamed a voice from the top of the entry. There was a general scattering and scrambling. The entry was cleared in seconds, leaving only Mick and Kitty. He pulled a piece of partly burned newspaper from a dustbin.

'Here, wipe that cat shit from yer face. It bloody stinks,' he told her. She tried, but merely smeared it.

'Give it us,' he snarled, and he snatched the paper and tried to clean her face, still making it worse.

'I'll tell me dad of you, and he'll kill you. He will, he'll murder you!'

'No, you won't,' said Mick. 'Because if he kills me, he'll get nabbed for murder, and he'll end up swinging from a Strangeways rope. Best keep yer trap shut, eh?' He gave her a friendly smile. 'Anyhow, I was only doing what King Arthur did all the time.'

'King Arthur?'

'Aye – him and his knights of old. Teacher was telling us they went round the country doing good by teaching people lessons, like I was teaching you. You won't go mooching in bins for clay pipes any more, will you?'

'No,' said Kitty. 'But I can still do me clog-dancing outside the Land O' Cakes?'

'I'll not deny ye that, for clog-dancing is tarts' stuff.'

Constable Kennedy turned into the entry. A great giant of a man he was, who had his thumbs in his tunic belt and bent his knees occasionally, very much as a comic policeman on the music hall. Kitty was adjusting her skirt, and maybe she was looking a little shy and a little guilty. Constable Kennedy grabbed Mick.

'You two have not been – ?' He thought for a second. 'Ach no, ye're both of ye too young for the shenanikins.' But he thought for another second. 'But 'tis possible, maybe, that ye've been playing with her with yer fingers, ye dirty little bastard.'

He grabbed Mick by the trouser braces, lifted him up, and hung him on a clothes hook on a backyard door. 'Let's hope the hook isn't rusty all the way through, and let's hope yer mother has sewn yer buttons on with good stout thread,' said the bobby.

The boy hung high on the backyard door, afraid of squirming. Kitty had to look up at him, and for a second he reminded her of Jesus nailed to the cross and her one of the weeping women looking up at him.

'Have ye touched this little girl?' boomed Kennedy. Eyes appeared at the bedroom windows of the dark houses.

'No, master! Spit on the Bible, master!' Mick yelled. 'Let me down.'

Kennedy laid his hand gently on Kitty's shoulder. 'Has that dirty little bastard up there been interfering with ye? Now, come on, 'tis the truth now.'

'No, master,' lisped Kitty.

'Then what was yez up to down this entry, and all them blooming kids o' the neighbourhood pouring out like beer from a pump?'

Once again Kitty saw Mick as the hanging Jesus, and to her Constable Kennedy was Pontius the Pilot.

'No, master! Please, master! I fell, and that's why all the kids come. And Jesus up there was trying to wipe cat dirt from me face, for I slipped and fell in the cat dirt, and the kids come to watch him wiping the cat dirt, because it was a brave thing to do with the cat dirt stinking and that.'

'Is that so, ye dirty little bleeder?' Kennedy asked the hanging boy.

'Aye, 'tis so,' gasped Mick.

'Well, 'tis the benefit of the doubt I'll be giving ye,' said Kennedy. 'But before I bring ye down from that door, I want ye to know what a murderer feels like before the big drop o' the trap door.'

'Yes, master.'

'So's when ye grows up ye'll not be after becoming a murderer and that.'

'No, master. I'll do me sums and learn me words.'

'And yer catechism?'

'Every morning, master.'

'Think on,' said Kennedy, and he lifted Mick down from the door.

The bobby twiddled the free fingers outside his tunic belt with the satisfaction of knowing he had put a boy on the right track, although it would always be registered in Kennedy's mind that the boy could be a potential rapist or murderer. He walked slowly up and out of the entry.

Mick strutted before Kitty with his chest stuck out.

'Did ye see how I handled him?' he said, and patted his chest like a chimpanzee at Belle Vue Zoological Gardens. 'Ye have to tell a few fibs to the bobbies to keep 'em sweet, like Al Capone does, and like King Arthur did.'

'I coulda got you hanged,' said Kitty. She began to walk away from him but she had to limp.

'I'll help you home,' said Mick.

'You'll do nowt o't sort,' said Kitty. 'And when they hang you, I'll come and watch, pushing a baby in a pram and eating a Rocca ice-cream for a penny.'

Mick hit his one fist hard into the palm of his other hand with annoyed frustration. 'I had to bloody do what I had to bloody do, and you bloody know it. You don't think for a minute that King Arthur would have allowed tarts to go killing dragons on their own if there was money to it? And I said ye could do the clog-dancing on Sat'days: what more d'y'want?' He calmed down. 'Look, Kitty, I'll take you to't Palmy on Sat'day afternoon. There's Tom Mix in

Dick Turpin and there's that new Mickey Mouse what teacher's seen and drawn for us on't blackboard in Religious Knowledge.'

'What's Mickey Mouse?'

'A bloody mouse.'

'I don't like mice.'

'Not a real mouse: a magic mouse what wears trousers.'

'To get hung up on doors by?'

'Aye – if you like.'

'Not today, thank you. I couldn't come to't Palmy with you for I'm going to be the Virgin Mary, and it isn't the likes of you the Virgin Mary would want to be watching Mickey the Mouse with.'

She limped away from him, and maybe she exaggerated the limp a little.

On May Sunday, Kitty was clean and radiant and smelling of Pears Soap. She was Queen of the May.

The church procession with its band and banners of saints dancing in the wind marched through the sooty streets of the parish. The bagpipes made the windows of the unending rows of terraced houses rattle to the vibrations of 'The Minstrel Boy' and 'Kelly, the Boy from Killane'. There were those who said it was only the dirt on the glass which prevented the windows from falling out.

After the tough, big-kneed pipers came the parish priest. He wore a large shiny top hat which was only ever seen on May Sunday and Whit Friday. People reckoned it was a special sacred top hat and went back to Jesus for the rest of the year: it certainly never appeared in the pawn shop, and priests were said to be very poor. Father Rourke did a hop and a skip from time to time: he was happy, and he raised his top hat repeatedly like a nigger tin toy in a toy-shop window. Sometimes he made a complete round-about twirl and bowed very deeply with his top hat, and made the crowds on either pavement applaud. Sometimes a few Protestants threw pennies, which he picked up and put in his pocket.

Behind Father Rourke came Paddy Byrne, aged eight or nine, about the same age as Kitty. Paddy swaggered, but he was meant to swagger because he was Marshal of the Parade. He was dressed as King Louis of France: his costume was white embroidered silk, beautiful white, beautiful silk, with knee-length silk knickerbockers tucked into white silk stockings. There were silver buckles on his sparkling black shoes: shoes, mind you, not boots. He wore a long yellow wig which trailed over his shoulders, and on his head a magnificent three-cornered hat trimmed with gold lace. On the front of his blouse was a large embroidered fleur-de-lis. Yellow gauze handkerchiefs dangled from his frilled sleeves. There were circles of rouge on his face. He was lovely, and women shouted 'Love' and 'Me darling' and 'Come here while I kiss ye, ye lovely boy!' Nobody in Ancoats but Paddy's father could have afforded to buy such a luxurious costume which could only be worn twice and was certainly of no use to a pawnshop afterwards: but then Paddy's dad was a bookie's runner down William Place entry, and there was speculation amongst many men as to how many of their sixpence-each-way bets Mr Byrne had pocketed in order to rig his son up as King Louis, which was a sure way of becoming earmarked for the holy priesthood in the years ahead.

There followed Kitty like a tiny and demure bride in her spotless white silks. There was such a lot of silk that she looked like a graceful white-foaming silent waterfall in a magic glen. Golden stars were stitched on her veils. Behind her she trailed a long train which was held by six page boys in black velvet suits and skull caps and white cotton gloves, with buckles, smaller than Paddy's of course, on their shoes. They held the train above the cobbles, lifting it high when mounds of horse shit from the police horses came into their path. Kitty had to sidestep the horse shit. People gasped and said she was a little angel.

Behind her came the altar boys carrying the large and heavy crucifix. Sometimes Kitty could see a back reflection of the boys and their crucifix in the windows of the butcher's shop, and the greengrocer's, and the fish and chip shop: and she almost wept for Jesus. The priest had often told the class of the pains of crucifixion, how the nails would pull and tear at the flesh so that when Jesus wanted relief from the pain of one hand it would put extra pain and pressure on the other: but these altar boys were swaying the dying Jesus at steep angles to the left and the right, and on the occasion that one altar boy lost his shoe, then hopped, then dashed back for the shoe, then hopped again as he tried to put the shoe back on, Jesus and his cross nearly fell in the cobbles. Kitty wondered what kind of terrifying hell a boy would be sent to for dropping the brass crucifix: even Satan would wince at having to face such a boy.

The bagpipe band stopped outside the church and played 'Faith of Our Fathers' and Kitty the queen led the way into the beautifully polished church. She had tried to polish the furniture at home to get it brown and glassy like the church wood, but it was impossible. The polish itself had a lavender scent, and this mingled with the haunting lingering smells of Sunday incense, wonderful warm incense, a smell to die and go to heaven with. The brasses dazzled, and they too seemed to have a smell, a sunshine smell, not that sunshine ever came near the church. But on this day of all days there was an extra smell predominating over the other smells of God: the smell of flowers. The church was filled with flowers; women who could barely afford food always bought great flowers at high cost for May Sunday, mainly trumpeting lilies of the field. The pulpit was covered with lilies.

The church might have been set in fairyland, or at least in a story-book with coloured pictures; it no longer existed in the Ancoats slums; it was far, far away and upon the clouds of a thousand incense Sundays. Kitty stepped up the spiral steps to the pulpit.

'Oh, Mary, we crown thee with blossoms today,
Queen of the Angels, and Queen of the May!'

The packed congregation sang loud and proud. Kitty was in heaven. Marshal of the Parade Paddy Byrne followed her up the spiral steps and placed a crown of flowers on the veil of her head. He was gentle and might have been Jesus himself: and Kitty was immortal. Paddy backed away. He tripped down the steps of the pulpit with a deafening clatter, and it seemed to Kitty he mumbled some dirty words, but only God would know that for sure.

Kitty was stunned. Apparently none of the congregation, including the priest, could have heard for they stooped their shoulders in prayer. But at the back of the church, Paddy's mother must have heard him, for her head bobbed up and looked around sharply. It reminded Kitty of the time she'd been on Shudehill Market, and the cobbles were crowded with large wicker baskets filled with hens, but one hen had managed to make a hole in the top of a basket, and her head suddenly appeared and looked sharply left and sharply right, and then it had looked at Kitty as if to ask 'and what am I doing in Shudehill market?' That was how Mrs Byrne looked over the shoulders of the congregation.

A bee came from one of the lilies under her nose. Kitty knew it was a bee because she'd seen pictures of them in comics. They said 'Buzz' and stung people who said 'Yow'. This one said 'Buzz'. It must have been fast asleep in the lily when it had been picked in the countryside beyond the tall chimneys: she'd heard of the lands beyond the tall chimneys. Kitty hoped it would sting her in front of the entire congregation. She would not say 'Yow' like the people in the comics: she would smile a blessing upon everybody. She would be brave, like she'd been when her mother's coffin was carried from the front door to the one-horse purple-plumed glass hearse and she'd known people were watching her to see her cry, but she hadn't cried: she'd joined the flat palms of her hands together with the right thumb over the left in prayer, and she'd looked down at her shoes. Perhaps the bee would sting her on the forehead and leave a stigma for ever and ever. But the bee zig-zagged away from her and flew over the heads of the praying people. Only the old women in shawls remained gazing at the darling little girl in the pulpit: the remainder took note of the bee's erratic flight, the young boys in particular.

Father Rourke strode down the aisle and opened the door to let the bee out, but it wasn't interested, perhaps because of the smell of the polish and the lilies. It continued its exploratory flight until Mick Dowd flattened it with a thud with his prayerbook.

'The Lord is merciful to great and small!' said Father Rourke for all to hear. 'Better the poor creature die a swift death in the church of God than be killed slowly by the soot and chemicals of

Ancoats.' And he slapped the back of Mick's head hard for using the prayerbook. ''Tis not what prayerbooks is made for,' he said in the boy's ear, then hit him again.

Kitty gave a special prayer for Mick Dowd. It wasn't fair, she told God: Mick was always getting into trouble because he was the boss of a gang, whereas Paddy Byrne was always washed and clean and held his mother's hand and people said 'The lovely boy'. Mick had killed that bee with bravery as King Arthur would have done, and perhaps he'd killed the evil bee to prevent it stinging her. She refused to tell God that she hated Mick for what he'd done to her in the entry.

The children began to sing the last hymn: it was the Lourdes hymn, the song of St Bernadette. The words were in Latin, but Mrs Giyaski had taught them some English words which fitted.

'I love little pussy, her coat is so warm,
And if I don't hurt her she'll do me no harm.
Ave! Ave! Ave Maria!
Ave! Ave! Ave Maria!'

The words came as a surprise to the old ladies in their shawls, and also as a surprise to Mrs Giyaski who had not expected it to be a chosen hymn. She hit Mick on the back of the head with her prayerbook.

It was all over. Her dad took Kitty by the hand and walked her home with a proud trot in his walk.

The house in Angel Meadow was darker than ever. The smells of glory had gone, and there was left the smell of mice, old newspapers, and firelighters from the cupboards, and from the backyard was the smell of the river over the wall.

Kitty brought the big brown stewpot from out of the oven at the side of the fire. She ladled a plate of hash for her dad and herself. They both sprinkled their plates with pepper to make the hash taste warmer. But before she sat down she took off her white silk trappings until she was only in her cotton vest and bloomers. Nothing must stain her veils: they'd be needed again on Whit Friday. Only Whit Friday wouldn't be the same as this glorious day of the parish walk, for all the Catholic schools of Manchester and Salford would be marching in processions with bands and banners to Albert Square, and each school would have its Virgin Mary, and there were many posh schools who would have posher Virgins: the Ancoats Virgin always got pity instead of applause on Whit Friday. And she herself would never ever be the Virgin Mary again, for next year it would be another girl.

Her father went out to the Ben Brierley to get drunk, and Kitty lay in bed before blowing the candle out. The house was quiet. She looked up at her picture of Our Lady and wept. She wept that she could not be the Virgin Mary and have an angel come down and tell her she was going to give birth to Baby Jesus and have the shepherds and the kings and the ox and the ass and the people of Ancoats watching her. And then she thought of Mick being hit across the back of his head with a prayerbook, and Mick hanging from his braces on a backyard door, and she giggled. Then once more she cried wet tears because she couldn't be the Virgin Mary. She wiped her eyes and she went to sleep.

The man, the jolly man in striped pyjamas, sat astride a huge Bovril bottle as he floated merrily on the sea. 'Bovril Prevents That Sinking Feeling' said the words across the large poster pasted up on the building. Kitty leaned against the wall of The Land O' Cakes to get her breath back, and she looked up at the advertisement. It had been up there for weeks and weeks, and often Kitty wondered where the man would end up if he kept on sailing on his Bovril bottle.

Sally Maguire, her best friend and assistant, also leaned on the wall, but she looked down at her shoes and not up at the man in pyjamas, which was understandable because Sally always said she was going to be a nun when she grew up.

'Are ye right, then?' asked Kitty.

'Aye,' said Sally.

Kitty began her clog dance and Sally accompanied her on the slates: Sally was good with the slates. Both girls sang:

'She's a lassie from Lancashire,
Lancashire, Lancashire.

She's a lassie I love so dear,
  Oh so dear.
Though she dresses in clogs and shawl,
She's the fairest one of them all . . .'

Men came to the door of the pub with pint pots in their hands, often being pulled back by young painted tarts who seemed jealous that these two little girls should take as much as a penny from their menfolk. 'Aw, come back to the bar, Paddy, will ye? They're gypsy kids and'll rob ye blind given half the chance,' was more or less the tarts' protest.

ELa The two little girls knew nothing about the travelling navvies and their Saturday-night tarts: they were only interested in the pennies which came their way. They worked hard. Their next number was 'Lady of Spain I adore you', and this gave Kitty a chance to change her type of clog dance, and Sally the opportunity to show how well she clicked the slates between her fingers. Men came to the door to watch the Lady of Spain, but the tarts played with the men's trouser buttons and coaxed them away: some of the men threw a penny when, if left alone, they might have chucked a threepenny bit.

The girls always knew when it was time to finish their dancing because the Salvation Army girls invaded the pub to sell copies of *The War Cry*. The big girls of the Salvation Army knew to a second when the men would be too drunk to move, and it would be easier for them to dip in their pockets for a penny for a *The War Cry* than stagger to the door to watch the dancing. By this time many of the tarts, having picked their man's pockets or borrowed money from him, had left the pub.

Sally said, 'Ta-ra!', and ran home with her half of the takings, but Kitty had shopping to do. Since her mother died, her dad had spent more time and money at the Ben Brierley. He rarely had any housekeeping money left from his wages, but Kitty always made sure he tipped the rent money from his pocket on Friday night: it would be the workhouse else. She bought food with her clog-dancing money, which was now less because she no longer dared sell clay pipes.

Shopping was best on the market off Swan Street on Saturday

nights. Meat could be bought cheap before it went rotten, and vegetables could be picked up from under the stalls; sometimes she could help herself from the open wicker shopping-baskets of housewives, for all vegetables were tipped loose into their baskets from the weighing pan. A carrot here, a turnip there, a spare onion, a couple of potatoes: they soon mounted up and filled her own wicker basket. The best place for stealing food was outside the tent of Ram Jam Singh, for all women were compelled to stop and listen to him.

'I come like a shadow, I go like the wind. Here today, gone tomorrow,' said he, but he was there every Saturday night without fail. He wore a turban and had a brown face, although it might not have been genuine brown, for some said it was cocoa and that if it rained his Indian rajah blood became streaky down his face.

He called himself the Indian Mystic and he did tricks with string, playing cards, and pennies. There was a coil of stout rope on one side of him, and a rounded basket with a lid on the other. Most people waited in the hope that he would do the Indian rope trick or charm a swaying snake from the basket, but neither Kitty nor anybody else had ever seen a boy go up a rope or a cobra nudge the lid off and do a dance. His performance was to persuade women to go inside the tent and have their fortunes told by his wife who was, he said, a direct descendant of the Queen of Sheba and had inherited all the wisdom of King Solomon. Women nudged each other to get inside the tent. Ram Jam Singh took their money, touched his forehead and said, 'Salaam, mem-sahib!' He was full of Ali Baba charm, which enabled Kitty to be selective and even help herself to luxury items like apples, pears and oranges. She always had to check her basket for food which she'd not been able to steal, and any missing but necessary items had to be bought with her clog-dancing money. She usually contrived to have a little money over for herself, maybe sixpence, and then she had to decide whether to buy humbugs from the man who stretched and twisted his own health-giving humbugs under the crackling kerosene lamps, or buy a large stack of American comics, or even have her fortune told by the Queen of Sheba lady. The American comics always won, for they were more permanent and could be read in bed by candlelight for an entire week of bedtimes.

This night she was lucky: she lifted some sausages wrapped in the *Evening News*. She and her dad could have them for Sunday tea; but she'd barely gone a dozen yards when she had to give them to a dog. The dog was being sold as a good watchdog, trained to the backyard kennel, but it was shivering and she knew nobody would buy it and it would end up being tossed over the bridge into the river when the market closed. 'Enjoy 'em!' she said, and the dog snatched them and ate the paper and all.

This was her Saturday world: the market, Swan Street, Ancoats Lane, and home sweet home in Angel Meadow. She was aware that Manchester was a big city and that other roads led to other districts with other people, but this had nothing to do with her.

On the way home she passed the glass cellars of the *Daily Express* where there were many electric lights, and men in blue uniforms carried long-stemmed oilcans, and a million unending miles of one long newspaper rolled and twisted fast from one giant roller to another, and needles on dials kept swinging from the left to the right, from the right to the left. And there was the man in his striped pyjamas still smiling on his Bovril bottle: maybe during the night when nobody was watching he'd reach the shores of Ireland, which was where her dad and his friends all sang about wanting to reach before they died.

It was very dark down Ancoats Lane. Men pushed their young tarts into black entries: sometimes two cigarette glows would dance in the dark of the entry, sometimes a man and his tart seemed to bounce their bums together in shop doorways. The stars were shining and could be seen shining because it was Saturday night and there was no sky smoke from the mills. Railway engines clinked and clanked wagons, and suddenly puffed as though in a forgotten anger; an occasional tramcar rattled, jerked and dinged. These were good sounds to Kitty, for they meant that the world lived and did things.

She was home and in bed before her dad arrived. She heard him singing the rebel songs, so she knew he was drunk but not too drunk. The back door slammed and she heard him pee-ing down the grid in the yard instead of using the lavatory, and him farting as he did so.

It had been a good Saturday night for she'd managed to steal some candles from a basket, which meant she could read and read and read to her heart's content. The front pages of the American comics always had Li'l Orphan Annie. Orphan Annie was Kitty's secret best friend. Annie lived in a wonderful house, which stood in a small garden, with each window lighted warm in red or yellow. She had a cheeky pup which looked up at her. The moon with sharp little horns was in the sky, and the night sky wasn't black, it was blue, even light blue, and the moon was yellow.

Sunday Kitty didn't like, she hated, and she felt guilty about hating Sundays. It was a day of the dead. No knockers-up tapped on bedroom windows with long poles, no mill hooters howled, no pavements clopped to the rushing late clogs of mill girls. No sweeps shouted 'Sweep!' and no scissor-grinders made sparks fly and shouted 'Knives to grind!' and no ragbone men blew Mons bugles and shouted 'Eeyagerbone!' and, worst of all, no Italian barrel-organs played in the streets, any of the streets, for girls, all the girls, to dance to. Where did they go to on Sundays? Did they sit before the fire and spit in the fire and wish they could sail Bovril bottles to Italy, Ireland or the ancient land of the Jews before Jesus?

The children had to go to nine o'clock Mass, otherwise they would be strapped on Monday morning first thing: and nine o'clock Mass was torture, it was purgatory, for there was no hymn-singing or organ music or incense-wafting. She'd once been to eleven o'clock Mass with her dad and it had been heaven, for the light-grey incense smoke had a beautiful smell which made her want to fill her lungs till they burst, and the organ played, and the choir sang in God's Latin, and lots and lots of the Mass had been chanted in magical Latin. She had felt that at any moment Jesus would appear on the altar and show the holes in his hands. But she doubted if Jesus would bother attending a miserable nine o'clock Mass, especially on a cold morning and with there being no knocker-up: besides, Jesus would know that the kids had all told lies in Confession simply because there was nothing to confess about. All that Kitty could tell Father Rourke was that she didn't like Sundays, but Father Rourke didn't seem to be all that worried about things for she got the same penance as everybody else, not one Hail Mary more or less. Perhaps they all said they didn't like Sundays.

She woke her dad up when she returned from Mass, and he slowly got himself dressed, searching and searching for his left boot until Kitty found it in the backyard near the drain: and away he went to eleven o'clock. Eleven o'clock Mass ended at twelve o'clock, at which time the pubs opened, and her dad would be in the Ben Brierley until thrown out, cursing and swearing, at two o'clock. It gave her plenty of time to light the fire, make the beds, and put the stew on.

Home he came, as ever in the best of humour and singing what Kitty could only assume was on-the-spot invented Gaelic. His songs, once the rebel songs had run their course, consisted of very little tune, and the words seemed to be 'a-rum-tee-tiddly-tee-tee-tee, tee-tee-twaddly-twaddly-tee-toe-tee' to which he did a little bit of a dance shuffle, and ended by falling against the table, thus allowing him to slither on to a chair and start to eat the steaming meal before him. After the meal, he staggered, sometimes on all fours, up to his bedroom, and within minutes Kitty heard the loudest of snores. He would be out to the world until half-past six, when he would get up, have whatever tea Kitty served him, and be back at the Ben Brierley for opening time at seven.

This was wonderful to Kitty. All the other little girls were forced to go with their mother or father or both to the cemetery, for everybody, including Kitty, had somebody lying in the Catholic cemetery of Moston.

The girls hated this dismal pilgrimage, for while their fathers looked around to see who had last taken up residence, and their mothers trimmed the graves with broken-handled knives hidden away for the purpose, they were sent to empty the jam jars of the old stinking flowers, prematurely killed by the smells of the chemicals from the chemical works outside the gate. They then had to walk to the lonely upright tap-pipe in the middle of the cemetery and put fresh water in the jars. If the girls met each other at the water tap they were not allowed to giggle because it was a solemn occasion: they had to pretend they did not know each other. Kitty was free, wholly, completely, bird-like free from this awful chore. Having washed the dinner things she was free for three hours.

She normally spent these three hours in a secret and exciting way; and away she now went, closing the front door quietly and making sure the key was tied securely in her handkerchief. She wandered down Ancoats Lane back towards town, and she turned down Newton Street, which was thrilling because it was the great never-shutting post office where even on Sunday people could buy postage stamps to send letters all over the world on waiting trains and waiting ships. Then she turned right through Stevenson Square, where tramcars gathered and talked to each other, and where people gathered and plotted rebellion. Hundreds of people stood around and listened to the spouters who said terrible things about the government: this was frightening but exciting, like going on the ghost train or the caterpillar on Belle Vue sports days.

She met Mick Dowd there by accident. He'd been trying to sell clay pipes because he'd taken over her racket, but he'd found that Sunday afternoons weren't much good for clay pipes. People who stood in groups to listen to nasty things about the government seemed to smoke Woodbine cigarettes, and he was on the verge of changing his racket to one of mixing with the crowds and begging for cigarettes, when Kitty spoke to him.

'Where's your gang?' she asked.

'Bloody cemetery, where else but?'

It was as true with the boys as it was with the girls, for families went to the cemetery and the boys were expected to pray for the souls of the departed, envying their sisters who went for the water. The boys, also like the girls, had to hold their parents' hands, and were always taken past the communal tombs of the priests with a view to interesting the boys in the priesthood.

'And ye'll see they're always buried in a group, which must be very friendly,' said Mr Keenan once to his son Bill.

'Furthermore,' added Mrs Keenan, 'a priest goes straight to heaven when he dies without customs or formalities.'

'So what d'y'think?' prodded Mr Keenan.

'I think I'd rather join the British Navy,' said Bill, and he was hit soundly over the head even though it was in a cemetery.

Mick's gang didn't like the Sunday cemetery, but Mick was free, as Kitty was free. He had no dad, only a mam, and his mam spent every Sunday after Mass and meal going around doing good. She went to houses where there was illness, and did things for the sick like washing them or cleaning clothes which they'd messed in or been sick over: sometimes she did things for the dead once they were dead. She earned a few shillings doing good like this, and kept a roof over her head and bread on the table.

Mick was supposed to go on his own and take flowers to his dad's grave, but he sold the flowers for a penny, and with his fist under one of his gang's nose threatened to half-kill the kid if he didn't say a quick Hail Mary for Mick's dad.

Kitty was about to walk on, but he grabbed her.

'Hey, tart, where you off?'

'Lewis's. To look in the posh windows and pretend I live in 'em.'

'Bloody barmy, that is.'

'Aye,' said Kitty. It was always best to agree with Mick, but she blushed that she had blurted out the truth about her secret Sunday trips to Lewis's windows.

Suddenly, from round the corner, as out of nowhere, a policeman appeared and brought his hand down on Mick's shoulder.

'No, master,' dithered Mick.

'No master what?'

'I'm not selling clay pipes a-Sunday.'

'I don't recollect bloody asking you, lad.'

Mick made a sudden cornered-mouse wriggle to run, but the bobby grabbed him.

'Come back, lad,' said the bobby, and then, as an afterthought, 'or I'll be having ye for hawking clay pipes on Sunday.'

'Who told you?' snarled Mick.

'You just did. But we'll leave it in abeyance for the time being. What I want from you, lad, is to be my deputy.'

Mick stood and stared with his mouth wide open.

'For what I'm going to do, lad, is nip into the backyard o' The

Grapes to slake me thirst, and while I'm gone I'll expect ye to keep that bloody mob o' bolsheviks and atheists in trim.'

'Me?'

'Aye – you and me big hat, lad.' The bobby took his helmet off and handed it like it was the Crown of England to Mick. 'This helmet stands for law and order, and that bloody lot over there knows it. Like a burning branch to a pack of wolves, it is. From time to time one o' them spouters'll spout summat detrimental about the King, the Prime Minister, the Archbishop o' Canterbury, the Pope in Rome, or the Devil in hell, and he'll like as not point in your direction as being the established order o' things. When he does, and that bloody lot looks round, just hold my helmet high to let 'em know they're under close scrutiny. They'll back, snarling.'

'Suppose they come after me to kill?' asked Mick, quite frightened.

'They won't, lad. But if they does, send this little lady to the backyard of The Grapes.' He bent down to Kitty. 'You'll find me in there, chuck, with a pint in me hand and ready to come if called.'

The bobby disappeared round the corner as fast as he'd appeared, and Mick stood there, knock-kneed with intimidation: just a small boy in a large square full of people, and holding a huge Roman-soldier kind of a heavy blue helmet.

'Right then,' said Kitty and was about to bounce away.

'Where's the fire?' asked Mick.

'In the grate at home. I'm off to me Lewis's windows.'

'Stay here with me!'

'And get killed in the rush when they charges you? I'll send flowers.'

'Listen, tart, I'm telling you to stay.'

'What's in it for me?'

'You can be me moll.'

'What's a moll?'

'King Arthur had one. Took her all over the place with him. He had to go out on bloody jobs like this all the time, and his moll always went with him.'

'I'd run a mile.'

Without warning or preliminary rumbling one of the spouters yelled out at the top of his voice and pointed to Mick: 'The Prime Minister'll have us at war. On the scrapheap for peace, bloody heroes for war. He'll have us at war: he will, he'll have us at war. Mark my words!' The crowd turned towards Mick.
'Up with your helmet!' shouted Kitty.
And Mick lifted the helmet high above his head.
'Keep it up there, you'll be all right,' she said. 'Oh, and if you ever get your hands free, wipe your snotty nose, it's running.' And leaving Mick sniffing and twitching his nose, Kitty skipped off to view the windows of Lewis's.
The windows were glimpses of heaven. There was a dining-room, and the great polished table arranged with plates, basins, dishes, knives and forks, and red wine in an ornamental glass bottle. There were beautiful curved-backed chairs around the table; there were bookshelves with brand-new books in them, and coloured paintings of sailing ships in full sail on rough blue seas around the wall. A large circle of lights and crystal glasses was suspended over the table; there was a standard lamp in one corner, with a huge golden shade and silk tassels; there were even little lights the shape of torches coming from the walls; there was a large, beautifully shaped wireless set on a table in the other corner. Kitty knew that if she died that very second, the Virgin Mary and one or two specially invited lady saints would suddenly appear seated at the table, and they would beckon for her to join them for a highly scrumptious meal, and maybe even allow her to turn the knobs and get a foreign station on the wireless set, and she would be able to step through the glass window without breaking the glass because she would be dead and an invisible spirit.
 The next window was a bathroom, and Kitty tried to imagine herself filling up the bath right to the brim with cuddly warm water and perfume, and stepping into it with a bathing suit on, a blue Bukta bathing suit. She'd never been in a bath in her life, and this would be a tingling, frightening luxury which would cleanse her spirit like getting a shock from a battery. Getting into the bath would be worth a hundred Confessions.
 She shuffled from one window of heaven to another, but she

seemed to develop a sort of sinking feeling, a sickly headache over the eyes which got worse and worse until she reached the gardening window. The pot rabbits seemed to hop, and the pot garden gnomes looked ugly and sneered. She was convinced there was an Egyptian mummy inside the garden shed, and it would, at any second bob up and stare at her. The pot birds looked evil: they would flap and fly and tear her eyes out. The lawnmower on the artificial raffia grass wanted to turn towards her, she knew it wanted to turn towards her: it wanted to turn and run her over.

Kitty knew she was going to be poorly, and she had to get home and go to bed and perhaps die in great pain: the kind of pain God liked people to have before he took them.

Somehow she got home and woke her dad up and got into bed, making sure she changed her knickers in case she died suddenly. It would be diphtheria. She knew it would be diphtheria because people said diphtheria came off the river, and the river was only on the other side of the wall from their house. Diphtheria, a beautiful purple shape with lovely music, would float down the Medlock, and the purple vapours, smelling like scent from Boots the Cash Chemists, would seep through the bricks and reach her nose, and then she would die in a terrible agony, only she wouldn't feel the agony because she would be unconscious. Hers would be a lovely funeral. All the little girls of Ancoats had lovely funerals. People would line the streets and weep for her. Some might even applaud at the loveliness of it all. She closed her eyes.

'Ah, now drink yer fine strong lemon tea, me darling.'

Kitty, weak as a half-drowned kitten, found herself propped up in bed with a bundle of pillows and cushions. She felt small and helpless and clean. Somewhere in the back of her mind were half-forgotten dreams of lions and tigers, frightening dreams which had made her sweat. The day looked grey and dirty through the window, it could be morning daylight or evening dusk. Mrs Dowd sat on her bed and held a steaming cup of lemon tea to her lips. It was bitter and Kitty shivered.

'Is it diphtheria?' she asked.

'Ach no, me darling, just a fever from the river.'

'And am I better?'

'Like as not ye're on the mend and'll be brownstoning the steps in a fortnight, though I don't mind telling ye there was a time when I thought 'twas me scented soap and cotton wool ye'd be requiring. But I burned a camphor ball in a teaspoon over a candle and I hung an onion up near the ceiling in the corner of yer room, and didn't the camphor chase all them germs from yer body? And aren't they all up there this minute, chewing away on the onion, which I'll be throwing into the river on me next visit? There's just a penny for the camphor and a shilling for me professional services, which I'll be holding me hand out to yer dad for come pay day; the onions and lemons are from yer own shopping basket; and all that is cheaper than a doctor's bill, is it not now?'

It must have been morning because the dark grey of the window became a light grey, and she heard the ragbone man's bugle from a few streets away.

Barely had Mrs Dowd left than Mrs Beckett of next door came in with a bowl of broth made from a sheep's head; and Mrs Fearnley of next door but one came in with some bread fried in dripping; and Mrs Roscoe called in with some sugar butties, because children needed sugar; and along came Mrs Compton with a cup of hot blood which her husband had fetched on his bike from the abattoirs. With all the hot drinks brought to her, Kitty became in desperate need to use the enamel po under her bed, but she had to wait until the house was silent before sliding out of bed, lifting up her mother's frock which she used as a nightgown, and sitting on the po to wee-wee. Once she heard a noise and was in such a panic of embarrassment to get back into bed that she knocked the po over, and then discovered it was only a mouse scratting. It was while dabbing the wet oilcloth that she noticed a shoe-box under her bed, which wasn't her shoe-box because she'd never had shoes in a shoe-box. Inside was a collection of clay pipes and a pencil-printed note which said, 'If you die, tell Jesus I gived you them pipes back for eternity. And my name is Mick Dowd.'

It was the beginning of a wonderful day, for the women called on her constantly and put the palms of their soda-rough hands on her forehead to test for temperature, and gave her Christmas things like blood oranges, pomegranates and grapes which they said had fallen from carts.

In the early evening, the sound she'd been waiting for for hours came with the downstairs thud of the front door, followed by 'A-rum-tee-tiddley-diddley-diddley-dob-dee, dob-dob-diddley-dob-dee-dee-dee!'

'And how are ye, me wondrous precious little darling?' said her dad as he pushed into her room. 'There y'are now!' He held out something wrapped in newspaper. 'And have I not been and got some sausages for the two of us to have with a few rounds o' fried bread. For when out I went this morning o' starlight there was you cool as a cucumber and sleeping like a top, and 'tis on the mend, says I, she is: and ready for the heftiest meal ye ever did see, so 'twas off to the German's I did go, with a ho and a ho and ho-tiddley-toe!'

Kitty slipped out of bed for she knew she'd have to do the frying.

'How long have I been poorly, dad?'

'Well now, me darling love, 'tis been days and days and days, and ye've been tossing and turning and burning and burning and coming out with a welter of strange words. But like St Patrick himself, didn't I blow away them lions and tigers and dragons and such things as was mithering yer mind.'

'Then what about school? And the rent?' She grabbed his arm. 'The rent? What about the rent?'

'Now that, me dear, was what they call providence, for d'y'see 'twas Whit Week, or had it gone from yer mind?'

Some awful truth waved through Kitty.

'So like the school was shutten down and that.'

'And I missed being queen o' the Walk?'

He sat down on her bed. 'Aye, 'tis so.'

Kitty sobbed tears on her dad's dirt-caked chest. He put his thick muscular arms around her. 'There now! Hush-hush, ma-cushla!' he said.

Kitty could hear all the bands of the procession: the men in leopard skins who banged and busted the great big drums and made shop windows rattle; the red-coated band leaders with their proud puffed-up chests who could toss their white-corded poles higher than the tram wires and catch them one-handed as they twirled back to earth; the silver trumpeters who were always shaking spit from their trumpets; and all the feet on the cobblestones of the city streets, and all with a bang-bang-bang. And the different holy brass hymn tunes from the different bands which played hide and seek with each other, so that 'Sweet Sacrament' would sneak down a side street and come bounding out and surprising 'Jesus, I am sorry'. And Kitty should have been the Virgin Mary of the Irish half of Ancoats (the Italian half carried an enormous Madonna covered in a million lilies) – but then, on second thoughts, she'd have been the poorest Virgin Mary of all the Manchester churches, and although people would have clapped their hands, they would have done it out of pity, and some would have said, 'What a shame!' So maybe it wasn't worth shedding many a tear for.

'Who took my place?' she asked.

'None other than your very own special little friend Sally Maguire, on short notice like, but with her dad having a win on the horses, the first in many a month, and him able to purchase from me them wonderful silk veils and dresses, and him giving me a pint of ale for your crown, for he's a decent enough man. And 'twas that financial transaction which put the rent money into the rent collector's leather bag, and him going off singing the song of the heathen and rattling the coins in the bag.'

Kitty fried the sausages on a bit of a fire downstairs, and she ate a few, but only a few, for she felt weak and soon had to go back upstairs to bed. Her dad, with all the thousand regrets of the world, had to go to the Ben Brierley, but before he left he carried most of the downstairs fire up to the tiny fireplace in her room on the shovel, and he left a bucket of coal. It was lovely to have a fire in her bedroom, such a luxury as never was or ever would be, and better than all the windows of Lewis's put together. Life was truly beautiful.

She was awakened the next morning by not one woman, not two women, but three women, all busying themselves in her bedroom. Mrs Beckett breathed on and rubbed away at the brass knob on the left-hand side of her black iron bedstead, and Mrs

Fearnley made the same motions on the other brass knob. Mrs Roscoe cleaned the ashes from the grate.

'There's a speck of fly shit or summat on yer knob, Mrs Fearnley,' said Mrs Beckett.

'Aye, and there'll be a speck on yer bloody nose, Mrs Beckett, if ye go poking it into other folks's business, for me knob's as bright and shining as yours.'

Both women, as though given a silent command, moved to the head of Kitty's bed and began the breathing and polishing of those two knobs with a rhythm which made Kitty feel she was riding a milk cart.

Mrs Roscoe held a spread-out newspaper across the fireplace, and holding it up there with the shovel, put her face almost to the floor and began blowing through the grate bars. There was a roar and a redness through the newspaper which signified that flames had started and the new coal and old cinders were doing their best to become a fire.

'For isn't the holy nun a-coming calling on you this very morning?' explained Mrs Roscoe.

Mrs Compton puffed and panted into the room carrying a bundle of patchwork quilt which she spread over the bed. 'There now,' said she, 'if there's one thing them nuns like looking for 'tis the results of hard work, patience and thrift, and many the month it took me making that quilt, and my hands cut to pieces with the needle.'

'The nun!' shouted Kitty. 'Have I time to warm a pan o' water on the fire for a wash?'

All women agreed there'd be no time at all, and they themselves bustled out of the room and away. Kitty jumped up, dashed downstairs with the po in her hand, swilled it out down the scullery sink, rushed into the yard with it, stuck it inside the lavatory, where the po would be safe and unseen because nuns never went to the lavatory. Then she swilled herself under the scullery tap, ran upstairs, dried herself on a shirt lying on the floor in her dad's room, dashed out, dashed back again and begun straightening up her dad's room because she realized the nun might look in by accident. She pushed his Sunday boots under the bed, straightened the army coats he used as blankets, noticed the large picture of The Sacred Heart was leaning at an angle and squared it up, then rushed back into bed, breathing heavy because of her rustling and bustling and dib-dabbing.

Within seconds she heard the gentle opening and closing of the front door, and smooth, almost silent, footsteps coming upstairs. She was afraid of nuns almost as much as she was afraid of priests.

The nun swished into the room, her broad starched headdress touching either side of the door. It was the nice nun; the one she was least afraid of; the one she liked; the small one with the pretty little face: Sister St Pius.

The nun smiled but said nothing. She sat on the edge of the bed and held her cool and delicate hand on Kitty's forehead. Kitty wanted to wriggle with sheer contentment. Sister St Pius then put her finger on Kitty's wrist and tested her pulse, while at the same time looking up at the ceiling as though looking for cracks or bugs or both.

'You've a temperature,' said the nun. 'And yer wee pulse is racing a little.' Then she gave the nicest of smiles. 'Och, but ye'll live.' The nun was slightly different from other people, for she was a Scotchie, and Scotland was a long, long way away, almost like Ireland. She gave Kitty a tickle under the armpits. 'Is there anything I can do for you, or be getting you?' she asked.

'No, thank you, sister. I've got everything.'

'Then ye're a lucky wee lassie, but I'll have to have a little chat with you.' She held Kitty's hand. 'Tell me, Kitty, now, is it not a wee bit difficult for your dad to be caring and minding for ye? Might it not help yer dad if you went into one of our very nice Catholic homes?'

'Orphanage, d'y'mean?' blustered out Kitty. 'Y'mean like Li'l Orphan Annie, only she didn't go to no orphanage but lived a happy life with a yellow moon shining, and a happy pup what smiled.'

'Och, our homes are designed for happy lives too,' said the sister. 'There's warmth from pipes even in the dormitories, which is where the little girls sleep, and there's warm-water taps, and there are splendid meals all cooked for you, and there are games like hockey and netball – och, they're wonderful! And there's nice uniforms, and the nuns teach the children, and some of the children move up to convents and high schools, where they're supplied with books and more uniforms.'

'I'm very happy here, sister, thank you very much.'

'That may be so, little bairn, but can your good father cope?'

Something triggered Kitty off. 'He doesn't drink beer no more! He hasn't drunken himself for a thousand years or more. Luke at this!' She gathered a handful of the patchwork quilt. 'Made this himself, he did! Aye, he did! So he did! Sat up at nights and cut his hands to shreds making it for me. And there was stories he was telling me all the time, about the kings of Ireland being nowt but laughing heads, and the cattle raid of porridge, which you wouldn't know of being a Scotchie.' She dropped her head on to the sister's broad white starched collar, and wept because she knew she'd hurt the nun, and the nun would be crying. 'Oh, I'm sorry, I'm sorry, I'm sorry!' she blubbered.

The nun wasn't crying, in fact the nun was covering a broad smile with her right hand as she smoothed the child's hair with her left.

'Just you go into me dad's room,' Kitty continued, 'and you'll see the Sacred Heart is dead square, honest it is. It started to slant this morning while he was saying his prayers, but he got up off his knees and made it dead square. He always keeps God dead square, sister!'

The nun got up. 'I'm sure your father is a good man, Kitty. But maybe you'll bear in mind – '

'Oh, I'll do that, sister.'

'And are you sure there's nothing I can get for you?'

'Aye, come to think of it, sister. Me dad's been begging me to read to him about King Arthur for it's wishful he is to be copying that man's deeds and such. D'y'think you could get me a book from the library about King Arthur and his clay pipes?'

'I'll call in on my way home,' laughed the nun. 'And I'll see that somebody drops it in for ye, wee lassie.'

'Thank you, sister.'

After the nun had wafted out of the room and the house, Kitty screwed her eyes up tight, made the sign of the cross, and begged Jesus forgive her for telling lies to one of his holy nuns. The neighbours rushed back. They'd taken it for granted Kitty was going to be taken to a home and were surprised she was still secure in her own bed. Mrs Compton gathered back the patchwork quilt, saying she hoped it had been noticed by the nun.

'I brought it to her attention, and that's no lie,' said Kitty.

That afternoon, shortly after a barrel-organ had played Irish tunes at the end of the street, the book arrived. She heard the front door open and Paddy Byrne's voice shout: 'There's a buke on't table for a sick girl!' then the door banged shut. She rushed down for it.

The book was full of a long kind of poetry which didn't rhyme by Alfred Lord Tennyson; but it seemed to be about King Arthur: well, yes, it was about King Arthur but there were so many strange names and long words that she soon realized Camelot was a snobby district nowhere near Ancoats. There was, however, one poem which rhymed and, in her opinion, could quite easily have been about her: it was of a lady who lived alone by a river. Kitty spent most of the time on her own in the two-up two-down by the Medlock. She never heard anything quiver from it, neither had she heard little breezes making it shiver. Sometimes she heard the men and boys hunting rats with bricks, and she heard the dirty words they shouted. There was a window, but it was impossible to look down on the river from it because the backyard came between. Through the window – even if she held the hand mirror up and looked through the window through the mirror – she could only see the rubber works. The window had to be kept tightly shut because her dad said the deadly germs from the river would come along in their tram-loads: for this reason the window was always very dirty and her dad only opened it and washed the outside when there was a thick white frost on a Sunday. He said the frost killed the germs, although Kitty often wondered why the germ smells didn't sneak in with the rubber smells because rubber smells managed to get in; or indeed she often wondered why the rubber smells didn't suffocate the germs.

But she was lucky now, for the book had made her the Lady of Shalott. And she loved a wonderful hero named Sir Lancelot who could dance a lot, chance a lot, glance a lot, and romance a lot. She blushed when she thought up the rhyme of 'romance a lot', because romancing meant him chalking their initials on walls, and he would have to write 'Sir L loves KN' and he might even have to draw a man's thing.

That night, when her father had built up the bedroom fire and left for the Ben Brierley on something as urgent as the Devil, she lay perfectly still and watched the red glows dancing and shifting on the brass bedknobs, and she imagined the bed was her magic loom with colours gay. She seemed to go into a warm and pleasant trance in which, muffled as cotton wool, she could hear barges chugging like the Belle Vue motorboats, funny as monkeys, brave as lions; and wedding bells, only the silent tinkling ones on wedding cakes, soft as marshmallow; and laughing girls laughing to market, new wicker baskets over their arms to fill with pumpkins; and the frosted breath of the solid funeral horse with its proud, purple plume, and the glass hearse with designs of straight lines and gentle flowers around the edges of the glass. Kitty held her breath, waiting for Sir Lancelot to appear. Then she jumped up, she jumped up fast, suddenly frightened. She was going to die as the Lady of Shalott had died. If she as much as caught a glimpse of Sir Lancelot in his shining armour she would float dead down the Medlock. She sprang out of bed, lit her candle from the fire, covered the brass bedknobs with her knickers and vest, and rummaged quickly through the American comics. She knew she'd be the Lady of Shalott again, she couldn't resist it, but she'd have to be careful and cover the knobs and never reach the stage of actually seeing the knight on his thick jewelled saddle with coal-black curls flowing from under his helmet, and his helmet and helmet feather burning like flames.

In a few days Kitty was up and about, and thinking of school on Monday.
 'Hey, tart, are ye all right like?' asked Mick.
 'Was nearly at death's door,' said she.
 'Aye, but ye didn't knock, wipe yer feet and enter.'
 'There's other times.'
 'Other times is other times.'
 'Aye.'
 'You got them clay pipes?'

'You want 'em back?'

'Giving's giving, isn't it, tart? I tried hawking them to't fellers, but there was no call. So like you can have your racket back, long as you tell Jesus I give it you.'

'I'll tell Mary.'

'She'll do. Don't say nowt about me being a bobby's runner in Stevenson Square, or I'll knock you skenning!'

'Right, kid! Okay, kid!'

She instinctively knew she could call him 'kid' which not even the toughest member of his gang could do, because he'd given the game away: he'd told her he wanted Stevenson Square hushed up.

Kitty had given thought to the stock of clay pipes while she'd been in bed. Maybe baccy was getting dear and men couldn't afford it, or maybe men were out of work, but she knew that kids could get pennies where grown-ups couldn't.

On Saturday morning she and Sally Maguire stood outside the gate of the University Settlement in Every Street where kids went to get free oranges and free flea powder: and, demonstrating with jam jars of soapy water, they sold pipes for bubble-blowing. The pipes sold at a ha'penny, but if anybody wanted the complete bubble-blowing kit with a jam jar of soapy water, it was three ha'pence altogether. They were sold out before the mill hooter at Butterworth's blew for noon and finish work.

*

'All I do is dream of you the whole night through;
With the dawn I still go on and dream of you.
You're every thought, you're everything,
You're every song I ever sing,
Summer, winter, autumn and spring.'

Kitty had worked out a new song and dance, and it made more money than the clogs.

She put an action to every word, but mainly she side-kicked as was the fashion of the new ragtime dancing. She always managed to touch her foot on the up side-kick whatever other actions she made. For 'dreaming', she tilted her head to rest on her closed hands, closed like praying at an angle. With 'the dawn', she yawned and stretched. 'Summer, winter, autumn and spring', she pointed to the sky, fluttered pit-a-patter raindrops, blew on her hands because of the cold, wiped sweat from her brow because of the heat. But always on 'you' she stretched her arm full out and pointed and wiggled her finger at one of the men watching.

Meanwhile behind her Sally waved the open palms of her hands as though pretending to wash windows in rhythm, and simply added, 'Boop-boop-a-doop!'

Ragtime was no dance for clogs, and the two girls danced barefoot. They had also smeared their lips deep with lipstick stolen from Sally's mother's handbag while she was on the lavatory. And they had flattened and kiss-curled their hair with lard supplied by Kitty. Men packed the doorway of the Land O' Cakes and when their tarts tried to get them to serious drinking at the bar they back-handed them and told them to piss off.

'And were there more than twenty-four hours a day,
They'd be spent in sweet content dreaming away.
When skies are grey, skies are blue,
Morning, noon and night time too,
All I do the whole night through is dream of you.'

For 'twenty-four hours', Kitty pointed up to the lighted clock of New Cross church. For 'skies are grey, skies are blue', she shaded her eyes with her hand like a sailor looking up for a sea-bird.

The group of men clapped and cheered the girls, and sixpences and even a shilling or two were thrown. The tarts said they'd send for a policeman quick, and Kitty and Sally put their clogs back on, gathered their coins and ran off. They knew it was criminal for them to pick up more money than a man whose body ran with sweat through swinging a pick for five and a half days a week.

Kitty glanced up at the man on the bottle, and he was smiling more than ever, which was a good sign because in a peculiar way she had come to look upon the man up there in his striped pyjamas as God, not God the gentle Jesus, but God the Almighty who did things with ancient Jews: and now he smiled approval and looked well pleased. They ran into an entry which had just enough yellow light from a street lamp for them to count their money by.

Sally was in a rush to take her money home and give it to her parents, for it was America money: her dad was saving up to go to America and become famous, although he'd not decided what to become famous at, but it didn't matter in America.

'I think I'd like to become a famous nun,' said Sally.

'I'd rather be a famous tart,' said Kitty. 'For every night is Saturday night, whereas a nun's only got a Sunday morning. One thing I'm not going to be is a mill girl, for a mill girl stands at a dozen looms until she's put up the spout, then she has to get married and grow wizened and have babies until she dies having the last baby.'

'What's up the spout?'

'I don't know, but it's what big girls get.'

Of all the Saturday nights, this one was going to be the best ever, and Kitty needed a lot of money. It was the last night of the wakes on Hilkirk Street Croft. Each night for a week she'd heard people arguing and swearing as they passed the top of Angel Meadow on their way to the wakes, and she'd heard them laughing and spitting, hours later, as they returned. There was no money for the wakes: it had gone on the rent, the gas bill and food, apart from what her dad needed every night. But she was determined to spend a couple of glorious hours on the wakes, and what's more she could stay till the hooters and bells made a noise for the shutdown, and still be home and in bed before her dad, and he'd never know how much money she'd spent.

There was no time this special Saturday night leisurely to stroll the market alleys and steal food from the baskets, she had to rush to strange shops and buy the food. She daren't go to shops where she was known, not with money, for they'd think her dad had stolen it and maybe report him.

She plonked her basket of food in the parlour and ran up Palmerston Street to where there was a red and yellow glow in the sky.

Long before she reached the croft she heard the poop-poop and clash-clash and dee-dah-dee-dah of the great steam organ, and the tune it was playing made her run all the faster, for the tune was 'All I Do is Dream of You'. Her heart pit-a-patted for she felt that the man on the bottle had sent an angel to the wakes to tell the organ to play 'Dream of You' as a hymn, for it was like a hymn, and the words were worded like a hymn. It was the Saturday night Annunciation to a girl who just weeks before had been the Virgin Mary in church: it was holy, and it was going to be exciting and full of beautiful blues and golds and music.

The wakes were surrounded by giant steam traction-engines, all puffing and chugging like a thousand kettles with angry and rattling lids. It was as though they were chained monsters from the past, and from them ran wires in the air and cables on the ground, all shaking and wriggling like serpents. The outside of the wakes smelled of steam like a railway station, but she'd no sooner stepped out of the cold darkness and over a few thick cables than her eyes were dazzled by a million coloured lights, and the smells were warm and of lubricating oil and cough candy. Everything raced round and round, faster and faster, with under-wheels rattling like thunder on boards. The green dragons tottered and swayed and chased each other to devour each other with long red tongues and large white teeth; the dobby horses jumped high like horses of heaven, up and down and up and down on their shining brass spiral rods; the chairoplanes whizzed higher and higher and carried the lovely kicking legs of big girls; the shuffling, swaying platform of the cakewalk was filled with men and women who tried to dance and held on to each other and laughed, or maybe the sliding platform made them dance; the frightening flying-boat stood on one end and then stood on the other end and the caged-in people screamed their lungs out. All these were too grown-up and frightening for Kitty; besides, she was too young and they wouldn't have allowed her on. They wouldn't even let her have a go on the money-winning stalls. The most popular money-winning tent was called the Stock Exchange: it was filled with machines on legs, and when their handles were pulled there rolled around in a little window words like 'coal', 'cotton', 'wool', 'iron', 'wheat'. If three of the same commodities came up in line, it was said that the market was cornered, and a stream of pennies tippled down the slot. 'Wheat' was the best payer, and Kitty would have loved 'wheat'.

And then her eye was taken by the baby doll on the rifle range. She needed it, felt physically hungry for it. It was a beautiful baby doll in a pink nightdress ready for bed. It had blue eyes, and the tiniest sweetest lips, and was almost the size of a real live baby. A man held a rifle out.

'Now come on, you brave boys what was at Wipers and the Somme, and them of you what has beheld the angel of Mons! Come on, them of you what has killed your share of Germans for King and country! Now's your chance to take home to the missus or the little girl a magnificent prize. Come on, you heroes with medals tinkling, show us how you did it! Win yourself a baby doll!'

Some men snatched the rifle, looked down the barrel, and flung it back at him because they said the sights were as twisted as a snake's arse.

Kitty didn't want the baby doll to be won and taken home by any rough man who had killed his share of Germans, for the two Germans she knew were nice people. He was the Ancoats Lane pork butcher who always gave her extra without her having the money to pay for it. He was a small thin man with a thick black moustache, with a straw boater hat dead square on his head, and an apron of thick white and deep blue stripes. His wife, whom he called Elsa, was fat and round. She had blonde hair, blue eyes, and was always smiling, and she wore a pure white coat. Whatever extra her husband put in Kitty's greaseproof paper, she always added another little extra. No, Kitty didn't want the baby doll taken home by men who had killed nice people like her Germans. Perhaps the baby doll was a German baby doll left orphan. She tried not to think any more about the baby doll: it would never be hers. Instead she turned to the sideshows.

At first nothing interested her. She didn't want to see the genuine mermaid, half woman, half fish. She had no wish to go giggling at the smallest midgets in the world as they undressed for bed. She had no desire to see Buffalo Bill's scout who had actually scalped Apache Indians in America's Wild and Woolly West. Neither did she want to stand and stare at Sacco, the bald-headed man who was fasting to death. She met some of the kids she knew tumbling out of Sacco's tent and laughing their heads off. One of the lads had taken up a butty to eat in front of him, and they called the man 'Sago' and asked him if he was fasting to death because he had a bald head. One of the kids said he was fasting to death because he was too mean to buy food, and that he bottled his farts to flavour some stew after the wakes had gone to bed. An attendant had chased them out of the tent. They pushed and jostled Kitty and asked her for a feel. She felt three or four hands feeling up her skirt and had to kick them away and spit on them. They laughed and pushed away with their arms around each other, and told Kitty to go inside and play with Sacco's trouser buttons. They disappeared in lights and steam and coke smoke.

The wakes had been a glimpse of heaven to Kitty, but her money was no use, just as it would be no use in God's real heaven. It must be awful for children who died and went to heaven because they wouldn't be allowed on anything. And then her eyes caught sight of a tent painted with stars and half-moons and it said, 'Consult Merlin'; the man who was Merlin wore a long gown, which was covered in cut-out stars, and he had a long white beard which went half-way down to his chest, and he wore a very tall conical cap, like the dunce's cap at school only ten times as high.

'I will read your future in the stars!' he said in a deep Father Christmas voice. 'The stars never lie!'

Merlin, Kitty knew, was King Arthur's very own special magician and this was a wonderful thing seeing him, or at least his representative, here on an Ancoats croft. Perhaps this was why the music had been playing 'All I Do is Dream of You' when she arrived, although now it was 'When the Love Birds Leave their Old Nest do they Fly to the East or the West?'

'Can I consult you, Mr Merlin, please?' she asked, and it took a lot of courage because there were a lot of people watching.

'Ho-ho-ho! Yes, my little child,' said Merlin. 'If you've got the consultation fee in full. I regret I cannot do half-price for children, for the future is the price in full.' He waved his long drooping sleeves towards the smoke-filled sky. 'Indeed, children should pay more because there is more future for a child than a grown-up.'

'Not if the kid gets flattened by a tram!' shouted some lad in the crowd.

'How very true,' said Merlin. 'And there'll be very little future for you, sonny, if I get my hands on your throat. Ho-ho-ho!'

There was laughter. Kitty dipped her hand in the coat pocket where she'd put her money. It had gone. The money had gone. Her pocket had been picked. Empty, empty, nothing!

'I've no money!' she told Merlin.

'Ho-ho-ho! Then you too have no future, my child, so sod off!'

The crowd laughed again, and Kitty sneaked away from his tent, and sloped into the shadows where she leaned up against the vibrating wheel of a throbbing traction-engine. After a time, when her eyes grew accustomed, she noticed a funny man sitting on the engine's platform. He was funny because he was dressed in coloured combinations, no trousers or jacket, like a picture of Punchinello on a toffee tin. The top half was blue with a large yellow S written on his chest, and the bottom half was red, but very tight to his knees and thighs. He had a bottle to his lips and was glugging booze down his throat, but he didn't look dangerous, so Kitty stayed staring.

A voice on a loudspeaker called for attention and announced that in a little while the greatest daredevil in the civilized world would mount the high tower, set himself on fire, then plunge head-first into a tank of flames. The voice went on to explain that Captain Swiftsure had learnt how to do this when he'd been an ace in the Royal Flying Corps and, after many courageous dog-fights with the famous Baron Von Richtofen had eventually been shot down in flames. Captain Swiftsure had always refused to wear a parachute because it took up ammunition space. In the meantime, the voice went on, there was still time for the lucky ones to collect a fortune on the slot machines.

Kitty looked intently at the man.

'That's right, little Wendy,' he said to her. 'Only my name isn't Swiftsure.' He proudly patted the left side of his breast. 'Used to fly Sopwiths in the RFC. Shot a few down in my time.' He flapped his arms, splashing liquor from the bottle. 'Like a dicky-bird high up in the sky. And now I do this every night except Sunday. And I'm shit-scared, little Wendy. D'y'know what shit-scared is? No, course you don't.' He guzzled at the bottle again, then mumbled a sort of song: 'So stand by your glasses ready and drink to the next man that dies! Hurray!'

An invisible finger at the back of Kitty's neck warned her it was time to be afraid. She pushed her way through the crowd which was making towards the tower. The tank, which stood much higher than her and was about the size of her bedroom, was covered over with a green tarpaulin. Already two men were untying the ropes which fastened the tarpaulin to the sides of the tank. At the back of that was the high tower which went up and up and had a long ladder leading to a platform on top. Suddenly a searchlight flashed on with a click and lit up the tower, and the tarpaulin was pulled off the tank. Something told Kitty she should run back and hold the man's hand and tell him he was a hero, a brave hero. Even Lucifer, accustomed to the flames of hell, wouldn't attempt such a daring feat every night except Sunday. But it was too late. A spotlight picked him up as he pushed through the people, now wearing a red swimming helmet and a black mask. He tottered with the drink: tottered like her father tottered after he had the drink taken.

There was a silence. Assistants went round the crowd with boxes collecting money, and the man on the loudspeaker shouted that every penny made the flames hotter and the water warmer. While the money was being counted, the great steam organ played 'Bye, Bye, Blackbird!' The boss man in a top hat gave a wave to Captain Swiftsure to let him know enough money had been collected to merit the death-defying leap. The organ stopped suddenly. A boy in the red tunic of a regimental drummer-boy tattoo'd a tattoo on his kettledrum, and Captain Swiftsure, holding a burning torch, climbed the straight upright ladder. His foot missed a ladder rung a couple of times, but the people laughed because they thought it was part of the act. The oil on the tank of water was lighted and flames licked up with a roar. Captain Swiftsure reached the platform, put something on his back, and was about to put the torch to it – but Kitty wanted to know no more, she didn't want to look, it was too much dare-devil, too much death-defying. She walked away.

Stallholders were leaning over their stalls to watch. The moon above Hilkirk Street Croft was large and yellow and round in the sky, and looked like a very high town-hall clock. It was cold.

There was a simultaneous sound of a splurp and a thud, a short thud which ended as a thud. A howl came from the people like the wind through ten thousand keyholes, followed by shrieking screams from women and groaning moans from men. He'd missed! He was killed! Kitty felt a sudden sweet death like a shiver and shudder through her body. The astounded and horror-filled faces of the stallholders still glowed red, so the flames were still dancing in the tank. They jumped over their counters and left their stalls and sideshows to join the crowd at the death place.

Kitty knew this was the time the traction-engines had been waiting for. The dragons were taking over, and they would move in and close the circle and flatten all the people who had given pennies for Captain Swiftsure to kill himself. She was terrified, and ran hither and thither, here and there, hitting against tent ropes and falling over cables and scratching her knees on mounds of furnace coke and finished clinkers, until she reached the lamplighted darkness of Palmerston Street. In her hands she was clutching the baby doll.

Word had spread, and people were rushing up to the croft before it was too late to see the body: they didn't notice the little girl and her doll.

She got hurriedly into bed, and hugged the baby doll. She was happy and frightened and excited, and she would never ever go to sleep again. Happy because she now had something to love and kiss and look after and to keep her company: frightened because she knew she'd stolen it, and Sexton Blake might track her down and send her to a bad girls' home where she'd be made to stand for hours in a bowl of ice-cold water. And what would her dad say? Would he take his belt off to her as some dads did to some little girls? But then there was the excitement of a beautiful sadness because she felt that in seeing Captain Swiftsure she had seen Sir Lancelot.

An ambulance bell clanged on its way to the croft, and she fell fast asleep.

*

Wendy became one of the family immediately, for Kitty's dad accepted without question her story that a man who'd driven an aeroplane in the war had shot bull's-eyes for the baby doll and won her, and then had just looked around for the first little girl in the crowd to give it to.

'Ah well, me darling, and isn't that just like them fellers o' the Flying Corps with their wings and that! All officers and gentlemen and swanks.' He put a finger to the tip of his nose and pretended to push his head back to show swank. 'But what a gentleman'd be doing in Ancoats is a matter for thought.'

'Perhaps he was lost.'

'And that'd be the only explanation.'

Her dad was so taken by Wendy that he sat her on the table and did a diddlum and a dance for her. And then Kitty said something without thinking, and for which she immediately wished her tongue to be cut out.

'I won't feel so lonely with her to talk to,' she said.

'Aw, me God!' said her dad, stopping his dance. 'Did ye say lonely?'

'No, dad, I said only. With only her to talk to.'

''Tis the same thing.'

'Aye,' she said, feeling awful guilty.

He bowed away from her, then bowed back to her in gestures of servility. 'Aw, me love, I'm sorry: oh that I am! 'Tis sorry I am, and 'tis sorry to be sure!'

'I'm not lonely, dad, honest I'm not. I have me buke of King Arthur and I can read it to her.'

'Aye, that's all very well and good ye having somebody to talk to, but who is there, will ye tell me, to talk to you by way of return? Answer me that, now!' He thought. 'There's summat'll have to be done about it, but what, I ask myself? 'Tis a conundrum.' He banged his head with his clenched fist in order to get his brains to swirl, then he clapped his hands with sudden inspiration. 'And hasn't yer old dad only gone and come up with the answer, the very ticket?' he said. 'And all ye'll need now, me little loved one, is a touch o' patience.'

And with that things went back to normal, and everything her dad had said, as always, was soon forgotten. There were other things to bother about.

To begin with she realized that Wendy had become the Lady of Shalott. The doll dare never leave the house because Sexton Blake and the bulls would arrest her for stealing, possibly even for kidnapping. And heaven knows what they would do to Wendy – probably chuck her at the back of a fire because she was stolen and sinful property. So Kitty had to keep Wendy indoors for ever, and therefore it was her duty to tell Wendy things about the world. She began by telling her the poem of the Lady of Shalott in order that Wendy would understand her position in life and know what was expected of her: it was like Wendy's catechism. And this was when Kitty received a great shock. She didn't have to read from the book, for she remembered most of the poem. It just slipped off the edge of her tongue, even some of the strange words: '*On either side the river lie long fields of barley and of rye that clothe the world and meet the sky: and through the field the road runs by to many-towered Camelot.*'

There were verses she'd missed out because she'd not been interested in them, but the verses which interested her and made the best rhythms she remembered.

The discovery of this memory was frightening, and the recitation to a stolen doll gave her the feeling of guilt which she now realized the big girls in school must have when nuns took them out of the class to disappear for ever and ever because they had been put up the spout, not that she really knew what being put up the spout was except that she guessed it meant having a baby full of sin. Nevertheless, along with this fearful feeling of having been half-way put up the spout there was a certain tingling excitement which caused her to wet herself a little, and she had to dab her thighs.

'*For ere she reached upon the tide the first house by the waterside, singing in her song she died, the Lady of Shalott.*'

She wasn't quite sure if her dad had forgotten his promise to do something about her loneliness, only once or twice over meals he'd pushed his nose to one side with his finger, winked at her, and said, 'Ah, you'll see.' She hoped he wasn't going to marry a widow or something.

About a week or two later, one night when Ancoats was fast asleep and the only sounds were the plinking and shunting of railway engines and their wagons, Kitty was awakened by bumps and thuds from downstairs. She was relieved when she heard her dad's voice. He seemed to be talking to himself, for he spoke in a loud whisper and there was never an answer.

'Will ye let go! Will ye get off of me bloody foot! Will ye bloody look where ye're bloody going! Do that to me once more and I'll break ye into smithereens!' It was as though her dad was wrestling with a monster from the haunted church, for he wasn't talking to a human being and that was for sure.

After a time she heard her dad coming up the stairs and puffing and panting like an old grampus. She was tired with concentrated listening and fell asleep, but at very first light she was awake and rushed downstairs. In the parlour on the table was a wireless set. A wireless set! But it couldn't be, because nobody in the world could afford a wireless. It must be a stolen wireless set. It stood, with a rounded top and fretwork representing the widening rays of the sun coming from a small half-sun in the bottom corner and it was so polished that if a fly landed on it, it would slide off and break its legs. It had three knobs, and the centre knob had a dial. She turned the centre knob, and numbers and names went round.

'There now, and isn't that something?'

Her dad's voice behind her made her jump, but of course it was five o'clock in the morning, his normal getting-up time: he had to be stripped to the waist and shovelling two furnaces by five-thirty.

'It's a wireless!' gasped Kitty.

'So it is.' He nodded at the wireless set. 'Top o' the morning to ye!'

'You don't talk to wirelesses, dad.'

'They talk to you, so you talk to them, 'tis the decent and mannerly thing to do. They're just like animals, me darling: they understand.'

'How does it work?'

'Sure that's easy. Will ye watch carefully, now?' He turned the dial knob. 'There y'are now, Daventry which is in England. But will ye keep watching.' He continued turning. 'There y'are now – Athlone: and that's our own beloved Ireland. Would ye wonder at that now? Here we can sit in the land of the stranger, of all people, and be hearing the pipes of Erin at the very second of being played and coming right through the walls without letting the bricks stop 'em. Isn't that a miracle?' He began to sing to the set. *'Merrily, cheerily, noiselessly whirring, spins the wheel, swings the wheel to the foot stirring.'* He turned the dial. 'And there's Fécamp which is in France. *Mademoiselle from Armentières, parlez-vous, Mademoiselle from* – ' He turned the dial. 'And there's Hilversum which is in Wales, though I don't know any Welsh songs.'

'It's supposed to sing to you, dad.'

'Well, you can't say it's doing very much of that right now, can you? I'm thinking it needs encouragement.'

'It needs other things, dad. I'll have to learn.'

'Maybe ye can take lessons somewhere. But come on now, there's me snack to be got up, else I'll be late, now.'

Every morning Kitty got up at five to get her dad's snack ready, like her mother had always done. It consisted of four cut slices of bread, each slice an inch thick, and something in between to make sandwiches of, like bacon or cheese or jam or sugar, depending on how much money there was in the house. And then there were two brews. She had to take about half a dozen pieces of newspaper, spoon on a large dollop of condensed milk, Carnation from contented cows, and the spoon scraped clean with a knife: and in the middle of the dollop pour two teaspoonfuls of tea-leaves, from the tin caddy with dogs on. Then she had to screw the papers up tight. When it was brew time at work, her dad would scrape the mixture into an iron kettle and turn steaming boiling water into it. The butties and the brews were put into a small wicker basket on which a lid fastened with an iron rod. Sometimes treasures from the middens were brought back home in this wicker basket. After this, Kitty went back to bed and slept until Singleton's mill hooter blew for eight-fifteen.

This morning she went back to bed overwhelmed with happiness and excitement. There might be rich fathers in this world who could afford to buy their daughters wireless sets for company, but her father loved her so much that he'd risked three years' hard labour in Strangeways prison by stealing one for her, and creeping down the entryways of the night with a heavy burden. Even King Arthur wouldn't have done that for Genevieve, sweet Genevieve. But she now had another secret to keep: she had to find out how to work the wireless without giving the game away that they'd got a wireless.

'I'll give anybody a penny if they can tell me how a wireless works,' she said to the lads. 'Just out of curiosity.'

'Nobody knows how a wireless works,' said Benedict Boyle.

'Oh yes, they do. Conjurers know,' said Mick Dowd, 'for they're boxes of tricks.'

'The priest doesn't believe in them, so it's best to pretend they don't exist, then you don't have to know how they work,' said Vincent Cochrane.

Kitty knew this to be true because the priest had said in the pulpit how evil they were because they brought Protestant church services and hymns into people's houses without bothering what religion they were, and there was one family in Ancoats, though only one family praise be to the Lord, who had been changed from good Catholics into wicked heretics by listening to the things said on the wireless.

But it was important that Kitty should learn how it worked: she was letting her dad down, for, he having provided the wireless, the least she could do was bring him the pipes from Athlone.

On Saturday mornings she waited outside the gramophone and wireless shops in the city, and when a couple walked in, she walked in directly behind them as though she were their little daughter. She stood beside them at the counter, and the shop assistant invariably smiled at all three: sometimes she was given a sweet by the assistant. But sadly most of the couples went in to buy sheet music for their pianos, and although Kitty gained a lot of information about the popular tunes of the day, she was afraid she would run out of music shops, that sooner or later a shop assistant would recognize her as the daughter of the Italian couple who had bought gramophone records of Caruso singing Italian songs, and would wonder why she was now the daughter of the Jewish couple who had called in to price violins. Fortunately there came a time when a man and woman bought a wireless and asked how it worked. The assistant removed the back and explained that it needed a 120-volt HT battery, which lasted six months if used sparingly, and it needed a 9-volt grid-bias battery, which lasted nine months, and it needed a 2½-volt wet accumulator which lasted but a few days, so most people had two, with one always being recharged at an accumulator shop. Kitty's accurate memory took a photograph of the terminal points. It was all very complicated and made her wonder how on earth a man could have invented such a contraption.

'Petty Colette is loved by all the college boys.' 'Shout till the rafters ring.' 'All the world seems bright and gay.' 'The daffodils who entertain at Angelo's and Maxie's.' 'What a glorious feeling, I'm happy again.' 'For I'm in the market for you-oo-oo-oo-oo.' 'Black Bottom, the new twister' and 'Charleston, Charleston'. 'And all the college boys love Petty Colette.'

Kitty, with Sally's help as always, soon put to advantage all the songs she'd picked up in the music shops, and Broadway itself could not have had the sparkling entertainment which the two little girls, all lipsticked and rouged, put on for the Irish navvies of the Land O' Cakes. Coins rolled and tumbled on each other like a wakes roll-a-penny.

Sally was happy because as a good little future nun she was learning in advance the anguish of handing her hard-earned money over to her father for him to become famous in Amerikay. Kitty was twice times two over the moon, for in next to no time she was able to buy a 120-volt HT battery and a 9-volt grid-bias battery from Lewis's. The very act of walking into that warm and well-lighted department store with real money in a real purse was a rewarding thrill. Unfortunately she'd had to steal the purse from Woolworth's, and it bothered her for she felt she should have stolen it from Lewis's where her money was being spent, but Woolworth's sold nothing over sixpence, and the wireless batteries were five shillings the big one, one shilling the little one, added to that the fact it was easier to steal from Woolworth's where everybody rooted around in a heap, whereas in Lewis's young ladies in black frocks would ask if they could be of assistance.

So far so good: the batteries were a piece of cake, but where, oh where, was an accumulator to be found? Where were there such shops as accumulator shops? Certainly not in Ancoats, where most shops seemed to display the three large balls of the pawnbroker. To find an accumulator might be an impossible task.

Some trigger in her brain detonated thoughts from the Tennyson book. It was the quest for the Holy Grail! *'And in the blast there smote along the hall a beam of light seven times more clear than day: and from the long beam stole the Holy Grail.'* She had found it impossible to read and understand, and yet she'd remembered lines like magic, as though some boy angel or girl saint had entered her head.

'O never harp nor horn nor aught we blow with breath or touch with hand was like that music when it came.' It rolled through Kitty's brain like a psalm from the Bible. She had told her dad about the Holy Grail and Sir Galahad and spinning-wheel ladies turning to dust and dragons and lions and swans talking and men growing wings, and her dad had put his head on one side like a pigeon inspecting a black beetle and said that it was the history of Ireland in a nutshell.

About as miraculously as anything in Lord Tennyson's poetry, a Jackie Coogan cap came to Kitty's aid – well, sort of accidentally it did, not as a miracle or anything like that.

It was noticed that Paddy Byrne wore a Jackie Coogan cap in the cemetery. It was presumably to show to his dead grandparents, because the observer remarked that his mother had brought it out from her leather shopping-bag with a diamond design as they entered the cemetery gateway, and had snatched it off his head and punched it down into the bag as they departed. None of the gang up till then had bothered about Jackie Coogan caps, even though this very large and floppy velvet cap had become the rage of kids throughout the civilized world: they were too expensive for Ancoats kids. Glass alleys, whip and toy, piggy sticks, garf rolling, cigarette cards and chewing-gum cricketers were within reach, they were cheap to obtain, lasted for years, and could be brought out of the gas cupboard when the season demanded. Jackie Coogan caps were out of the question.

But that wasn't good enough for Mick Dowd, who snapped his fingers for Dermot MacMahon. Now Dermot was a wandering boy. He disappeared from home for days on end, and his parents simply shrugged and said, 'He'll be back.' Dermot had strange tales to tell of his wanderings. For one thing, he knew the city of Manchester like the back of his hand, whereas the rest of the kids only knew Ancoats, the market, and a long tram ride to Moston Cemetery, sometimes a horse and carriage ride if a parent had died. Dermot had been and returned safe from the district where the mysterious Jews lived: he'd seen their magic writing and heard their strange dragon talk. He'd been to Strangeways prison and heard men choking their last gasps while being hanged by the neck for murders. He'd been to the Ship Canal and seen giant steamers so crowded together that they touched each other nose to tail, and were filled with Chinamen in pigtails. Indeed he'd been on board many of the Manchester liners and begged to be signed on as a cabin boy, but he'd always been marched down the gangplank and kicked up the arse. He knew that the city ended at the River Mersey because he'd swum across the river and found grass and trees and birds singing in the bushes, and he knew that behind the singing bushes were Ancient Britons who covered their naked bodies in blue paint. Dermot knew the posh districts where there were parks with lakes full of tiddlers and jacksharps and ducks begging for bread, and these areas, he claimed, were where boys wore Coogan caps. Mick Dowd appointed Dermot MacMahon as his scout to lead the gang to where Coogan caps might be captured.

When the gang saw a boy wearing such a splendid cap, they surrounded him with a great noise. 'Hey, kid, your buttons are undone and your dick's hanging out,' and 'Hey, kid, there's a hole in your trousers and your arsehole is peeping through,' and 'Hey, kid, there's lice creeping down your hair on to your forehead.' All these things were shouted to the victim at the same time, which confused him; and then somebody would grab his cap and shake it, and the rest of the gang would stamp their feet as though killing the hundreds of lice which had toppled out. 'It's swarmin! We'd better gerrit to nurse who'll gerrit purrin paraffin!' they would shout and run off with his cap with the victory whoops of Red Indians who had taken a scalp.

Soon every member of Mick's gang wore a Coogan cap, and it became known even as far as the Italian quarter of the district that the success had been brought about by Dermot MacMahon's knowledge of the territory. Kitty saw him as Sir Galahad.

'What d'y'want an accumulator shop for?' he asked, after she'd approached him.

'For a bloody accumulator,' she replied.

'Aye but – '

'Aye but me bum! Ask no questions you'll be told no lies.'

'What's in it for me? A feel?'

'A shilling.'

Such an amount of money staggered him. 'Bloody hell! For twelve pennies I can get twelve feels from twelve different tarts: twenty-four if they'll do it for a ha'penny.'

'Aye, but not from me. Is that okay?'

Dermot swung the peak of his cap to the back of his head and strode wide strides down Palmerston Street to let her know he was on the quest.

A few days later he whistled her shrill between his two fingers, and she ran running.

'Found one,' he said, polishing his fingernails on his jacket like Tarzan would do on his leopard skin. 'But it's a tram ride.' He explained how she'd have to catch the 51 from the haunted church, and get off at Ardwick Green, and turn here and there, up and down, left and right, and there in a little back street, hidden away, was an accumulator shop with a big window all painted yellow. 'And I reckon that's worth a bob,' he concluded, holding his hand out. 'What's more, tart, for another ha'penny I'll let you put your hand up me trouser leg.'

'I'm too old to play with toys,' said she, and giving him his shilling she skipped away.

The journey was more exciting than anything Mrs Giyaski had told her class about Amundsen, Shackleton or Scott, or perhaps more appropriately about Livingstone and Stanley going up the Zambezi.

There was a black man on the tram, and she'd never seen a real black man before: neither apparently had the tram guard for he made great sport of the man, and winked at the other pasengers for support.

'Ever been on a tram before, Sambo? 'Course not, they're

canoes where you come from eh? Umba umba umba!' He pretended to paddle a canoe. 'What's for tea tonight, Sambo? Stewed missionary? Walla walla umba!' The guard held up his hands for the passengers not to panic. 'Keep calm, everybody!' he shouted. 'This tram is being followed by crocodiles.' He put his hand to his ear. 'Dem der drums is telling me dat Ardwick Green is infested wid man-eating lions and tigers.' From time to time he patted the black man on the head and gave him a friendly wink and a grin. Kitty had to put her hand over her mouth so that the black man would not see her laughter, but she had to burst out laughing, as did most of the passengers, when the guard recited:

'I wish I was a nigger boy from far across the sea
Where lots of other nigger boys would come and play with me,
With elephants to ride upon, and tigers fierce to chase,
I'd never have to go to school or wash my hands and face.'

Just before the tram reached Ardwick Green an elderly man with half a dozen books under his arm boarded and sat down with a puff and a grunt next to the black man.
'Hello, doctor!' he said.
'Thank heavens!' said the black man. 'So this tram is going to the university after all! I was beginning to think it was on the way to the Zoological Gardens.'
The tram guard began emptying the confetti from his ticket punch, and straightening the many brightly coloured tickets in his clip, and examining the outside pulley rope, and leaning out to make sure the tram was still on the tram lines, whistling a non-musical tune between his teeth throughout.
Ardwick Green was the wonder of creation. There was a cinema much bigger and posher and redder than the Palmy Picturedrome. It was called the Coliseum, and right above the entrance, to advertise *Hell's Angels*, was an almost life-sized poster of a two-winged aeroplane with circles shooting deadly machine-gun bullets one after the other at another two-winged aeroplane with a cross. It was magnificent, but she had to take her eyes away when she thought of Wendy's dad. Absolutely next door to the cinema was a great high palace called the Ardwick

Empire. This was a real music-hall theatre. Lit up in red lights were words which could be seen from the moon, and they said: 'Will Fyffe, the Ship's Engineer, singing "I Belong to Glasgow".' Beneath were smaller names of singers, acrobats, high-wire cyclists, and a professor with his performing wonder-dogs.

People queuing up to go into both places were being entertained by a jazz band of ex-servicemen wounded in action; and there was a glowing stove of hot chestnuts looked after by an Italian in a large hat, with an ornamental black moustache which curved like a music symbol; and a barrow of greengroceries owned by a man in a brown coat who shouted, 'They're lovely!' Ardwick Green was five main roads, all with trams going up and down them and clanging their clang-bells and making blue sparks from the overhead tram wires. She had to be careful and go up Stockport Road and not Hyde Road, as Sir Galahad had warned.

Eventually, after twisting and turning, running and walking and occasionally hopping, she came to what must be the accumulator shop. It looked quiet and almost ashamed of itself. Its large once-upon-a-time shop window was painted yellow except for a margin of clear glass near the top which only a giraffe could look through. She had to hide behind a lamp-post and wait for a minute or two in case it was a Chinese laundry, because Chinese laundries painted their windows, but she saw a man leaving with a square jar which he carried by a handle, and she felt fairly confident it was an accumulator and that this was the accumulator shop.

It was dark inside, but wonderful. Merlin's tent on the wakes could not have been more magical. Ram Jam Singh's hut on the market could not have been more mysterious. There was a strong smell of sweet dark vinegar, the holy incense of wireless. Indeed it felt more sacred and nearer to heaven than the church itself at twilight Benediction. A stable had brought God into the world, and it was this back-street shop which was in touch with the stars in his heaven.

All three walls of the shop were lined with shelves, shelf upon shelf: shelves almost to the ceiling, shelves down to the concrete floor: and all these shelves were crammed like soldiers on parade with accumulator jars, and all joined by wires. There were rhythmic plinkings and bubblings, although it would be impossible to bet money on which accumulator would plink next. In a corner an immense jar was seated in a basket like an Easter egg in a straw nest. Near a door were dials like the top-halves of clocks, with needles shivering slightly in the dials. There was a small glass window between the shelves on the back wall, and Kitty detected movement in it. This must be the kitchen in which the accumulator man lived. But superimposed over all this was music playing from a wireless set she couldn't see: then there was the sound of motor-car traffic, and a woman's voice called 'Violets! Lovely sweet violets!' and a voice shouted 'Stop!'

The glass-panelled but curtained door of the kitchen opened and the accumulator man shuffled through. Kitty wanted to scream and run away, for the man was horrible and ugly. The left half of his face seemed eaten away and twisted, causing that corner of his mouth to turn down. His left eye seemed white, still, fixed and blind like the eye of a codfish on a marble slab. He was bald on that side too, although there was plenty of hair on his right side, and his right eye looked loving and kind, and the right side of his mouth curled upwards in a smile.

'Don't worry, little lady – I won't eat you!' he mumbled, and it was a mumble, not a talk. He touched his scars. 'Done with sulphuric acid when I first started in accumulators. The big jar was on a top shelf and fell on me.' He laughed a nice laugh. 'One of the first casualties of wireless, you might say. Never had it with the crystals. I'm like Squashy Motor. D'y'know who Squashy Motor is? He's the hunchback of that whopping cathedral in Paris. They did a play about him. I get all the plays. And all the plays of Mr Shakespeare: I bet you never heard of him.' He pointed to the large bottle in the corner. 'That there's sulphuric acid, and I pour some in every accumulator.' Kitty thought what a brave man he was to have been half-eaten by the acid and yet still continue working with it. It was like having a dragon in a bottle which could spring out and devour him any time.

He must have read her thoughts. 'I'm very happy being an accumulator man,' he said. 'Oh, very happy and contented. Here we are, in this room, in the middle of London town with Big Ben telling me the time. And in me kitchen I can make toast by the fire and be in Paris and listening to the can-can dance what brassy ladies show their frilly bloomers to, and I can do a boiled egg to have with me toast. And in me bedroom is Berlin with lots of oompah-pah and "Bull and Bush" bands. And I can eat fish and chips with plenty of salt and vinegar to opera from Italy. And on a very clear night, when all the stars is polished and sparkling, I can pick up America, very faint and going and coming, but America. And while I do sausages, Mr Christopher Stone comes through the walls and plays gramophone records without me having to wind the handle or change the record. And I'm open on Sunday for people what is urgent, and I like being open on Sunday though you get a lot of hymns. The world comes through them walls.'

Kitty felt that any girl would want to marry an accumulator man, even if ugly with acid, for she could close her eyes and listen to the music.

She finally got around to asking if she could buy two accumulators. She was in luck: he had two second-hand ones because the previous owner had been converted to electricity from gas, and they'd bought a wireless which ran off the mains. He charged half a crown each, and the charging-up price was twopence a time, so she took a charged one, and left the other to be wired up on charge. She walked the long way home with it because she was afraid the rattle and jog of the tram might splash sulphuric acid down her and burn her knees away: and she didn't want to get home until dark so that nobody would know they had a wireless.

From memory she connected up the batteries and the accumulator, and music came. It was so thrilling she danced, although it wasn't dance music, and she brought Wendy down and sat her on a cushion on a chair near the wireless to listen. She could hardly wait for her dad to come home from the Ben Brierley. He was, of course, three sheets in the wind.

'There y'are, dad – Athlone!'

It was a man talking, but he wasn't talking English, and her dad banged his fist down on the table. 'And, would ye know,' he shouted, 'a man leaves his beloved Ireland, and what do they do behind his back? Sure they start talking foreign, that's what they do. They've become bloody heathens and scallywags, so they have!'

An English voice came on to say they'd just heard the news in Irish.

'Irish is it? Sure 'tis a wonderful language is Irish, and don't I wish I knew a few o' the words,' said he, with tears coming into his eyes. 'And would ye now obtain Gertie Gitana for me, my child?'

'Who's Gertie Gitana?'

'Who's Gertie Gitana? Is that a question I'd ever thought to hear? There's yer blooming head filled with the Virgin Mary, the Mother o' God, God bless her, and yet more blessed is Gertie Gitana. Oh a lovely lady, and 'twas her who gave the world "Nellie Dean", a fitting end to an evening's fine entertainment.' He switched the wireless off and began singing to it:

'There's an old mill by the stream, Nellie Dean,
Where we used to sit and dream, Nellie Dean.'

Kitty clutched Wendy and went up to bed, leaving her dad still singing.

'And the waters as they flow seem to murmur sweet and low, You are my heart's desire, I love you, Nellie Dean.'

Kitty knelt down by the bed, crossed herself, and prayed to the Virgin that she might grow up to be one of the ladies who said, 'Violets! Lovely sweet violets!' on the wireless; and she prayed that people would not convert to electricity so that the accumulator man would live happily ever after; and she prayed for all black men, tram guards and performing dogs.

Mrs Giyaski was in the middle of telling the children how the little girls in China had their feet bound up tight so that they would grow up with tiny feet, and that the boys played with kites and had a kite festival, and the girls played with dolls and had a doll festival, when two nuns walked into the classroom and whispered to her, smiling around at the children as they did so. Mrs Giyaski pointed to Jane at the back of the class, and the smaller smiling nun walked down between the desks, held out her hand and asked Jane to go along with her.

The little girl screamed, 'No, don't let them! Please don't let them! I'm sorry! I'm sorry!' The nuns had to hold her and carry her out of the classroom still screaming, 'It wasn't me what did it, but I'm sorry: I'm sorry to God! Let me go home!'

The class of girls fidgeted their bums on their seats with excitement. One by one, each giggling girl made a circle with the pointing finger and thumb of her left hand, and pushed the outstretched pointing finger of her right hand in and out of the circle very fast. This was always done when a girl was dragged out of the classroom. Kitty, along with the rest of the girls, made the finger movement out of tradition, not knowing the meaning. She even stood up to let the class see how quickly she could jerk her fingers. But on this occasion, Mrs Giyaski looked away from the sad business with the nuns for a second and caught Kitty in the act.

'Come out here, you dirty, filthy, disgusting little girl!' she shouted. Suddenly, the excitement which had been in Kitty's shoulders and arms with the warmth of a Thermogene pad rushed down to her knees and feet. She felt her knees weak and trembling, and her feet tingled as she walked to the front. She couldn't understand what she'd done which was so filthy and disgusting: and it was no use asking Mrs Giyaski because Mrs Giyaski always made it worse for girls who pretended to be innocent.

The teacher indicated for her to hold an arm fully stretched with the palm facing upward. She brought the black leather strap with its many thongs out of her desk, and swung it over her shoulder. She didn't strike immediately but looked out through the window as though there was something to see: and then she lashed the strap down on Kitty's hand. It hurt and made her hand feel dead and was like the earth stopping still with all its classrooms and pictures and wooden floors. The teacher nodded for her to raise the other arm. Kitty wanted to beg forgiveness for whatever it was she was being punished for, but she held her hand out automatically. Once more the leather came down and split her hand into numbness. She returned to her desk feeling that her hands had been sewn inside cushions, which they sometimes did to girls who couldn't stop scratching their heads. There were tears in her eyes, but Kitty was glad they didn't roll down her face, which would have caused the girls to laugh at her in the playground for being a cry-baby. Mrs Giyaski then went on to say that the Chinese grew rice which they ate with chopsticks like darning needles.

'What's it about?' she asked Sally after school.

'What's what?'

'That!' She made the finger movements. 'And getting the strap for being filthy?'

'It means being got done,' said Sally. 'And Jane was done. It was in't paper. Rape it said. Look!' she went on, and she made the circle with her finger and thumb. 'That's what we've got between us legs. And this – ' She held out her straight finger, ' – is what fellers and lads have, and they stick it in us.'

'That's daft!' said Kitty. 'Lads've just got little blobs they pee through.'

'Ah, but when they grow up they become big and stiff as iron pokers. Haven't you heard the big girls talking about getting poked?'

'I always thought it was a sort of punishment.'

'Perhaps it is. Perhaps it's God's punishment for us being girls.'

'There's nowt about it in't catechism, so you're telling a pack o' fibs!' shouted Kitty with triumph, for the catechism was the beginning and end: but her victory lasted less than a second when she realized what all the chalk drawings on street walls and lavatory walls were truly about. 'Have you been poked?' she asked Sally.

'Aye – once. Just the once like. By me dad, but he'd been drinking at a funeral and was very drunk. Me mam chased him round the house with the carving knife and threatened to cut his throat and called him the limb of the very old Harry. She made him get on his knees and swear to the Blessed Virgin he'd never do owt o't sort again. And she made me kneel down and cross meself and swear I'd not breathe a word to a living soul.'

'You've just told me,' said Kitty. 'And I'm a living soul.'

'Aye, I know. And I'll have to mention it at next Confession for breaking me oath.'

Suddenly Kitty didn't want to go near Sally any more, and felt repelled because Sally was dirty and filthy. She felt that if she touched Sally, Sally would feel cold and goose-pimply, and it would be the coldness of contagious sin like chicken-pox. Sally may have sensed Kitty's feelings for she walked away.

'Dead rotten when it's your dad,' Sally sniffed. ''Cos it takes away Father Christmas for ever.'

Kitty was angry that Father Christmas had been brought into it, because nobody believed in Father Christmas, and yet everybody did. It was easy to say you didn't believe, until it got to Christmas Eve and you looked up at the sky and felt you'd better get to sleep fast in case, just in case, although nothing really had happened when you woke up, but Sally had no right to shatter a belief which perhaps wasn't a belief. She wanted to run to Sally and put her arms round her shoulders and tell her there was a Father Christmas: but she couldn't. Instead she called her back, 'Hey, Sally!' and when Sally looked round, probably expecting Kitty to sympathize, all she saw was Kitty pushing her finger into a finger circle and laughing, 'Pokey-pokey!'

But on her own Kitty was far from laughing: she was frightened and disgusted to a sick feeling in her toes and stomach, and wished she could float down the river and be gently dead.

There was a small bolt on her bedroom door. It had never been used and had been painted over with dark oak varnish several times and couldn't be moved by hand, but she nudged it loose with the rolling pin. From now on she could lock herself up from her dad: she would be safe, and he could not, in a drunken mood, take away her Christmas.

There were other men she immediately became mortally afraid of and knew she'd have to avoid on pain of death.

She frequently bought penny bags of broken biscuits from the Co-op stores, and a lot of these crumbs were given to the Monkey Man. He was an ugly dwarf, and it was said with reliability that he was half ape. He looked like a monkey. His hair grew in a V down his forehead; his ears were large and round and stood out; he had a split lip and his teeth protruded. But whoever had him always sent him out smart, dressed like a little toff: it was obvious his keeper obtained the best of clothes from the penny bazaars put on by churches in the better areas. Pinned to him was a beautifully hand-written label which said, 'I am harmless. Please do not hurt me.' He could clamber smack-smack up a lamp-post and swing on its arm, and sway and swing with the one hand until he could grab the other arm. Most people gave him sweets and toffees. The girls only threw stones at him when he tried to climb lamp-posts on which they were swinging with ropes. Kitty knew he had to be avoided.

Back Entry Bertie would also have to be given short shrift. He lived in the back entries and never left them. They said he curled up and went to sleep, even in the rain and frost, down a back entry. He wore an over-long army greatcoat; he rarely washed or shaved, and stunk to high heaven of his own dried shit. Kitty's dad said the poor bugger was shell-shocked, and thought the entries were safe trenches and everywhere else was no-man's-land. The lads had great sport with him, and would save some of their Guy Fawkes fireworks just for the howling fun of catching him napping and tossing a loud banger at him, when he would screech and claw like a tom cat hanging from a clothes-line. After these attacks, when the boys ran away punching each other out of pure fun, Kitty would sneak down and give him some broken biscuits, and he would sing to her, *'It's a long way to tickle Mary, it's a long way for Flo,'* but she now realized it was a dirty song, and he might do dirty, filthy, disgusting things. From now, he had to be avoided like the plague.

More and more she became dependent on poetry books, which she read to Wendy after she had bolted the bedroom door. She liked Mr Wordsworth who didn't talk much about men, but spoke about little Lucy who had died: this poem made her cry. And she liked Mr Longfellow's 'Hiawatha' because she could see herself as Minnie Ha-Ha, the wife of a clean and brave warrior leader who lived only in the forest of a book, and no harm could come in a book.

She loved her wireless set, particularly for Saturday Night Music Hall and the play afterwards, although she mistrusted it when a man was speaking on his own, feeling that the real man might be waiting for her in the scullery, which had no gas light. Nevertheless it was a pleasant routine every Saturday morning to go to the library, and then make the tram trek to the accumulator shop, all in preparation for Saturday night. Music Hall was always on late enough for her to do the song and dance at the Land O' Cakes and her market shopping and stealing. She had no fear of the accumulator man: perhaps because of his connection with radio waves in the invisible air. If anything, he seemed afraid of being in the shop with her because he always kept the shop door open if he had occasion to talk to her about the comedian who played a violin but never played it, and the man who played motor-car horns, and the two cads from college, or whatever.

There was a play one Saturday about a girl's dad dying, and it made her feel sorry for locking the door against her own dad. It bothered her every time she put the bolt in the socket; in fact putting the bolt in the socket was a dirty act like the fingers, and she felt she was doing a dirty act on her dad. It mithered her.

Something urged her to visit her dad at work. He would be stone sober then, and she might, but only might, be able to explain to him that she bolted her door for fear of bogeymen and nothing else. Of course he'd laugh and say there were no such things as bogeymen, and if there were they'd be able to walk through walls and doors in any case. If only as a penance, she felt compelled to call on him at work, and as long as she didn't tell him why she'd called, there'd be no argument to that.

In order to give herself an excuse, she deliberately forgot to put her dad's brew papers in his basket. About eight o'clock she set off up Palmerston Street to the district across Ashton New Road known as Holt Town. She'd never been before, and all she knew was that her dad worked at the Refuse and Cleansing Department Yard off New Viaduct Street. People called it the Shit Yard, but it wasn't a shit yard because, as her dad had often pointed out to other men, sometimes with his fists, the yard only disposed of the muck from the middens. The work was dirty, he'd say, but the money was clean.

Finding the yard was easy, for there was a muck cart heaped high and pulled by a great heavy lion of a horse rattling up Viaduct Street.

'Are ye going to the muck yard?' she shouted to the horseman.

'I am that,' smiled he.

She held up a brew in each hand. 'I'm looking for me dad, for did he not forget his brews this morning?'

The horseman extended his muscular and tattooed arm. 'Then up ye get, me love and ye'll arrive there like a queen.'

She seemed to fly through the air like a top twanged from a diabolo. The queen reference was good to Kitty, for they were doing Queen Boadicea in history, and, standing in the muck cart, she felt like the great British queen riding her chariot.

'Where's yer dad from?' asked the horseman.

'Angel Meadow.'

'I didn't ask where he hoped to end up, I asked where he came from in the old country. Like I'm from the City o' Cork on the banks o' the sweet River Lee.'

'He's from Kilkee in the County of Clare, and he learnt to swim by holding on to a cow's tail and making it swim the River Shannon.'

'Did he now?'

'Aye – he did.'

'Kilkee man, d'y'say?'

'Aye.'

'Then 'tis the boilers he's on?'

'Aye.'

The horseman said no more but picked up a comic and began looking at it. The horse knew its own way to the Refuse and Cleansing Department Yard, and headed towards the mighty gasometers which stood like castles.

They arrived at a wide entrance, and the horseman lifted her down with the same lightness of the top returning to the diabolo string.

'As the Scotchies say, I be taking the high road and you be taking the low road, me lovie. Just ye be telling the Tipperary man in the hut 'tis the Kilkee man ye're seeking.'

The one cobbled road inclined upwards, and this was the one

the horse trundled and clip-clopped up, making sparks on the cobbles. The other cobbled road declined downwards towards an enormous brown wooden shed – indeed everything was brown, dusty comfortable brown.

The Tipperary man pointed to the bottom of the giant's shed, which was not a bottom at all: the shed seemed to be standing on nothing but iron pillars, it was a gap. Kitty had never been down such a wide roadway of cobbles before: it was like walking on a wide river of rocks. Half-way down there was a bridge, and when she dared look over it there was a black stream which must have been the Medlock. Pipes peed out green, yellow and red steaming liquids. By looking up, she could see where the horse and cart went. The horse pulled and heaved to the top of the shed – except, just as the shed had no bottom, neither did the shed have a top, it just fenced in a mountain of cinders, clinkers, ashes, rags, tea-leaves, charred newspapers and all the other things people threw in their middens. The cart tipped its load on the top of the mountain, then the horse turned and clip-clopped down again. Everything Kitty saw was rusty brown, and the air was filled with millions and millions of brown and golden particles.

'Me own darling!'

Kitty looked in the shadows of the shed gaps and there was her dad, stripped to the waist with black and brown streaks of sweat running down him. She walked timidly towards him, holding out the brews. 'I forgot to put them in your basket, dad.'

Her dad click-clicked with his tongue and shook his head from side to side. ''Tis the eighth wonder o' the world, Joe,' said he. 'Me daughter walks these many miles into a strange land so that her old dad can have his mug o' tea.'

Joe was a black man, and Kitty nearly giggled at the thought that he'd never have to go to school or wash his hands and face because the dirt didn't show on his body like it did on her dad's. He had great white teeth, all perfect teeth, not half rotted like most men's; and he gave her a smile which almost lit up the shadows. 'Which he share wid me, else we'd both go raving like dem hydrochloric dogs,' he said, sticking a very red tongue out and pretending to pant like a dog.

'What part of Ireland are ye from?' her dad asked Joe, giving him a nudge and a wink.

'Kingston, sir.'

As they talked, her dad scraped a brew from the paper with what she guessed was an old bayonet into a large teapot or kettle, it was hard to tell which, and he turned a tap of hissing steaming water into it. Joe meanwhile washed two large chipped enamel mugs at another steaming tap.

Throughout this, midden rubbish continued to slide down the mountain, and one or another of the men would belt a furnace door open with a shovel, spit, and then shovel half a dozen shovelfuls of rubbish into the almost-white and sparking furnace. They had four furnaces to keep fed and, as they shovelled, more and more rubbish slid into the gaps left by the shovels. There were two dead boilers, and Kitty guessed they'd been given a holiday in order to be boiler-cleaned, a job her dad sometimes had to go in on Sundays for.

Her dad and Joe, just the two men, were fighting to keep this mountain from growing.

'What'd happen if you was both poorly-sick and there was no one to stop the mountain growing?' she asked.

'Then it'd grow and grow till it became so high it would cut out the sun, and it'd always be night,' said her dad.

'And der'd be de Great Plague and de Black Death and de locusts like it say in der Bible,' added Joe.

Kitty had a sudden sniffing of pride for her dad and Black Joe from Kingston. Every hour of the day they were saving the city, and the city didn't want saving for it kept filling its middens; the conditions were like being in the real live hell, God's own Devil's hell, for when a furnace door opened the heat sucked her lungs out, and the faster they shovelled at the base of the mountain, the quicker the giant heap was replaced on the top by strong horses climbing into the sky. But the two men, the mick and the nigger, were happy as sandboys, and they both did a song and a dance which consisted of 'Oh, ye bugger ye are, ye bugger ye are, a bugger a bugger a boo,' which was repeated over and over again like a skipping-rope song. Eventually they both sat down on the refuse, with more and more dust sliding down behind their backs, and her dad opened his basket and gave Joe a butty while they sipped the tea.

The shed and the mountain and the furnaces and the two men and Kitty seemed to shake gently all the time to a *chur-chur-chung, chur-chur-chung, chur-chur-chung*. Kitty felt it was Lucifer's pulse beating. Later she guessed it was the making of potash, for once, over a year ago when she'd been a very little girl, she'd asked her dad what he made at work because all school dads, at least those working, made things at work, and he'd said potash, which she'd thought at the time was a giant cauldron of Irish stew, perhaps for the dads who weren't working.

When it was time to leave, Kitty walked up from this yawning throbbing chasm towards the sun, which due to the millions of brown dust specks was a round red ball. Gradually, nearer the street level, the dust lessened and the sun became too bright to look at. It was a nice day, and Kitty felt she had ascended into heaven. She wondered what naughty things Jesus had done for him to have descended into hell to begin with. Why was it necessary? Perhaps he looked in to make sure the tortured souls had not forgotten their brews.

The year was at the spring, the day was at the morn. A horse with an empty cart was clip-clopping away from the high road and she shouted up to the horseman, 'Can ye give me a ride, mister? Me dad's a muckman like you.'

'In that case, mavourneen, hop ye on to me golden coach.'

She flew on to the cart platform.

'A muckman?' asked the horseman.

'Aye. He's Kilkee.'

'Kilkee, is it? What drinks in the Ben Brierley?'

'Aye.'

'Will ye tell him Limerick Larry was asking after him?'

'I'll do that.'

'Aye,' said Limerick, to conclude the introductory part of the conversation. 'And now will ye tell me what yer wishes are? Is it to fly up in the air in this horse and cart like the old woman on her broom who went ninety times as high as the moon?'

'Just across Ashton New Road, please?' said she, and she felt as bursting proud as the day she'd stood in the pulpit as the Virgin

Mary. The forgiveness of sins, said the Creed: and she would not bolt her bedroom door again because she'd learnt there were good men and bad men, and her dad and Black Joe were live heroes who would grow into dead saints.

'If I had a talking picture of you-oo – Boop-boop-a-doo!' Kitty put more and more enthusiasm into her singing and dancing, and 'you-oo' gave her plenty of chances to point to men. She needed more money, for her responsibilities were growing. Now that she knew her dad shared his brews and snacks with Black Joe, she made more brews and twice as many butties: she even went to the special tea-shop with its shelves filled with large red and gilt tins and bought five penn'orth o' Darjeeling because she felt that most of the many names of teas were genuine nigger-land names. She spent more money on German meat, and she became more selective in the stuff she stole from the market shopping-baskets. As she told Sally, 'Once there was only me and me dad to take care of, but now I've got me dad and a wireless set and a nigger and a baby doll.' She had to buy cotton remnants to make new clothes for Wendy. 'Oh, it's all too much!' she sighed, putting the back of her hand to her forehead, not meaning it, but loving it. She pointed personally up to the happy man astride the jar. 'And it's all right for you just sitting on a bottle day and night. Some of us have cares!'

Since her descent into the muck yard, and her subsequent ascent into the sunshine, she had learnt to forgive, yet she still found it difficult to forgive Sally. Sally, perhaps sensing this, boop-boop-a-dooped with more determination than ever, obviously boop-boop-a-dooping to please Kitty. The trouble was that Kitty didn't quite know what to forgive Sally for. She knew her dad's sin had been to poke her mother, and she, Kitty, had been put in her mam's belly as a baby for punishment; but although her mam was resting up in heaven, her dad was down below paying for his sin in the Corporation Yard. He must be forgiven and prayed for. But she couldn't sort Sally's sin out, unless it was for telling her what poking was all about, in which case it might be a joint sin because she had listened to Sally, even asked her questions, so perhaps Sally's sin was that she'd made Kitty sin by listening to dirty talk. Anyway, in spite of all Sally's boop-boop-adoops Kitty didn't want to touch her. In any case she had to rush through the market and then home quickly for the man with the monologues was in Music Hall.

On Monday morning the nuns carried Sally out of the classroom, and Kitty hated everything and everybody, for why did the girls always scream they were sorry: why didn't they spit in the nuns' faces? The girls bum-wiggled with excitement, and Kitty slapped the girl next to her hard in the face with her knuckled fist because she made poking finger movements.

'Come out to the front, you wicked, violent, horrid wretch!' shouted Mrs Giyaski. Kitty stepped proudly to the front. She was going to get the leather strap for Sally.

'Can I touch yer bum?' asked Paddy Byrne on the morning of August Bank Holiday.

Kitty spat in his face.

'I love you,' he said, wiping the spit from his eyes with the sleeve of his jersey.

'Aye, well go to't doctor's. He'll give you a bottle for it. Sides, you're going to be a priest, and priests aren't supposed to muck about with bums and that.' She was about to skip off when Mick Dowd came up and thumped the top half of her arm with a brass knuckleduster which he'd got from swapping twenty cigarette cards of cricketers. It would bruise blue. 'Hey, tart, what you talking to him for?'

''Cos God gave me a tongue,' she said, and pulled it out at him, then she put her thumb to her nose and wiggled her fingers. 'Fat Bacon!' she sneered.

'I'll bloody mollycrush you for fat baconing me!' he yelled. He grabbed her wrist and twisted her arm up her back, holding her shoulder with his other hand so that she couldn't swing away from the pain. 'I'll twist it till yer bone cracks in two,' he said. 'Less ye tell me what ye was talking about.'

Kitty was in pain, a ripping, burning, searing pain, and she feared he would break her arm or her shoulder.

'He wanted to touch me bum! I spit on him!' she sobbed. 'Give over hurting, please!'

He put his knee in her back and sent her sprawling into a wall, which scrawped her nose and made it bleed.

Paddy Byrne made a fat bacon at him as he was about to run off but Mick jumped on Paddy like a kangaroo cotton gin with many arms flailing many fists, separating some of the pimples and skin on Paddy's face. He might have gone on pulverizing Paddy but Constable Kennedy appeared from nowhere like the genie in *Aladdin*. He grabbed Mick by the seat of his backside, leaving Mick to kick and sprawl like a spider when somebody holds a lighted taper to its web in the lavatory.

'Well now, and if it isn't the spalpeen what's going to grow up to take the eight o'clock walk,' said the constable.

'I was only telling me bloody tart that she love me!' shouted Mick.

'Love is it? Is that what it is? Sure I'd hate to be in the shoes o' them you took a disliking to. Come on, me brave hero, it's a good tanning ye'll be getting down the back entry where we'll not be disturbed by man or beast.'

'Hey, tart, say summat! Say summat!' begged Mick as he seemed to swim like a frog in the bobby's grip.

Kitty skipped and flapped her arms.

'*Let me fly, says little birdie, mother let me fly away.*' And with that, she skipped and flapped down the street like a good fairy off to do a good deed. She was pleased she'd remembered the cradle song from Mr Tennyson's, no, Lord Tennyson's poem; and she felt like Pippa in Lord, no, Mr Browning's poem, except the hillside was filled with crowded black crowded houses and there was no lark on the wing, only a pigeon fluttering on the cobbles because a kid had catapulted its wing, and it was waiting for somebody to come out with a coal hammer or a shovel and belt it out of its misery.

August Bank Holiday was good even though it meant a thunderstorm at night: at least God was in his heaven: not like Good Friday. How she hated Easter when all the millions of chimneys on all the hills poured black stems of smoke, a forest of smoke, up to heaven, enough smoke to make God and all his angels cough and need lozenges. God was away from heaven for three days every year on account of getting crucified. On August Bank

Holiday he was at home and no doubt resting for the air was heavy and dry.

Her dad found the holiday difficult, for on this dry-as-dust day he had to go easy with the money in his pocket in order to have enough for essential booze on the normal Saturday night and Sunday dinner. Kitty found him at home singing to the wireless:

'Mellow the moonlight to shine was beginning,
Close by the window young Eileen was spinning,
Bent o'er the fire her blind grandmother sitting
Was crooning and groaning and drowsily knitting.'

He looked up. 'Ah, me precious darling, sure the wireless is a gift from God, is it not? Did ye know when I first clapped me peepers on yer darling mother – may she rest in heaven – she was spinning the wool on the wheel? Ah, sure this sacred jumble of wires and bits o' things has brought it all back.'

'Then why don't you switch it on, dad, and it'll be even more better?'

'Because if I did, it'd tell me things I'd not want to be bothering me head about. But by talking to summat which ye know has the brain, it helps bring back the happy memories. *"Land of song, said the warrior bard, Though all the world betrays thee, One sword at least thy right shall guard, One faithful heart shall praise thee."*'

'Hey, dad, that's poetry.'

'It is indeed, me very own love. I'm a poet and don't know it.'

It blushed and flushed her that she'd got the gift of memory and poetry from her father, and it worried her stomach that the sins of the fathers are visited on the children, and maybe learning poetry was a passed-down sin. Her dad cleared his throat: 'The sun is shining in the sky, and I'm feeling powerful dry. All I can do is scrat and think how nice 'twould be to get a drink.'

Kitty couldn't resist it. She applauded him as she herself was applauded on Saturday nights. He winked with delight. 'The last bit was by me,' he said, 'but the warrior bard was by another feller altogether.'

Kitty ran upstairs and unearthed a shilling piece which she'd hidden under the base of a small plaster statue of St Francis of

Assisi, who had his nose smashed because she'd once had to throw the statue at a mouse. She ran down again and gave it to her dad. 'Take this, dad, before you burst, here's a bob to slake your thirst.'

Her dad spat on the coin before putting it in his pocket, and the two of them burst out laughing. He bowed deferentially to her, and touching his forelock backed slowly out of the house. She saw him through the window doing a brisk bog-trot on his bright and merry way to the Ben Brierley.

The thunderstorm came as promised that night, and the rain sounded like the impatient steam from a stood-still railway engine, the lightning zip-zapped and lit up the picture of the Virgin on the wall, the thunder was so cracking splitting loud that she felt she was the only person in the world and was growing bigger and more get-attable every second. Wendy was frightened and she had to cuddle her close. And then the storm ended suddenly: there was a draught of cold air cutting under the door, and there was the safe and reassuring yowl of the all-night tram, which was God's city rainbow sound that he would never ever again flood the world.

The air cleared, and she could hear the Medlock gurgle in flood, but not flood enough to swill the street. It was with the feather-stretching pride of a Boggart Hole Clough peacock that she got up at five o'clock: the morning was going to be toe-tingling long, an hour was going to be three hours, and three hours was going to be for ever, because that afternoon Mrs Giyaski was taking the class to the Opera House in Quay Street as a long-planned summer holiday treat. It had cost the sum of one shilling at a penny a week, paid over each Monday morning; the shilling she gave her dad had been hidden away to buy ice-cream, salted peanuts and a Vimto. However, by running errands for the neighbours she managed to raise twopence, with which she bought twopenn'orth of scented cachous. She didn't like going to her normal toffee shop, Miss Daly's, because there seemed something naughty about scented cachous, but she'd read somewhere that ladies went to the opera in fur coats and foxes and expensive flashing diamonds, and scented cachous seemed the next best thing for a little girl who sometimes didn't have two farthings to rub together. She got them from a shop way up Palmerston Street where she wasn't known from Eve.

As it was school holidays, the kids had to make their own way to the Opera House and wait outside in punching, kicking, swearing, sneakily-smoking groups for the arrival of Mrs Giyaski. One or two charabancs rolled up to unload children in school uniform with designs on their caps and breast pockets. These children were naturally called all the names under the sun. When Mrs Giyaski arrived, the kids yip-yapped around her like dogs in the dogs' home at feeding time. 'Follow!' she ordered, and they entered the theatre, the lads wiping their noses on their sleeves, the girls twiddling handkerchiefs between their fingers, and all looking at different things. Kitty was filled with the same kind of awe as she had been on her visit to the muck yard: she was in a place which was mighty and powerful. The front ticket hall had a smell of daffodils, not cemetery daffodils but fresh-cut ones from the watering-can shops; and there was a ticket smell, almost like tram tickets only nicer and richer. Even as they walked through, a lady like a servant walked through with a spray gun spraying more daffodil smell.

They climbed up a winding stairway, and up and up. At first there were jokes about Mount Everest, but then the boys and girls became out of breath and had nothing more to say but pretended to push down on their knees to help them climb each step.

When they finally poured out into the real theatre Kitty was frightened. It was so high, yet so beautiful and fairy palace like. The ceiling was even higher and was painted with cherubs and red roses, and great frightening chandeliers hung down from between the cherubs, long pieces of glass or maybe diamonds hung down between a hundred electric lamps. The walls beneath her held audiences like trays of cotton bobbins in a haberdashery shop, and the balconies were of golden baby angels with round bellies, and there was a lot of dark red velvety plush everywhere. There were electric lights dressed like candles sticking from the walls. There was a constant and growing hum-drum buzz-buzz gabble-gabble from the millions of school kids below. It was an all-schools matinée, and Kitty guessed that the kids below paid more money and came from the better schools in the posher privet-hedge districts.

The red and golden curtain of the stage was down, down, down, so down-down-down and small that it made Kitty dizzy looking down at it.

She was aware from the gossip and chit-chat that most of the kids were satisfied that they'd been and climbed and seen the inside and looked down, and would now be quite happy to go back home and play The Farmer Wants a Wife and German and British war-fighting in their own streets. A number of boys, who always carried a pocketful of stones to aim at cats or birds, began flinging them over the balcony, causing a patch of half a dozen white faces to look up, upon which they tried to spit for bull's-eyes. Only Kitty seemed excited at the thought of the opera ahead. It was called *The Bohemian Girl*. Some of the kids down below had programmes which fluttered white, and she would have given a million pounds for a programme, but the only two programmes in the top balcony were held firmly by Mrs Giyaski and another teacher from another school. The two teachers sat together and talked, which was why the boys were able to drop stones.

The lights faded out, not quickly like from a switch but slowly, like dying peacefully. The curtain lights brightened like coming to life, and then violins and other musical instruments from the orchestra below but in front of the curtain began making little squeaking noises like kittens being drowned. Kitty's bum slid backwards and forwards in her seat with excitement. The boy seated on her left had the smell of much-used Lifebuoy soap, which was a clean smell, and he seemed a shy and decent boy, but a voice told him to piss off else he'd get his knackers in a pan, and he shuffled away to let Mick Dowd sit down, who stunk of hot day and road pitch.

'Hello, tart!' said Mick, but she looked away at an illuminated Exit sign.

Almost immediately he pulled a large fat cigar from his inside jacket pocket, and he bent his head between his knees to light it. 'Ten pence,' he said. He puffed at the smoke and it had a Yates's Wine Lodge smell. The lad next to him, and various other lads, asked him for a puff. 'Ha'penny a puff,' he said, and soon the cigar was being passed around under the seats, and ha'pennies were rolling into Mick's hand.

'And I suppose King Arthur was doing that all the time?' asked Kitty, being sarcastic.

'How else d'y'think he kept his crown from being popped at uncles?' said Mick, shaking his head with arrogance, and fluttering his hand for the lads to hurry along with their puffs and ha'pennies. 'Pass along the tram, please!' he whispered in a loud whisper.

The curtains opened on red, orange and blue: on a light brown castle which could have been inhabited by all the trees and lamps and happy things of Hans Christian Andersen: on gay peasants, merry courtiers, happy soldiers and dancing gypsies in dazzling colours. Kitty opened her eyes wide in order to take it all in. It was more brilliant and sparkling and promising of expectation than any shop window at Christmas.

And then one of the lads coughed, genuinely because of the cigar; this was followed by daft coughs, silly coughs, mock coughs and squeaky girlish coughs. One lad parodied 'The Penny Bazaar' song by singing, 'At the end of me old cigar ah, ah – ah, ah!' and another kid shouted, 'Choke up, chicken!' There was a loud shush from below like the Irish Mail getting ready to leave Exchange Victoria, and the boys shushed back like a little Ancoats shunting engine.

It was a great pity that Thaddeus the Pole, and the hero, was a very fat man. A slim young man might have got away with it, but an elderly grey-haired fat man didn't ring true, not with the Ancoats boys.

'It's Fatty Arbuckle!' shouted one of the lads. 'Hello, Fatso!'

'Somebody bring the Flit gun on stage. Fatty Arbuckle's kakied in his keks and the stink's worse'n a gas attack!'

'It's going to ruin my bloody cigar trade, this is,' Mick whispered in Kitty's ear.

A thousand white dots of faces looked up at the gods. 'Silence!!' boomed Mrs Giyaski, and her voice was so loud and commanding that for a second there was a silence on the stage as well, and the orchestra leader had to begin again by tapping with his stick. But at least there was silence, and Mick put his cigar out, saying it would do for later when the lads began gasping for a draw. Kitty wriggled herself cosy to watch the stage again. It was magic, and it was grown-up: it was real love and not friendship. She'd been to a pantomime at the Round House and the fairy had stepped forward with an 'Oh yes it is – oh no it isn't' backchat to the audience, but no gypsy did this, for this was the genuine theatre, and the people on stage had twinkling eyes and meant what they said.

At the end of Act One there was an interval and the big lights went on. Most of Kitty's class, thinking it was all over, stood up ready to shuffle out and home, but Mrs Giyaski ordered them to sit, and they sat. A girl in long black silk stockings appeared from the entrance with a tray and a flashlight. 'Chocolates, cigarettes and minerals!' she called, then changed it to 'Chocolates, nuts and minerals,' but she screamed and yelled 'You dirty bastard' when one of the lads put his hand up her clothes, and she was never seen again, which made Kitty all the gladder she'd given the bob to her dad because she'd not have been able to spend it. Trouble was she didn't dare suck a scented cachou, not with Mick next to her: it would have been different with the Lifebuoy lad.

The second act was more and more bewitching because little Arline, who was the daughter of the Count but didn't know it, had grown into a beautiful young girl in a way in which Kitty wished to grow. Arline was so convincing that Kitty even began to wonder if perhaps she was the long-lost daughter of royalty: it was a nice thought anyway. Arline then sang a song which was more beautiful than any hymn ever sung in church, and Kitty wished that she might have sung such a song on the day she'd stood in the pulpit crowned as queen of the angels, queen of the May.

> 'I dreamt that I dwelt in marble halls
> With vassals and serfs at my side,
> And of all who assembled within those walls
> That I was the hope and the pride.'

Mick submerged to relight the cigar, and Kitty prayed he

wouldn't. She also prayed that Fat Thaddeus wouldn't appear again, but she knew he'd have no alternative.

> 'I dreamt that suitors sought my hand,
> That knights upon bended knee,
> And with vows no maiden heart could withstand
> They pledged their faith to me.'

If only the roof of the Opera House would open on hinges like a Queen Victoria tea caddy and she could float up and up with all the world as an audience praying and pledging their faith to her. She felt her feet lifting.

'Here he is! Follow the bouncing ball!'
'It's Harry the Hippo!'
'Stick a pin in him! He'll pop!'
'Silence!!' There was a sudden hit-smack silence.

Thaddeus walked to the front of the stage. 'I'm sorry!' he said. He was clearly hurt. Most of the children downstairs clapped and cheered him for his bravery, but the kids in the gods booed and laughed. Mrs Giyaski's feet thumped down the steps of the aisle. 'Who's that wretch smoking?' she demanded.

'Not me,' said Mick, and he flicked his lighted cigar over the balcony. It sparked like a firework among the children below.

'Fire!' shouted a voice.

The house lights came on, and several uniformed attendants took red fire buckets down from their hooks on the walls.

'Out!!' screamed Mrs Giyaski. 'Every one of you – out!' She bundled the herd out of the theatre and down the stairway, holding tightly to Mick's jacket collar. Some giggled and said he was in for a police birching.

Down in the ticket hall, a woman was operating an electric vacuum sweeper on the carpet. The girls became interested because they'd never seen a vacuum sweeper before, and they begged to stay and watch. It had a bulging blowing bag on its black iron handle, and there was a small light on the part of the sweeper where the brush bristles should have been, and it lit up bits of cigarette ash and paper which did a dance before being swallowed up underneath. Kitty knew the girls would talk about the vacuum sweeper for weeks and weeks, all saying they would marry a man who would buy them one; and she knew the lads would be laughing at Fat Thaddeus and Mick Dowd's punishment. Only she had been interested in *The Bohemian Girl* and now she'd never know whether Arline ended up in marble halls with knights kneeling like Sir Lancelot and saying they loved her. She hated the class for being what they were.

But she knew one thing, and she told Wendy all about it. When she grew up, she wanted to be an actress, a famous actress, a very famous actress.

Kitty put herself down to run the girls' half-mile, and her immediate friends had signed up to run the hundred yards, two hundred and twenty yards, high jump and long jump.

Miss Plunkett, the physical training teacher, who was tiny where Mrs Giyaski was immense – everybody said they'd got their jobs mixed up – came in to congratulate the girls who had volunteered to give their best for St Anselm's in the annual Manchester Schools' Sports Day at Belle Vue. Mrs Giyaski smiled benevolently at the class after Miss Plunkett had walked into the door and fumbled her way out, and for the handwriting lesson immediately afterwards she wrote the most beautiful upstroke downstroke writing on the backboard – 'And it's not for the sake of the ribboned coat, or the selfish hope of a season's fame, but his captain's hand on his shoulder smote – Play up! Play up! And play the game!'

None of the girls of course had the slightest intention of running in any of the races they'd put their names down for: it was a means of getting into Belle Vue for nothing. Once inside they would complain about bellyaches, headaches, bad feet and sore knees, then limp away through the entrance to the Zoological Gardens and amusement park.

As Kitty and her pals were hobbling away, the loudspeaker called desperately for any contestants from St Anselm's.

'Ah, well!' said Bridie McBride. ''Tis the school's name that's getting a mention, and that must be good publicity if ever there was such a thing.'

'Aye,' said Kitty. 'And isn't it the pity we can't get the man to mention the church's penny bazaar on Sat'day, then all would be forgiven.'

The boys had obviously worked the same dodge, for there were plenty of them mooching around in the amusement park, hands in their pockets, looking for lost pennies on the ground. The girls split up and Kitty wandered into an Amusement Only building next to the lion house. There was a thick crowd in there, and it was gathered around the large For Amusement Only case called 'The Early Morning Execution'. Kneeling before it, and the reason for the pushing crowd, making many rapid signs of the cross and moaning in anguish, was Mick Dowd.

A penny in the slot lit the prison up, and a group of warders and a priest moved along like clockwork to the tower, then disappeared into the tower. The tower bell went ding-dong eight times, and the tower wall swung open on a hinge, and there was the prisoner with the rope around his neck. The trap door opened, and the prisoner was swinging, swaying and twirling on the end of the rope.

'Ah, me grandad! Me poor grandad!' moaned Mick, and beat his chest.

'Did he take the walk?' asked a voice in the crowd.

'Oh, he did that!' wailed Mick. 'And all for the cause of old Ireland. Wasn't it a rebel they said he was? God Save Erin was the last words he said before the long drop.' And Mick groaned loud and made yet another quick sign of the cross.

'Just one more time,' said a sympathizer in the crowd. Twopence was given to Mick by way of consolation, and another penny was put in the slot, and the whole mechanical performance began again.

For the first time Kitty felt sorry for poor Mick. It seemed such a shame that people would pay pennies just to gawp at a poor lad being reminded about his grandfather's death. She wanted to put her arms round his neck and give him a penny, but she'd no money.

After a time a man in uniform broke the crowd up and told Mick to skedaddle quick while the going was good. Mick came to Kitty.

'I saw you gawping, tart!' he said.

'Was your grandad hanged like that?' she asked, full of sympathy.

'Heck, was he buggery! He was a dirty old man what sat in the corner by the chimbley and spit in the fire, nearly putting it out at times, and he farted like bloody Big Bertha, and me mam said he deserved hanging. Me other grandad pissed off to Amerikay.'

'You was putting it on? Acting then?'

'Aye, and giving 'em more for their money than watching that bloody daft little doll twirling on a piece o' cotton.'

She had a sudden admiration for Mick because of his acting, but she daren't think so, and she couldn't say so. Anyway, when he rattled the coppers in his trouser pockets and said, 'Let's go on things!' she didn't hesitate to follow him, but she wouldn't touch his hand for it was knobbly with segs.

They went on the Caterpillar, the Dodgems, the Big Horses, the Chairoplanes and the Canadian Rapids. They weren't allowed on the Figure of Eight and the Scenic Railway, and she refused to go on the Ghost Train because she knew he'd put his hand up her skirt as soon as the skeletons came on. Mick spent his money, and Kitty decided to go home.

'Why?' asked Mick.

''Cos I'm fair clemmed,' said she. 'That's why.'

'Why didn't ye say yer belly thought yer throat was cut?' said Mick. 'Stick close, tart! Us'll get some food.'

She followed him into the huge cafeteria. Dozens and dozens of people were bringing food on trays to the long oilclothed tables. A man and a woman sat down and unloaded their tray.

'Hey, tart, d'y'see the meat pie that feller has?' asked Mick in a loud voice. 'It's what's left of that keeper what was half eaten by a lion yesterday. They managed to save bits of him.'

The man stopped his action of taking a knife and fork to the pie.

'And that fish what the lady's going to eat was sicked up by a penguin.'

The woman also stopped her knife and fork in mid-action. The couple looked at each other and put their knives and forks down. 'Sod you, sonny!' said the man.

'Only kidding! For amusement only!' said Mick.

'Harm's bloody done, in't it?' said the man, and the couple walked out.

'Right, tart, ease your weight, and get stuck in,' said Mick, rubbing his hands with achievement. 'Fish for you, meat pie for me.'

Kitty picked at the fish, but she felt a bit sick. She got some apple pie and custard when Mick in a loud voice referred to it as being diarrhoea from the monkey with the scabby arsehole, but she felt even sicker, until she had to run to the ladies' lavatories holding her mouth. She was very sick, and knew she would never eat apple pie and custard again as long as she lived.

She was all set to go home, but coming out of the lavatory from the other door she saw the colourful mock town on the island in the boating lake. It was larger than life: some of the wooden cut-outs were as big as churches, only they weren't churches because their tops were shaped like onions. They were supported by scaffolding and platforms. It was for the nightly magnificent firework spectacle, none in the world like it, called 'The Massacre of Cawnpore'. She'd heard about it. It was shooting and killing, and then the British redcoats charged on and there was more shooting and killing, only it wasn't real killing because nobody got killed. She'd often heard the nine o'clock bang from the backyard in Angel Meadow when the wind was in the right direction. Mick said he'd protect her from the bangers if she stayed to watch the magnificent spectacle: she would have stayed in any case because it was real-life acting on a real-life stage.

'What's Cawnpore?' she asked him.

'What's what?'

'Cawnpore. Them what gets massacred.'

'Englishman's name for wallah-wallahs,' he said. 'They've nicknames for everybody what isn't English. Like they call us micks, don't they?'

'Aye – why do they call us micks?'

'I don't know,' said Mick. 'But cawnpores is easy. Pores is holes in yer skin, and corns is what grows under people's feet.' To give an example, he started limping and trying to talk in an old man's voice. 'It's going to rain 'cos me corns is killing me.' Kitty laughed.

'So y'see,' went on Mick, sticking his chest out to show his point had been made, 'corn pores is what Englishmen thinks is under their feet and to be walked on, and tonight they're going to massacre the poor bleeders.'

As darkness turned grey things black, the crowds gathered in their thousands, and a band played and the crowds sang 'Rule Britannia', 'Land of Hope and Glory', and 'We're the Soldiers of the Queen, Me Lads', but they were Protestant songs and made Kitty feel she was in a strange land.

There was a sky-shattering explosion, the one she heard most nights from home, which told her it was time to go on up to the chip shop for a ha'p'orth o' scrapings and a ha'p'orth o' mushed peas, because that was when the chip shop man usually had a pan-load of fish batter scrapings and squashed squelchy peas to distribute cheap to what he called the starving kids.

And then the frightening banging and shooting began, and the wallah-wallahs made nasty noises and their victims squealed, and the crowds cheered when the redcoats and Scotchies ran in. The windows in the onion buildings glared Bengal-match red; cannons banged flash red and yellow; rifles flashed white bangs; wallah-wallahs dropped screaming dead; the Union Jack was hoisted to many cheers.

Searchlights came on, and a voice on the loudspeaker called, 'Ye Dead Men Arise!' and all the massacred wallah-wallahs jumped up and waved to the crowds as they ran off.

Kitty too retreated. She'd no wish to be going under the dark Fenian Arch on her way home with Mick Dowd, for he'd try to feel her, and even if he didn't feel her on account of her not letting him, wouldn't he tell the lads at school he'd been up her skirt, and she could never prove he hadn't. Besides, she was a heroine – she'd imagined herself leading the charge of the Scotchies, and she'd known the crowds were cheering for her leading them – and a brave heroine like Boadicea has to be on her own.

On her way out she lifted a newspaper from a litter basket. It would be something to read in bed: maybe it would have things to say about the magnificent firework spectacle. She ran down Hyde

Road, turned at the tram sheds where a few trams were still yowling at each other before going to sleep, and she was down Pin Mill Brow and into Angel Meadow in no time at all. She was home long before her dad.

She sat up in bed and told Wendy about Belle Vue, including a pack of lies about lions and tigers just to excite her. 'And now ye must be off to the land o' Winkin, Blinkin and Nod, while yer mammy reads the paper.' She kissed Wendy, tucked her down, and opened the newspaper.

And reading the paper was like the Archangel Gabriel of the Annunciation talking to her. Her eye was caught by '*Ancoats*' and it wasn't in connection with crime either: it had something to do with the Horsfall Museum, just up Ancoats Grove from where she lived, and with a Children's Theatre attached to it. She'd never heard of a Children's Theatre, but then, as the newspaper article said, it had been closed for many a year. She moved the paper nearer the candle.

A schoolmaster from a school up the road was going to reopen it and put on plays for the children of Ancoats. He said the boys in his school were enthusiastic but his trouble would be finding girls. '*Would you like to be another Lily Langry?*' the Archangel Gabriel asked. '*If you're a schoolgirl and live near the Horsfall Museum and would like to act upon the stage, call upon Mr Davies any Thursday night.*'

She didn't sleep very much that night. The next day she missed school dinners in order to run to the museum. She asked the man in uniform if she could take a peep at the theatre.

It was more holy than the stable at Bethlehem. It was like a great barn with rows and rows of forms. The floor was scrubbed-white wood. The yellow curtains were closed on the stage like a shut eyelid; but above the stage there was a painting. It was of a knight in armour, bearing a lance and rushing to save a tall conical-capped lady in distress from being eaten by a dragon. She needed no further sign.

Mrs Becket, Mrs Fearnley, Mrs Compton and Mrs Roscoe approached Kitty in a group, all with their hands under their pinnies, and informed her that she was growing into a young woman and would have to muck in: this in spite of the fact that Kitty was only ten years of age and it was less than one week after her visit to Belle Vue when she had been considered a little girl.

Kitty had made up her mind to become a famous actress and intended applying to the Children's Theatre like the newspaper told her. She was aware that a certain amount of wickedness was involved in her ambition because the Children's Theatre was run by Protestants, or at least a municipal school, which was saying the same thing, and maybe this sudden thrust into womanhood by the neighbours was the Blessed Virgin's warning.

'If you want to act like a woman, then you must wash the clothes like a woman,' the Virgin was perhaps saying to her.

What mucking in meant was that she was now expected to take her turn at doing the Monday morning washing. Up till then she had done her own and her dad's and hung them to dry in the backyard, all nice and private, and in her own sweet time. But now she would have to use her copper boiler every fifth week, and her washing, like it or not, would have to be displayed on the street clothes-lines for all the world to see.

The copper boiler rested upside down in its brick cot and fireplace. Kitty always thought of it as being upside down because the large dome was about the size of the dome on top of a railway engine near the funnel. She had used it to keep things cool in during the heavy summer months; it kept butter hard, milk from going sour, and bacon from smelling.

At the bottom end of the brick tomb was a small fire grate, and at the dark, silent time of four o'clock in the morning, Kitty had to open a bundle of firewood, screw up newspapers which she'd gathered from the tram-stop litter boxes, light the papers, and lie flat on the stone scullery floor to huff and puff and get the fire started. This was the beginning of a duty which would be hers every fifth Monday. Each neighbour would take turns and thus save money on firewood, coal and soap.

Steam was beginning to fill the scullery by the time her dad got up: she had already put his brews and butties in his basket, so she had time for a quick word with him while he saucered and blew his tea.

'I'm going to be a famous actress, dad,' she said, and she was as relieved as when she'd told the priest she'd sworn at the cat. At the next Confession she told the priest she'd lied about swearing at the cat because she'd not got a cat.

'Are ye now?'

'I am.'

'Indeed.'

'Aye.'

'Then 'tis proud of you I am for it runs in the family.'

'What does?'

'Being a famous actor and that.'

'You what!' She was staggered.

Her dad touched his nose and winked for secrecy. 'Let's go into the scullery and I'll tell ye, my love, for I'll not be blathering me blooming life history in front o' that wireless set, for it knows too much already.'

They went into the scullery and could barely see each other because of the steam.

'The blooming toffs pay a hundred pounds for the likes o' this,' said her dad, wafting himself, 'for 'tis known as a Turkish bath and is calculated to take away all the fat and make ye young and beautiful and rich into the bargain.'

'The acting?' said Kitty impatiently.

'Aye, 'tis in the blood right enough, herodititty as the saying goes. For did not me, the very man what stands afore ye here and now, and yer own beloved father, once sing in the opera at Convent Garden?'

'You never!'

'Oh, I did an' all. And 'twas brought about by the funeral of Queen Victoria herself.' He paused to twirl his pointed moustache. 'For there was me in them self-same Irish Guards what that fat old lady had but formed a year earlier, and us doing the slow march behind her coffin through the streets of London, for 'twas at Windsor Castle we was on duty at the time, and enjoying many a pint of ale when off duty we were. And that's an important point to remember.'

He rubbed his fingers in soap from the slop stone in order to wax his moustache with pride.

'Oh, 'twas proud of us the officers were, most of 'em being gentry, would ye know. And after the funeral this young officer, a man of nobility if ever there was one, says we're to be given a reward for our smartness and discipline, and the reward was to report every night to the Convent Garden theatre instead of doing sentry-go. And us would be required to sing in grand opera.'

'Grand opera! You, dad!'

'Say I'm a liar! May I drop down dead if me lips speak a lie. 'Twas by an Itie named hurdy gurdy Vurdi or summat like that. Haven't I heard the same music played on the barrel-organ? And 'twas a drinking song, and we had to wave tankards and make singing sounds to the music.' He swayed his tea cup.

'Here I am on a tram
And I don't give a damn
If we slam another tram
With jam on ham.'

'Was them the words, dad?'

'Ach, not at all. I made 'em up. Y'see, they was singing in Itie at the front so what the hell did it matter what we was singing in the back. But 'twas a most disappointing opera.'

'Disappointing?'

'To say the least, me darling. For in them tankards was nowt at all but cold tea.' He made the sign of the cross with the cup in his hand. 'May it never happen to me again as long as I live. Cold bloody tea it was! A reward was it? Punishment it was! If we'd been back on sentry-go at the Castle would we not have been supping all the ale our bellies would hold? I tell you, me darling, after a couple of weeks we was all waving and singing:

We are dry, and we'll die,
That's no lie,
If we don't get a drink bye and bye,
We sigh, tiddley-eye
Tiddley-eye-tie-tie.'

He grabbed his basket, kissed her and left the house. He was still singing his Italian opera and doing a bit of a dance up the street, which embarrassed Kitty no end for it would wake the neighbours before the knocker-up did.

> 'Got no fee but cold tea,
> Not for me,
> 'Cos you wouldn't give that to a flea,
> Monkey's pee tiddle-ee
> Tiddle-ee-tee-tee.'

He turned the corner into Palmerston Street, the singing was lost, Kitty was relieved. She started the business of cutting a bar of soap into flakes and tossing them into the steaming copper. The house filled with steam, and everything became wet.

Next job was to roll the zinc dolly tub in from the yard, tip out any black beetles, ladle out some boiling soapy water from the copper and put handfuls of her neighbours' washing into the dolly. Neighbours' washing had been dumped in heaps in her scullery the night before. And then she reached for the wooden peggy. It always reminded her of a five-legged man whose bum had been built too near the pavement: old women said it was like a milking stool. There were five small legs on a round top, but from the round top grew a long straight neck like a wooden giraffe before they put the spots on. And at the top of the neck were outstretched arms like those on a lamp-post: above that, a round knob for a head.

Kitty jerked the arms backwards and forwards like doing the Cuban rumba; they said the exercise was good for a woman's hips. After that, she brought out the zinc scrubbing board and scrubbing brush and scrubbed up and down on collars and brown streaks on men's combinations and women's bloomers.

> 'Peggy in the dolly tub,
> Get rid of the muck,
> Give 'em all a jolly rub,
> Extra one for luck.'

She sang the thousand verses of the washday song until it was time to mangle the clothes. She scrubbed them and tossed them and slapped them in the slop stone where the tap was aways running to rinse them. And after that they were fed through the heavy mangle in the backyard. It was a ferocious thing. The two great rubber rollers had to be tightened by a huge hand screw on the top of a wide arch of iron; it was like a picture in her history book of William Caxton's first printing press. The large turning wheel was also of iron, and about the size of a bicycle wheel. It was like having a fierce dragon in the backyard always ready to devour. The two rubber rollers could flatten her like a pancake if once they caught hold of her fingers.

> 'Knickers in a tangle,
> Yours and hers and mine,
> Put 'em through the mangle,
> Hang 'em on the line.'

She sang the thousand verses of the washday song until it was time to hang the clothes out. Putting up the lines was the only time the women were offered help by the men. No matter how hard the women had to struggle with the mangle wheel, the men who had no work to go to just sat and watched. It was only when the lines were needed to be hooked across the street that a man would stand on a chair and reach up to the hooks between the bricks. After that bit of assistance, it was still the woman's job to stand on the chair and peg the clothes on the line. The favourite shout of the men whenever a pair of bloomers was hung out, or if in reaching up the woman showed her bloomers, was 'Up she comes and the colour's red!'

The three or four men in the street made no exception for Kitty, except that somebody produced a rickety pair of wooden stepladders because she couldn't reach the line from a chair. They still tried to look up her frock as she reached. Twice they were able to shout 'Up she comes and the colour's red' although it wasn't for Kitty's thighs: it was when she pegged up Mrs Fearnley's knickers, for Mrs Fearnley was a good-looking woman who winked and clicked her tongue on the side of her mouth when she passed men, and men guessed she wore knickers and not bloomers.

Once the clothes were fluttering and flapping on the lines, Kitty ran to the morning Mass before school. She was just in time to throw herself on her knees before the statue of the Virgin Mary before the priest shuffled on to the altar. Her earnest prayer was for there to be no sootfall, because if there was a sootfall it would be from her scullery chimney. She had never lit the copper boiler before, it hadn't been lit since her mother died, and she guessed the scullery flue would be thick with soot. Some said a sootfall was an act of God, but the chimney sweep said it was because people were too bloody tight to spend sixpence. Whatever, a sootfall meant that all the clothes had to be washed again. 'Oh, blessed Virgin, please keep the sky clear from soot, and let my washing dry clean and dry, and I'll light a candle in your name on Friday night.'

Women had been known to drag a woman out of her house if her chimney had caused a sootfall, and tear her clothes off, and the men would laugh. 'Oh, blessed Virgin, if there's no sootfall I promise to join the Children of Mary when I'm old enough.' She was on the verge of promising the Virgin that she would not go to the Protestant's Children's Theatre on Thursday, but she stopped herself in time: in any case, it occurred to her in a flash that if she made a lot of money as a famous actress in the future she might be able to buy millions of candles, perhaps even a small chapel, for Mary.

A fair breeze blew over Ancoats, and when she ran home at dinner-time the clothes were getting healthy and dry, and she was able to gather in some of them, watched by the out-of-work men who sat on their doorsteps to watch the clothes drying. Even had there been a sootfall the men wouldn't have budged from the steps. 'Keep an eye on 'em,' she'd said to one man. 'Aye, I'll do that, lass,' he'd said, and she knew that would be all he would do.

She ran home after school to gather the rest of the clothes which had blown dry. There had been no sootfall, there was no pigeon shit.

'I kept an eye on 'em, lass,' said the man.

'Aye,' said Kitty.

The clothes were folded in heaps for the women to collect. After tea it would be ironing time for them all. Fires had to be lit even in midsummer for the cooking, and irons were placed against the bars of the grate. The handle was gripped with an iron-cloth because it was hot. The women then spat on their irons and rubbed them in dry soap before sprinkling their clothes with water like a priest's blessing.

Kitty banged her iron down with great pride. This had been her first-ever street-washing day, and she had now become a woman; it gave her confidence for Thursday.

But on Thursday she was a timid little girl again, at least to begin with.

'Children's Theatre?' said the one-armed, one-legged uniformed attendant.

'Aye,' she said, afraid to say "sir".

'Through them doors,' he snapped, jerking his thumb to somewhere underneath a beautiful staircase.

The doors were hard to open, and the one door swung quickly back into place after she'd sneaked through. The brass handle hit her in the middle of her back and made her stumble into the wonderful barn of the theatre as though she was somebody who was not right.

The groups of boys in the theatre turned to look at this object who seemed to have been thrust in, but they were Protestant boys and she didn't know any of them. One of the lads in one of the groups beckoned her. 'Hey you!' Kitty meekly obeyed and shuffled to his group.

'Show us your bum!' he ordered.

'Shan't!' she said. She wanted to run away and get lost for ever. She didn't care if the brass door handle broke her ribs as she ran away. She hoped the theatre would burn down. But she wanted to be a famous actress, and she knew she had to stand her ground.

'Let's see your bum,' she said to the boy.

'Hey, Ratbag, she's bloody right,' said one of his mates, giving him a thump.

'Sod off!'

'Are you frightened?' asked Kitty.

Suddenly, like animals, the others pounced on him. There was swearing, kicking, punching, scratching, and tearing of sleeves and pockets. The group parted like the dirty petals of a cemetery flower to the yellow sun, and they were holding Ratbag so that a pale bum was showing.

'Not much of a bum, is it?' said Kitty, plucking up all the courage she could.

'I'll kill her! I'll bloody swing!' The gang restrained him, and then suddenly they fell away. A teacher, presumably a teacher, had walked into the theatre. A smart young man with a shining forehead and hair greased back, an old sports jacket with leather elbow patches, a blue, green and white striped university tie with coiled snakes on, cycle clips still on his trousers, an old well-wax-polished brief-case bulging with things.

Ratbag held his hands down below in front of him for he had a short shirt. The teacher brought a script out of the brief-case and flung it at the boy. 'Catch! You're the Red Prince!' In catching it the boy had to show what he'd got.

'Not much o' one o' them either,' added one of the lads.

Scripts were distributed from the brief-case, and the lads walked up the stage steps and disappeared behind the scenery of a woodland, reading their parts as they went. Kitty looked up at the teacher. He raised his eyebrows at her, which was the same as asking her name.

'Kitty Noonan, sir.'

'I'm Thomas Davies,' he said, smiling and shaking her hand. Nobody had ever shaken her hand before. His hand was smooth, and she sensed that it smelt of Pears Soap.

'And I'm a Roman Catholic.' She thought she'd better mention that in order to give him a chance to order her out, which was better than being discovered as a spy later on, and probably made to show her bum as punishment.

'Funny, I never noticed,' he said, then realizing the joke might be over her head quickly added, 'I don't think it matters a great deal on stage. However, I must warn you there are one or two other girls who wish to be considered, so I'll have to give you each an audition.'

He gave her two large pieces of paper with typing on. 'Learn these and come back in a fortnight's time and we'll see how well you do.' He gave her another gentle smile and explained they were speeches by a rich heiress named Portia in William Shakespeare's *The Merchant of Venice* and she is disguised as a doctor of law and is defending Antonio the merchant against a harsh contract. She had read the name Shakespeare in books, but this was the first time she'd ever heard anybody say the actual name. No priest had ever made Kitty feel so blessed as did Mr Davies when he handed her the papers. This was placing her back in the pulpit of lilies on May Sunday. She was determined to call in at the library on the way home and borrow the entire play because it was important she should know all about Portia in order to become Portia.

As she left, Ratbag was on the stage, only he was no longer Ratbag, he was the Red Prince in his robes, and he looked like a prince, and he spoke like a prince. The theatre was magic.

Her dad came home from the Ben Brierley on Saturday afternoon looking like a giant tin tortoise. Kitty was behind him, returning from the accumulator shop, and she didn't recognize the giant tortoise as her dad until he turned at their door and banged and clattered the great tin shell against the doorway until it fell away from him with a noise like thunder in a railway station. Round faces appeared at windows.

''Tis galvanized,' he said.

'Oh, aye!' said Kitty.

He'd bought her a large tin bath, long enough for a person to lie down flat in. She'd never had a bath in her whole life, and had made do so far with sponge body washes, but obviously now that her dad had found out she could light and use the scullery copper, and the scullery chimney was not blocked with soot and rats' nests, he felt she was fully competent to get a couple of buckets of water warmed up for herself like any lady in the land.

'Aye – galvanized,' he repeated. 'Else would I have bought it if it wasn't?'

He had difficulties getting it through the door; there was much banging and clanging, and Kitty blushed with embarrassment that the entire street would know sooner or later she would be taking all her clothes off to lie naked in a bath before the fire. She must never let anybody know what day or what hour otherwise they'd be thinking about her and imagining.

Her dad wrestled and swore the bath into the backyard, where he hammered a six-inch nail into the wall, causing black brick dust and dirty whitewash flakes to fall, and upon the nail he hung the bath from the handle on its wider end.

He would never need the bath, for like so many men and boys of Ancoats he swam in the Droylsden Canal on occasional Sunday mornings: some cycled up, some took the tram, some walked. Although there were palatial cotton mills on one side of the Droylsden Canal, the water was pure and warm, and many large goldfish swam in it. The mills took in pure cold water at one end, and pumped out pure hot water at the other. Hundreds of men swam naked in the canal on Sunday mornings, and no woman or girl dared go near the area. It was said that a girl had once hidden and peeped but had lost her eyesight and needed a white stick for the rest of her life. No man ever tried to catch a goldfish from the canal because it was said he would die of drowning.

Kitty was afraid of taking a bath before the audition in case the hot water sapped her strength and took away her power of learning lines.

'The quality of mercy is not strained, it droppeth as the gentle rain from heaven.' She not only learned her lines but tried to put an action to every word, like fluttering her fingers above her head for 'rain'. She even took this enthusiasm to school with her. The class had to learn The Creed and she was first to put up her hand.

'Then come to the front and recite it for us,' demanded Mrs Giyaski.

For 'suffered under Pontius Pilate' she winced and placed her arm to protect her face as though being hit. For 'crucified, died and was buried' she held her arms wide, then let her head drop on one side. For 'descended into hell' she pretended to be walking down steps until her head disappeared under the desks. At this point she was stopped abruptly by Mrs Giyaski who gave her the strap on both hands with great severity for committing the abominable sin of sacrilege and turning the most sacred Creed into a pantomime.

About that time, both of Manchester's newspapers, the *Evening News* and the *Evening Chronicle*, were carrying a story on their front pages about the Angel of Arms Hill. Not one or two but dozens of people had seen this white angel as they had been seated on the Bury train and Cheetham Hill trams. The city was a little frightened, and people looked up in the sky a lot.

Kitty was sorry for the angel. Perhaps it was lost, and Manchester was too cold and damp for a lost angel, especially one which was used to the warm climates of heaven and the Holy Land. And then Kitty got to wondering if perhaps the angel was looking for her, maybe with an announcement that God wanted her to become a famous actress.

However, according to both newspapers the mystery was solved. The railway line between Exchange Station and Bury had only recently been electrified and this caused many overhead flashes, like the trams. And, by coincidence, only recently a white marble angel had been erected as a tombstone in Arms Hill Cemetery, so the flashes lit up the angel. That was what the newspapers said, but Kitty didn't believe one word of it. The angel was there, waiting for her to come to him. It was her obligation; Sir Galahad would not have hesitated.

She set off one evening after her dad lad left for the Ben Brierley. There was enough tram fare to get her to Rochdale Road and back, but she'd have to walk along Queen's Road or cut across Barney's Field.

Now Barney's Field was a fearful place; her dad had once walked her across it. It was large, and a million smoking big chimneys could be seen whichever way she'd looked, and the black town hall, like the Devil's castle, could be seen on the skyline. It had dirty valleys going here, there and everywhere like the blue veins on an old woman's face. Through the deepest valley ran the many railway lines from Exchange Station, and there were always puffs of locomotive smoke passing each other, often giving a whistle to each other.

All the cats and dogs in the world came to do their mess on Barney's Field. Quite often there were gypsies with their caravans and horses. It was the gypsies that made Barney's Field a frightful place because it was said they stole children and sold them to wily Afghans.

Another valley, deep, black and hidden like the railway smoke valley, was the valley of the River Irk. Kitty hated the name Irk because it had all nasty rhymes but no nice ones. It should have been a beautiful little river; it always had many rainbow patches floating down it, whereas her own Medlock was dull, moving mud, but the Medlock was hers, it was her home river. The Irk, she felt, was Satan's stream. It was known for a fact that new-born babies were wrapped up in brown-paper parcels and thrown in it. There was a story Mrs Giyaski had once started to read them about a baby washed down on an Irk flood in a wicker cradle, who was rescued, and grew up to be a boy who went to the Manchester Grammar School, which was a Protestant school; the girls had argued in the playground whether he would go to hell. Maybe the boy had been baptized as a Catholic and snatched and put in the river by Protestants, like Moses in the bulrushes who was turned into a Jew. There were no complications like this about the Medlock, for the Medlock ran near the Hilkirk Street market where there were toys and bargains galore, and the men said funny things to make people laugh as they sold their pots and pans, and the Medlock was where the yearly wakes were put up and heard music like 'Bye Bye, Blackbird' and 'The hippo-hippo-potamus, he can beat the jolly lot of us'. The Medlock was the river to Camelot.

She had mixed feelings about crossing Barney's Field on her own, and was tempted to turn back home and let the angel find her in Ancoats. But then if the angel was waiting to speak to her it would expect her to risk fearful dangers, so she clenched her fists and marched forth across Barney's Field to meet the angel at Arms Hill.

Mrs Giyaski said that Barney's Field was what Manchester had started from, being a settlement for the Ancient British where the little Irk met the big Irwell because in those days it was a good place for spearing salmon and trout. Well, the Ancient British must have been dirty buggers because there wasn't much field to the Field, maybe occasional clumps of hard, sooty grass, most of it being gravel and ashes and clinker, rusty tin cans and broken bottles and smashed pots, splintered bones crawling with flies, broken fireplaces, ripped boots, dog muck and cat muck, and maybe human muck for some of the mounds of muck were covered with decaying newspapers; there were squashed petrol tins and red rotted oil drums and flattened Sharps toffee tins, old stays and corsets with wire bones sticking through, and bloomers ripped into shreds, sometimes a long-dead rotting cat with its eyes and teeth popping out through a half-furred skull. There were flies, some with a touch of green, some with a touch of blue, around all these things.

She kept her eyes on the far-off street-lights of Cheetham Hill Road. There was a crescent moon in that part of the sky opposite the town hall silhouette.

Suddenly, as she dipped down into one of the deeper gullies, a man seemed to come from nowhere and flung himself on top of her. Her face rubbed into some cat muck as she fell down. He put a rough, salty hand to her mouth and kept it tight. And then she felt his other fist and hand going up her clothes, and his knees wriggled her legs apart. She moved her head, but he banged it hard with his head. 'Keep still less you want yer throat cutting,' he growled in her ear. 'I've an open razor handy, dead sharp.'

She was now paralysed with fear. She felt her knickers being pulled down, and then she felt something awful hurting her between her legs and tearing her apart. It didn't last more than a few seconds, then she felt a hot sticky glue around her thighs. The man jumped up, fastening his trouser buttons. He flung a penny down at her. 'Ta, chuck. Buy yourself a wedding ring.' She peeped a peep at the man, still afraid that her throat might be slit. He skipped gaily up the gully slope and was away.

She lay there motionless with her face in the cat muck for a long time. She knew she had been poked and was now no better than cat muck, no better than the other girls in her school who had been poked and taken away. She lay until it grew nearly dark so that nobody should see her, for nobody must see her. As she got up, she noticed small feathers sticking to her clothes: they were dragon feathers, for she'd seen pictures of dragons and they had huge wings loaded with millions of small feathers.

She ran and ran, puffing and panting and sobbing, tripping over bricks and cans and making her knees bleed. She was relieved that her knees bled, for then she knew she was wounded, really wounded, and that she was alive. It was necessary to run over the Queen's Road railway bridge, but then she ran down again to the Irk because she had to wash the cat muck from her face, it was stinking and she wanted to be sick with the hurt of the stink and hell and nothing. But the water was oily, and her face smeared brown and began to smell of rubber.

She had to keep running otherwise people would notice her and throw half-bricks at her for being a gypsy. Eventually she reached the civilized corner of Queen's Road and Rochdale Road and there was a lit-up shop with plate glass windows called Swan's Pianos. This was where she should have caught her tram, but she dared not catch a tram for the police would catch her and hang her. She criss-crossed the side streets and back entries like a cat on the prowl.

Swan's Pianos – it made her laugh amid her blubbering because her dad had once taken her on a Sunday tram ride and he'd pointed down to Swan's Pianos and said he didn't think swans could play pianos; and then he'd gone on looking for things to make her laugh.

'Will ye look there – Tiger Sauce. Now what, I ask ye, would a tiger put sauce on? Maybe sausages. What kind o' sausages? There y'are now – Wall's Sausages. Now who'd want sausages made out o' walls? Sure the bricks'd break yer teeth. 'Tis maybe tigers like brick sausages with sauce on.' And he'd spent the entire trip doing an I-spy for funny names, like Zebra Metal Polish, Bird's Custard, Robin's Starch, Kiwi Boot Polish, Lyons Café, which Kitty knew wasn't spelt like king of the jungle, but she wouldn't humiliate her dad as he made everything into a story. 'Now a zebra always likes to polish its silver spoon before having some delicious custard made by a dickie-bird and served by a lion wearing a neat pinafore what'd been starched white and stiff by a cock robin, and isn't all that a fact?'

She ran and ran, and bumped into people and lamp-posts and letterboxes. She passed her dad's yard and wished she could be taken up the slope by a big horse and dropped into the burning furnaces until there was nothing left of her, and all the time she said, 'Tiger Sauce! Tiger Sauce! Tiger Sauce!' out loud.

The door of her house was never locked, for there was never anything to steal, and she pushed herself in. She needed a bath, a galvanized bath, a burning bath, like a bath in accumulator acid, but only her dad could reach the galvanized tin bath from the nail in the backyard.

She brought the fire back to life and put the kettle on, then tore her clothes off, not daring to look down between her legs.

When the water was hot, she poured it in the floor bucket with some carbolic soap, and scrubbed and scrubbed underneath her legs until the bristles of the scrubbing brush came out red with blood. Throughout, the tears rolled down her face and down her chest.

Suddenly she was tired, oh so very tired. More water went into the kettle, this time to sponge her face and body. And then she went hot with fear and shame, for she remembered she'd left her knickers in the dirt of Barney's Field, and although nobody had ever seen her knickers, everybody would recognize them as her knickers.

Her vest, frock and socks she burned in the fire, prodding them down with the poker until they disappeared under red coal and formed soldiers. She had to open and shut the front door to waft out the smell of burning cloth. She would have to say she'd been ironing and forgotten the iron.

There were nice clean linen clothes to change into, and she combed her hair, and then she went up to her room, stood on a chair and spat on the glass of the large blue picture of the Virgin Mary.

'You watched!' she snarled at the picture. 'You watched, and did nowt to help me!'

Then she felt afraid as though the roof of the house was going to lift into the sky. She grabbed a clean handkerchief and began polishing the glass. 'I didn't mean it! I didn't mean it!' she wept.

She lay in bed stiff and straight like people did when they were dead. A separate bedding of coats was made for Wendy on a chair because Kitty didn't think she was pure enough for the doll to sleep with. She could hear the darkness of the night sucking in and out like a concertina full of holes.

Her dad came home singing about bayonets and the British. She heard him say goodnight to the wireless set before he clumped upstairs and shut his door and dropped his boots on the oilcloth.

And then the black torture of the night began. Her brain seemed to bulge, and she was afraid of looking at the Virgin's picture in case the Virgin's eyes, lit by the candle, were looking reprovingly at her.

'She has heard a whisper say, a curse is on her if she stay to look down to Camelot. She knows not what that curse may be, and so she weaveth steadily, and little other care hath she, the Lady of Shalott.'

As Portia, she stood before the caskets of gold, silver and lead. *'Go draw aside the curtains, and discover the several caskets to this noble prince.'* The prince was the Red Prince Ratbag. Kitty had learned all Portia's lines.

And she knew the Lady of Shalott by heart. *'For often through the silent nights a funeral, with plumes and lights, and music, went to Camelot.'* She knew that outside on the cobbles of Angel Meadow a horse with grinning teeth and purple plumes and a glass hearse with lines and designs were waiting for her.

The Red Prince opened a casket and it was filled with red rusty corned beef cans and stinking cat muck with flies.

'You see me, Lord Bassanio, where I stand, such as I am.'

'Out flew the web and floated wide – the mirror cracked from side to side – "the curse is come upon me!" cried the Lady of Shalott.'

'O my God, I am heartily sorry for having offended Thee, and I detest all my sins, because I dread the loss of Heaven and the pain of hell.'

The candle flickered. She'd been afraid to blow it out.

'That light we see is burning in my hall. How far that little candle throws his beams! So shines a good deed in a naughty world.'

She blew out the candle so that the Virgin couldn't see her, even if she stuck her tongue out at her; then she closed her eyes tight in case the Virgin had eyes which lit up in the dark. She thought of the feathered man throwing her a penny to buy a wedding ring.

'*If you had known the virtue of the ring, or half her worthiness that gave the ring, or your own honour to contain the ring, you would not then have parted with the ring.*'

A train pooped its whistle.

'*Lying, robed in snowy white that loosely fled to left and right – the leaves upon her falling light – through the noises of the night.*'

'*For ere she reached upon the tide the first house by the waterside, singing in her song she died, the Lady of Shalott.*'

'*She has a lovely face: God in his mercy lend her grace,*' said a woman's voice of the Virgin.

She woke up to a grey morning. It was tippling with rain, and she could hear it slashing into the Medlock. The weight of her guilt fell down on her like a ton of bricks.

Once her dad had danced off to work, she knew exactly what she had to do. She dare not go to the priest, for he might lock her in a dark convent – she must go to the nice nun, to Sister St Pius. The nun might protect – in any case, it was better to surrender herself than be dragged kicking and screaming from the classroom. She dare not think of what might happen to her dad with her taken away, she would have to become a nun and pray and pray and pray for his soul, but if she confessed the truth her prayers might carry greater weight than if she tried to bear out a lie and carry on as if nothing had happened. Prayers from unrepentant sinners were just swept up and emptied in God's midden tin.

She washed Wendy and put the doll's best clothes on, and half an hour before school-time the two of them rang the bell of the convent house adjoining the church and school. The hall with its smell of carbolic and furniture polish, its tiled floor, its large lady saint statue, was a cushion of rest and peace.

Outside were the dulled sounds of Ancoats, a ragbone man and a chimney sweep calling out their trades, the iron shoes of carthorses clopping on the cobbles, children singing that the farmer wanted a wife, a grinding tramcar, a man singing about the love birds leaving their old nest, a bicycle bell, a dog barking, the rattle of a midden tin, a woman's laugh, a train whistle – but they were just sounds and not connected with real live people, sounds which were all part of the cushion of silence.

Sister St Pius shuffled out of a room, from which there came a smell of bacon, smiled, put her hand on Kitty's shoulder and ushered her into another room. It was a small room and seemed taken up by a bookcase filled with fat books; there were two easy chairs, an upright chair, a small table, and an aspidistra in a pot with a painted picture of a little girl feeding a little boy cherries. The nun made Kitty comfortable in one of the easy chairs.

'Well now, Miss Kitty Noonan, and how are ye today?'

'I'm very well, thank you, sister.' It was not right to ask nuns how they were, for nuns were not supposed to be anything.

'And your father?'

'He's very well, thank you, sister.'

'Good! Well now, and what can I do for you?'

'Do you know of a nice clean girl in a nice clean convent who would look after Wendy?'

'Wendy?'

She held her doll up. 'This is Wendy.'

'Oh, hello, Wendy!' The sister took hold of the doll and smiled at it. 'And why would ye wish to part with such a nice wee person as Wendy, may I ask? Och, she's a canny wee lass.'

'Because I'm filthy, sister, and no longer a suitable person to look after her.'

'Are ye now?' The nun placed her free hand on Kitty's hands. 'And why is that, will ye tell me?'

'I was poked, sister.' Kitty burst out crying.

The nun seated Wendy on the upright chair. 'Will ye just bide a wee while?' she said to the doll; then she shuffled her chair near to Kitty and put her arm around her. 'There now! 'Tis all right!'

'But I'm a wicked sinner! My tongue is black, and my forehead'll soon turn black, and the Devil, like the black, shiny joker of the playing cards, will come laughing for me.'

'You were sinned against, my child.'

'No, sister! I had it coming, sister! I pinched Wendy from the wakes when a man was getting killed. And I want to act in plays for the Protestants. And I caused my class to laugh when I recited the Creed. It's all my most grievous fault!'

The nun gave a slight smile, a little like the Mona Lisa, but it went in a second. 'Ah, I've heard about the Creed. It was over-enthusiasm, and maybe, wee lassie, that's your problem.'

'So will you find someone to take care of Wendy when they take me away?'

'My child, let's keep it a secret for the time being, eh? I shall pray for you, and that may help a little. But you must save your pennies, and when the fair returns give the people the full price of Wendy. D'y'hear me now?'

'Yes, sister.'

'The play-acting? Well, between you and me and the gatepost, I see no harm in it. But you must remember at all times that you are a Catholic, you must be extra special, you must be the best actress on the stage, so that people will ask who you are, and others will say "Why, that's Kitty Noonan, she's a Catholic".'

'Yes, sister. But I was poked, sister.'

'The word is "raped", my wee one. But my guess is it was all over and done with in a couple of seconds, for the kind of men who do such things are immature and near enough impotent, which ye'll not know what I'm talking about but means they're near enough to being sick infants. It is your dignity which has been hurt more than your body, and that's the sin of pride which was the downfall of Lucifer.'

'But you can't know what – '

The nun put her finger to Kitty's lips.

'Can't know – is that it? Oh, but I do know.'

'You, sister?'

'Oh, yes. And do ye know what I did? I prayed for the poor man who raped me. And I felt so much the better. Wait here, will ye now?'

Sister St Pius got up and left the room, and the room became cotton-wool quiet. Kitty wished she could remain in the room for ever and ever, for she knew she'd never grow old in that room. There was a small crucifix on the wall but she averted her eyes because she did not feel clean enough to look straight at it, although in truth she felt a little cleaner than when she'd first arrived, like having a swill under the tap before using the soap.

'They always make you wait,' she whispered to Wendy. 'It's like at the doctor's, and is part of making you well again.'

And then some awful thoughts came to her. It was as though the restful little room had become a mangle, and the silence grinding was the rubber rollers, and the nun had gone outside to turn the wheel, like St Catherine's wheel. Sins would drip from her.

There was the sin of the Fry's Cocoa. She didn't count the food she stole from the baskets on Saturday nights because that was to live on, and God meant people to live otherwise they wouldn't have been born, but once upon a time she'd taken a tin of Fry's Cocoa. Her dad didn't like cocoa and made fun of it: 'Frying cocoa, did ye ever hear of such a thing. It shoulda been Boils Cocoa for ye boil tea. Ah, *mo chroidh*, 'tis a funny old language is the language of the English.' So she'd made herself a cup of cocoa each night and taken it to bed with her like rich people did. The cocoa was a luxury, and therefore it had been a sin to steal it. She wondered if she should confess to the nun while she was at it. And not many weeks ago she'd told the teacher she was going to run in a race for the school just in order to get into Belle Vue without paying, where she'd eaten cheated food, and if nobody paid to get into Belle Vue the animals would starve to death because they wouldn't be able to buy food for them, and they wouldn't even be able to pay the keepers to go out and steal from baskets for the lions and tigers and elephants.

Her mind went back to the cocoa. It might have been bought to save a child's life, like in the story Mrs Giyaski had told them about a child named Little Nell. 'This child needs Fry's Cocoa or she will die,' the doctor may have told the grandfather, and the grandfather may have sent a neighbour to Tib Street Market. Little Nell might be dead and lying in a pauper's grave because Kitty had stolen her cocoa. It was no wonder she had been punished on Barney's Field.

The door frightened her: it opened suddenly, and in rushed Sister St Pius. She gave Kitty a string of rosary beads.

'Here ye are, my wee one. These are very special rosary beads. And they're yours.'

'Thank – '

'Och, dinna thank me, lassie, because I'm going to ask you to say these beads every day of your life for the poor man who hurt you, and for yourself for stealing Wendy, and maybe anything else ye may have helped yourself to. Will ye do that now?'

And anything else! The nun knew! 'Oh, I will!'

'D'y'give me your most solemn assurance?'

'Oh, I do! I do!'

'Well, away ye go to lessons.'

'The quality of mercy!' said Kitty, crossing herself.

'Aye – it droppeth as the gentle rain from heaven,' smiled the nun. 'Be on your way, Portia!'

She was free! It was like breaking-up time for the summer holidays, it was like the end of Mass, it was like Friday afternoon, it was like Big Ben on the wireless. She could feel the beads tingling in her hand with holiness. She was late for class and raced across the playground, nearly tripping over a walking pigeon. Mrs Giyaski asked her where she'd been, but she wouldn't say. The strap was pleasant. It tickled her hands, and she secretly thanked the Virgin for giving her the strap.

Kitty knew she'd have to change her ways. Somehow it now seemed sinful to steal from Saturday night shopping-baskets, and her stomach turned over at the thought of dressing up and singing and dancing to entertain men from the Land O' Cakes: she felt herself blush hot when she remembered how some of the men had told their tarts to piss off because they wanted to watch the little girl dance. She also blushed tingling when she recollected how she'd pointed her finger and beckoned and winked at men as she'd sung, 'I'm in the market for you-oo-oo-oo.' What she'd done in fun and innocence had become twisted and darkly significant.

Unfortunately it was necessary for her to collect money for rent and food because her dad would always need most of his wages for booze.

She had a quick brain, and the answer soon came to her. She was already recognized as a woman by doing her washday stint, and deeply and secretly to her black shame she had become something of a woman on Barney's Field. Added to that, she had her mam's foot-treadle Jones sewing machine, the head of which had been encased in its polished coffin of a box with one handle since her mother died. She had never done any treadling, but she could thread a needle because, with her mother's bad eyesight even with Woolworth's glasses on the end of her nose, she'd had to thread needles for her from as long as she could remember, and it wouldn't take her long to learn how to put coloured patches together.

The women of Angel Meadow worked at home on their own machines for Becky Mandelberg of Cheetham Hill Road; they made patchwork quilts, and every Friday afternoon pushed what they'd made in an old pram all the way to Becky Mandelberg's shop, which wasn't a shop because like the accumulator man's shop it had its plate glass window completely painted over except near the top. Two women always went with the pram: maybe it was because money was involved and one could always keep an eye on the other. The men in Angel Meadow would never help. They wouldn't be seen dead pushing a pram, even if that pram contained a real live baby, and that baby was their own flesh and blood.

Kitty put it to the women that she'd like to make some patchwork quilts for Becky Mandelberg, and she'd be prepared to push the pram after school, no matter how heavy, all the way to Cheetham Hill and back. She knew that Sister St Pius would be pleased because she would have to push the groaning pram of quilts down Queen's Road with Barney's Field across the road on the left going, and on the right coming back, and that would be like Jesus carrying his cross to Calvary every Friday and not just the once.

They agreed, and she became a quilter.

The work was beautiful, because the squares were of the most vivid colours and designs, and it was exciting to choose whether to put a bright red square next to a bright yellow one or a midnight-blue one with gold stars. Occasionally she put the wireless on, even though this meant an extra trip to the accumulator shop. If the music was lively, she worked fast: if it was dull and dreary, she worked slowly, and switched it off because slow work meant less money. It was not worth the cost of an extra accumulator charge.

It suited her down to the ground. She worked at her treadle by the river: she was the Lady of Shalott, and the cotton squares were fields of barley and of rye, and only reapers, reaping early in among the bearded barley, heard a song that echoed cheerly. The song she sang, and now felt entitled to sing, was the Quilters' Song:

'Red, blue and green
In my sewing machine,
I work till me fingers is stunned,
And what I am paid
For the quilts that are made
Pays the Penny-Week Burial Fund.
When I fade and I wilt
And lose all me gilt,
Tell the funeral man not to dally,
But bundle me up in me old patchwork quilt
And bury me out of the tally.'

It wasn't as nice as her dad's 'Spinning Wheel' song, for in his song the young maiden sneaked out into the garden and the arms of her lover, but she saw romance in her work when she imagined a newly married husband saying to his newly married wife, 'Oh, darling!' – she'd heard the word 'darling' when Mrs Fearnley had taken her to the talkies at the Gem Picture Palace. 'Oh, darling!' the newly married man would say. 'What a beautiful, spiffing patchwork quilt. Tomorrow morning we will have tea and buttered toast in bed before going to Mass.' And they would live happily ever after.

She worked hard on the quilts at night, and she was good at them, she had very little unpicking to do, but after a few days she was told off by the women of the street for putting a centre design on her first batch of quilts because they reckoned once Becky Mandelberg found that designs could be done she would ask for designs and not pay a ha'penny extra.

A newness came from the oldness in Kitty's life. She was the

Lady of Shalott working on her loom, albeit a Jones treadle machine. The river was just outside, and it occurred to her that down the river was Camelot in the shape of the many-towered Horsfall Museum. Now that she was learning lines for an audition there, she felt she had the right to walk through its main doors any time she liked. The river was at the foot of the hill on which stood the museum.

Inside it was everything come true. '*I dreamt that I dwelt in marble halls,*' she sang aloud with sheer joy.

'We'll have none o' that, lass!' said the one-armed, one-legged uniformed attendant, stepping out of the shadows. She didn't care. There were marble pillars and arches which touched fingertips at the ceilings, and the ceilings were high, and the corridors broad, and the rooms even bigger than classrooms.

'You evidently like it in here,' said a gentle female voice. There was a lady standing behind her, a beautiful elderly lady, like the lady she'd imagined in the story Mrs Giyaski told them of Tom and the Water-Babies.

'Yes, miss,' she said, and didn't know whether to give a little curtsey.

'Come on, I'll show you round.' It made Kitty's toes tingle that a clean and clever lady should take the trouble to show a small girl around such a palace and, gently though the lady talked, Kitty expected any moment to get a whack on the back of the head and be ordered, 'Get out!'

It had been a manor house in the days of Good Queen Bess, the lady told her. In those days it would have stood in lovely countryside: trout, maybe even salmon, would have been caught in the crystal clear River Medlock, and timid deer would have nibbled the rich grass of Angel Meadow. Men would have walked these rooms in doublet and hose, maybe just returned by horses and carriage from London, where they'd met Drake and Raleigh, and probably been entertained by a new play at the Globe Theatre by a young man named William Shakespeare. The last reference thrilled Kitty because she was learning the lines of Portia by this same William Shakespeare.

As the lady talked, she escorted Kitty through the many rooms which were positively filled with pictures and models. There were flowers, birds, Jesus talking to fishermen, trees, ladies with bare tits swimming in a pool full of water-lilies, a spinning wheel, Crompton's spinning mule, Arkwright's spinning frame, Hargreaves' eight spindles, Kay's flying shuttle, Cartwright's power loom, Jesus talking on a hill, wise men bearing gifts, a man talking to a camel, a large wire-netted coop of live, fluttering, twittering budgerigars with a red map of Australia fastened to the wire, and a plaster bust of Homer. There were so many things, she couldn't remember a hundredth part of them. They didn't go in the room marked 'Athens'. The lady thanked Kitty for coming, and asked her, please, to come again.

Kitty stood outside. It was black and grey; only the red and cream tramcars gave moving patches of colour. Maybe twenty big chimneys tried to touch the clouds, and half of them made clouds of their own with black and dirty brown smoke drifting sideways and upwards to mingle with the real clouds. A man peed down a gutter grid, a man pushed a handcart with a wardrobe on it, a Corporation man cleaned another gutter grid with a giant spoon scoop, tipping his black, smooth, stinking, plague soup into a large midden on wheels with a handle to push, two cats hissed, spit and fought, a window cleaner on a bicycle with ladders balanced over his head and on his shoulders, and a bucket between the rungs of the shorter half of the forward balance, whistled that happy days were here again. Kitty wept tears for the manor house with all its treasures.

She went straight into the small-home sanctuary of her little church. There were no special prayers for manor houses but she remembered a couple of lines of a poem she'd read. She knelt down, made the sign of the cross, closed her eyes, joined the palms of her hands. '*The mistletoe hung in the castle hall, the holly branch shone on the old oak wall. The baron's retainers were blithe and gay, keeping their Christmas holiday.* Amen.' It seemed fair enough for a prayer because it mentioned Christmas.

'Hey, tart!' Mick Dowd's voice ripped her back to reality as she left the quiet church. 'You, tart! I want you, tart!' The word 'tart', which hadn't bothered her a few weeks ago, now hurt, and she wanted to spit on Mick.

'Tart, I'm bloody talking to you!' This time he grabbed hold of her and waved his clenched fist under her nose. 'I saw you coming out o' that museum just now. You was mixing with Proddy-dogs, wasn't you?'

'Are you sure?'

'I guess bloody eggs when I see bloody shell.'

'Aye – six or maybe eight, I didn't count.'

'No bloody tart what's going to marry me mixes with bloody Proddy-dogs!'

'You asking or telling?'

'I'm bloody telling, tart. And I'm going right in that bloody museum this minute and knock them bleeding Proddy-dogs skenning one be bloody one.'

'I'd think twice if I was you, 'cos happen they'll pulverize you, 'cos they're little coloured birds called budgerigars and they'll peck yer nose and peck yer bum, and they're definitely not Catholics.' She skipped and flapped her arms. 'Chirp-chirp! Flap-flap!'

He rushed at her. 'I'll bleeding swing! I bloody will! I'll bleeding swing!' he yelled, and he rushed right into the belt and belly of Constable Kennedy.

'Ach, ye'll do that all right, me spalpeen,' said the constable, 'and the sooner the better to my way o' thinking.' He picked the boy up and carried him to a lamp-post. 'Hold on to that arm!' he shouted. Mick instinctively grabbed hold of the arm, and the policeman let go and stood back.

'If I let go I'll drop and get killed!' yelled Mick.

'Well, it'll happen to ye one o' these fine days and that's for sure, so I'll be saving the country the price of a new black mask for the public executioner. Did I not hear ye telling this pretty little lady that it was desirous of swinging ye were?'

Constable Kennedy walked away, leaving Mick swinging by his arms. As from nowhere, half a dozen lads ran up, held hands and danced around the lamp-post.

'Guy Fawkes, Guy – hit him in the eye,
Tie him to a lamp-post and there let him die.'

'Help me down!' he yelled.

'Why don't you spread your wings and fly down from your perch,' said Kitty. 'Them budgerigars are doing it all the time.'

Ratbag she knew, but on the night of her audition she was introduced by him to some of the others. There was Snotrag, Kakikeks, Shagnasty, Catshit, Jumbo and Augiduck. It surprised her that Protestants had such nicknames, for Catholic boys had no nicknames, not really nicknames, for Paddy was a friendly way of saying Patrick. Perhaps it was because Catholics took on saints' names and it wasn't very nice, and could even be dangerous in heaven, to muck around with saints' Christian names; whereas Protestants, who she assumed were strangers from strange shores like Saxons and Vikings, going by her history book, took other names like Broad Axe, Tall Ship, Whale Killer, The Red, and The Unready. It was obviously traditional for Saxon and Viking Protestants, but nicknames apart, they were just as dirty and scruffy and friendly as the Catholic boys: they all told her not to worry about the audition, that she'd be okay, that there was nowt to worry about. Jake, they said.

Mr Davies strode in through the thumping doors. By clicks of his fingers the stage curtains parted, and red and amber lights silently flooded the stage. Somebody backstage rumbled the thunder tin, but another click from Mr Davies's fingers stopped the thunder. He took his university cap and gown from his old but polished brief-case, and put them on Kitty.

'Might as well get as near the real thing as possible,' he said. 'Curtains, stage lighting and costume. In your own time, away you go.'

Kitty climbed on to the stage. It was her stage; every corner of it was hers – the lights and the floor planking were hers. It was Lewis's shop window at Christmas. She had no hesitation in walking from this side of the stage to the other, like the Bohemian Girl had done, or standing at the very front of the stage and looking at the audience, like the Bohemian Girl had done. As Portia, pretending to be a learned doctor of law, she saw the audience as the courtroom.

'*It is twice blessed* . . .' She held two fingers up high. '*Him that* gives . . .' She held out her hands to give. '*Him that takes* . . .' She held the hands to receive. And so she acted line by line, word by word. '*An attribute to God himself; and earthly power doth then show likest God when mercy seasons justice.*' She raised the college mortarboard high above her head, like the parish priest did his top hat when leading the processions. The mortarboard was raised again when she spoke of the laws of Venice and the State of Venice. After a time, she no longer knew what she said or did but just knew pleasantly that she was saying and doing things.

Suddenly it ended; she had said it all. The lads down below in the half-coloured dark clapped their hands. Waves of warmth rippled through Kitty's body. And then the coloured lights went off, and the white lights came on; it felt cold and the theatre looked shabby.

'Thank you,' said Mr Davies, and he took away his cap and gown. 'Very good!' he added, but not, she thought, with any wild enthusiasm. 'Well now, Miss Noonan, I've got a few more girls to audition, and in fairness I'll have to hear them before announcing my decision. But I promise you'll be receiving a letter from me.'

Somebody rattled the thunder sheet. Almost immediately Mr Davies's attention was diverted. 'Did I ask for thunder? Who's creating the blasted thunder?' He sprang up on to the stage like an athlete, without touching the steps. 'Cathcart, are you thundering?'

'No, he's only farting,' said a voice from the darkness. Mr Davies appeared to ignore the remark.

Kitty sneaked quietly out of the theatre. She moved the door very slowly so that it wouldn't squeak, bump or bang. She dabbed her eyes, for she was beginning to cry. The nice lady of the Water-Babies approached her, but she wasn't a nice lady any more, she was a nasty lady. Why had she shown Kitty all the wonderful things in the museum? Why had Mr Davies let her see the theatre? None of them wanted her. Perhaps because she was a Catholic. She'd become Irish, that's what she'd do, for she was Irish. She would never try to become English again, for everything they sang in the songs about the English was true.

'Sod off! Sod off!' she shouted to the Water-Baby lady.

'Enough o' that!' shouted the one-armed one-legged man

coming out of the shadows. They were all against her. She ran out of the museum.

Down Ancoats Grove and all the way to Angel Meadow women were stood arms-folded and low-voiced; it was unusual; summat must be up for every woman of every house was out on her step. As she turned into Angel Meadow the women smiled and looked relieved to see her.

'Where've you bloody been?' shouted Mrs Fearnley.

'Bloody nigh hairless!' said Mrs Becket.

'I can't say,' said Kitty, still on the verge of tears.

'Aye, well you'd better say in future – you'll be tied to the table leg else,' said Mrs Compton.

'Why – what's up?'

'What's up?' bawled Mrs Roscoe. 'Sky's bloody up, that's what's up.'

'Is it dad?' A terrible thought hit Kitty.

'Not less he's been drowned in ale.'

'Then what?'

'Little Jane Barczok in your class, weren't she?'

'Aye.'

'Not no longer. Found dead with her throat cut on Barney's Field.'

Kitty put her hand to her throat. She felt faint. Her legs didn't seem to be there. Fear hit her like a brick in the belly.

'I know nowt about it! Nowt at all!' she screamed, and ran in, leaving the four women scratching their heads in puzzlement.

Inside the house, she put the kettle on the hob and was instinctively about to start the dead-and-alive process of scrubbing herself between the thighs with hot water, carbolic, and the floor scrubbing brush, but she stopped herself. Jane Barczok wasn't her, yet she seemed to be joined to her; it had happened to Jane who was only two desks away from her in class, and who had had the strap for flirting pellets only that morning. Fear made her teeth dither. Suppose the freshly-made ghost of Jane Barczok was waiting for her up in the bedroom with her throat all cut, and pointing to her throat in order to accuse her of not telling the police about the man, for she had seen enough of him to give a description, and even had a hunch where he could be found. Jane would be alive if she had gone to the police, but that would have meant the girls in class poking straight fingers through their circled ones, and the old nuns dragging her out to be put in a place. She didn't want to be sent to a place away from her dad and her home and her Wendy, and made to say prayers all the time. Besides, the nice nun had given her some rosary beads to pray for the man who had raped her, and to pray each day, which she'd done, and it wouldn't be a scrap of use praying for the man and informing on him at the same time.

And then another trembling fear rushed in on her. Suppose, hiding behind the door in her dad's room, the murderer himself was waiting with his razor opened to slit her throat because she might be able to describe him to the police. There could be Jane's ghost in her room, and the mad murderer in her dad's. She dare not go upstairs, so she decided to sew a few quilts until her dad came home from the Ben Brierley. But the sewing did not help because Portia's words came from the vibrating needle.

'*You must prepare your bosom for his knife,*' and '*Have by some surgeon, Shylock, on your charge, to stop his wounds lest he do bleed to death,*' and '*Shed thou no blood, nor cut thou less nor more but just a pound of flesh. If the scale do turn but in the estimation of a hair, thou diest.*' '*Thou diest!*' repeated the trembling needle. But the voice of the treadle was the voice of Mr Davies – 'I've got a few more girls. But you'll be receiving a letter from me.'

'Enough o' that!' shouted the treadle wheel in the gruff voice of the attendant. She dare not run out into the night street because her throat would run straight into the open razor which would burn like a hot wire because it was so sharp.

Her dad staggered in through the door, and she felt a shock, not expecting her dad but the killer.

' 'Tis not from work I've just come, is it?' he asked, surprised and blinking at seeing Kitty on the machine. 'For the life of me 'tis convinced I am that but fifteen minutes ago they bolted the door of the Ben Brierley.'

Kitty said she'd not been able to sleep so had decided to earn a few pence rather than toss and turn. Her dad gave the treadle wheel a spin.

'What's the sound that I hear at the window I wonder?
The little birds chirping the holly branch under.'

He then did a most unusual thing. He put his arm around the wireless set and gave it a kiss. 'Goodnight, me little lovely,' he said to the wireless, and he put his arm round Kitty's shoulders. 'And come on, me darling, for 'tis away ye must be to the land o' Winkin, Blinkin and Nod.'

Kitty expected a nightmare night, for there had been horror, and there were things to be done in the morning, but, cuddling Wendy, she slept like a top.

For one thing, when Kitty set off next morning early to see Sister St Pius, she left Wendy at home snuggled down in bed: she now trusted the nun. She had to get things straight in her mind, and the nice nun would help. Only that morning, Mrs Fearnley had looked in to say it was all in the paper, and that the only clue the police had was that there were feathers: they called it the Hawk Murder, the Hawk of Barney's Field. Kitty now knew for certain who the Hawk was; she had thought about it, and double thought, and tested herself, but she was dead certain, and now she was certain, she didn't know what to do about the rosary beads. It was easy to say beads for souls unseen like those in heaven, purgatory, Canada or Australia, where her uncles and aunts were, but it would be very difficult saying beads for the man who chopped hens' and turkeys' heads off in Shudehill Market while they were still alive and kicking, for that's how she remembered him. 'Which one?' 'That one.' 'This one?' 'No, that one.' 'That one?' 'Aye, that one.' 'Come here chuck-chuck-chicken! Ching-ching-Chinaman, choppy-choppy-chop! Chop!'

That's how it was, and she'd hated him when she'd seen him doing it, and she'd hated the swanky people who'd chosen their Christmas turkeys while they were still going gobble-gobble.

It had been difficult saying the rosary before she'd remembered him, but now it was impossible. Perhaps there was something wrong with the beads, even tramcars broke down; suppose the beads weren't working properly and had made the Hawk worse not better, and had maybe led to Jane getting her throat cut? If she told those same beads again another little girl could get herself murdered; it might be that saying a Hail Mary on the wrong bead could mean 'Up she comes and the colour's red.' She needed the nun's guidance.

'Is Sister St Pius in, please?' she asked the old nun who answered the door.

'Who?'

'Sister St Pius.'

The old nun looked puzzled, as though she'd never heard the name in her life before.

'I'll make enquiries. Bide awhile.' The nun half closed the door. This was strange. Kitty stood. There was a beautiful smell coming from the brewery, it was either hops or . . . Her dad had told her but she'd forgotten. Her dad had said, 'Rats like malt, and frogs like hops,' and he had hopped on one leg in order to make sure she knew it was a joke, 'about the frogs, eh? Hopping and that.'

Way up on top of one of the big chimneys were two steeplejacks working on a platform; they were only dots; they would be killed if they fell, killed like the flying man in the burning tank on the wakes. Her toes tried to curl up in her shoes, and she couldn't watch any more for fear they fell.

'She's gone.'

'Oh!'

Another old nun had come to answer.

'Sister St Pius has?'

'That's right, child. Gone.'

'Gone?'

'Is there anything I can do, my child? Do come inside.'

Kitty backed away. Will you walk into my parlour, said the spider to the fly – oh, no, thought Kitty, they'd nab her given half a chance.

'Gone where?'

'That I can't say.'

'Then I'll call again, thank you very much.'

Kitty curtsied and backed away, and curtsied again, then turned and ran like hell across the playground.

She was the first in class that morning, but being first in class made no difference; she couldn't concentrate. What had happened to the nun? Had they sent her to another convent, perhaps in China, perhaps in Outer Mongolia, because they'd overheard her saying she'd been raped once upon a time? Had they stopped her being a nun? Whatever, it wasn't fair, because she needed the nun, and nuns were supposed to be where they were needed. She didn't know what on earth to do with the beads. Something told her to drop them down a grid and run away, but if they were holy beads then God would punish her summat dreadful; and if they were killing beads she daren't use them. She daren't swop them either. They would swop easy because any fool could tell they were ancient and expensive, but it would be the worst sin ever to let a classmate, thinking she'd got a knock-down bargain, pray on beads which might make the Hawk kill again.

She had a sickly headache and wanted to go home, but she couldn't tell Mrs Giyaski because Mrs Giyaski would send her to the school clinic with a card to be stamped to prove she'd been, and the first thing the clinic would do would be go through her hair with a louse trap, they always did. Mick Dowd had told her how his finger was hanging off and he was bleeding to death, but they insisted on the louse trap and the paraffin before they would save his life, for they said his head was 'lifting'.

The minutes thumped into her head until the dinner bell clanged. She ran home, narrowly missing being hit by a tram in Every Street. At home, she wrote down a description of the man, and she said he'd done a dirty thing to her, that he'd threatened her with the razor, that he worked at the hen cages nearest the bookstall on Shudehill. She did not give her name and address. She wrote "Police" on an envelope, and she took the price of a twopenny-ha'penny stamp from the gas bill money vase with the chipped handle on the mantelpiece next to the orange and white pot dog which she always pretended guarded it. She didn't post the letter in the pillarbox in Every Street on her way back to school but ran very fast to the one in Pin Mill Brow, which made her puff and pant back at school.

They did Alfred the Great in class, but she only really paid attention when Mrs Giyaski told about him burning the cakes in a peasant's humble cottage. She guessed Alfred was a Saxon because only a Saxon would call himself 'the Great'.

She wondered if the nice nun had been 'taken' suddenly, but made a pact within herself that if neither of the two steeplejacks fell from their big chimney before end of school then everything would be okay and honkydory. The two dots were still up there at four o'clock, and so all should have been right with the world, except she felt more frightened than ever. When she saw Constable Kennedy coming up Carruthers Street she dodged down a back entry in case he recognized her as the girl who'd written the anonymous letter; and when she saw the priest coming up Every Street she dodged down another back entry in case he felt she'd done something terrible to make the nun disappear. She daren't look up at the big chimney in case the two men tumbled while she watched. She couldn't seek sanctuary in the museum because the man in uniform might grab her with the treble strength of his one hand and turn her over to the Water-Baby lady for shouting a swear word at her. Somewhere on the long way round near the haunted church she made a positive decision; she jumped all the pavement flags, being resolved, honest to God, that if her foot went on a crack, the future would be very bad for her. After four or five jumps, her right foot spawled across a crack.

*

> 'It ain't gonna rain no more, no more,
> It ain't gonna rain no more,
> So how in the heck can I wash my neck
> If it ain't gonna rain no more.'

Two navvies from the town hall gas department heaved up cobbles with their picks outside Kitty's home because somebody had reported smelling gas. It was seven o'clock on Saturday morning, and too early for men to sing in the street, and that made Kitty all the more miserable. She lay fully dressed on her bed and thought about the years to come. Old Moore's Almanac had said there would be droughts, and the two singing navvies confirmed what Merlin said: life was predictable. It held no great shakes of a future for Kitty Noonan.

It was this awful purgatory time of growing up and passing the years away; if only the years could be wound up and made to roll fast like a gramophone record with a dog watching. In a few years' time she could become what they called a whore. Some of the bigger girls at school said they got sixpence a time, and then when they'd picked up the tricks of the trade they could get a bob a time. 'A shilling, I'm willing!' the older girls would say to the men outside the pubs. And then later they could become prostitutes and get half a crown a time, but they had to rub round red rouge on their cheeks, and put bright red post office lipstick on their lips and big brass ear-rings on their ears and white powder on their faces, and they had to paint their fingernails and toenails red, and they had to change their names, for she knew a sixteen-year-old girl named Bridie who sometimes called herself Dolores, which probably meant they became Saxons; and they stood in lines with white handbags at Lewis's arcade, and ran away when police paddywaggons came.

She didn't really want to become a whore or a prostitute but she felt that because of what had happened to her she was half-way there.

On the other hand she could become a nun, but recently the sudden disappearance of Sister St Pius had frightened her. It was the fear that a mother superior could wave a wand like a fairy godmother in a dark forest of snarling trees and cause a nun to be sent to Tibet, and probably half-way through a prayer.

It was okay for boys. They could run away to sea as cabin boys and sail the world and come back as captains, or they could take a moggie-moonlight cat and go to London and become Lord Mayor and rich; but there were no such opportunities for girls who wanted to run away from home. But then again, even the thought of leaving home and her dad pained her, for her dad would surely die of starvation and a broken heart if she left him. It was no good becoming a mill girl either, for mill girls went pale and died of consumption. She didn't know what she'd have to do.

It seeemd almost God-sent when Paddy Byrne knocked on the door and asked if she'd come with him to London Road Railway Station to help him take train names. The railway station was a smashing idea because she would find out what places trains went to, and it would give her some choice.

They walked past the museum, but she wouldn't look at it. They walked on past the stables of a hundred horses under the never-ending railway arches. All the horses were out working but most of them would be home for Saturday half-day and dinnertime, and she wondered what horses thought about at weekends; perhaps they didn't think, perhaps they just chewed hay, but on the other hand they might be waiting and hoping for King Arthur and his merry knights of the round table to come laughing and joking and jumping on their backs and galloping off to rescue damsels, like the painting above the theatre stage. She stamped her foot with anger at having thought about the Children's Theatre.

After that came the sweet smell from the Danish Bacon Curers' warehouse by the Ashton Canal: it was a salty bacon smell. She'd often peeped inside but never seen anybody. She half expected to see Vikings with horns on their helmets because the Danes were written in the history book as Vikings, and they might have sailed up the Ashton Canal and established a bacon-curing warehouse. King Canute, who tried to stop the sea, was a Dane, and he fought King Alfred, who burnt the cakes.

She nudged Paddy. 'Look inside and see if you can see a Viking, but don't let them see you looking.'

'I can see nowt,' said Paddy.

'They're there – you can smell their pigs being cured.'

'Cured o' what?'

'Whatever pigs get.'

The business of the Vikings ended as they turned into Store Street, for at the end of the cobbled slope was the secret entrance to the station. It wasn't really secret, because it had stone steps, a wooden handrail, and dirty white tiles around the round walls, but nobody ever used it. It was on the Ancoats side, and perhaps nobody from Ancoats went on trains. It came up at a glass pillbox at the top of the long wide sloping approach.

The front of the station had columns like she'd once seen on a mantelpiece clock which was supposed to be a Greek temple. But the station was unlike a Greek temple because it was spinning and busy and noisy and shouting and hissing and clanging with a thousand big milk cans. The cans were the size of Kitty, and sloped towards their necks, and their lids were like the splendid caps worn by Chinamen.

There were galloping young horses pulling red two-wheelers painted 'Manchester Evening News'. There were taxi cabs, looking like black concertinas on wheels: they chug-chugged and went 'honk!'

There were old Jews with black bushy yet shabby beards, and black wide-brimmed hats, and long coats tied with rope; and Irishmen with clothes much too small, showing odd socks, and with hats precariously on the sides of their heads, and sometimes licking their thumbs with the tips of their tongues to show they were ready for a pint of beer or a fight; there were Italians, looking a little like the Jews except they didn't have beards but long black curling 'sideboards' or hair twisting around their cheeks, and curly black moustaches like the kings on gambling cards.

Inside the station it was black and grey, and serpent-hissing with steam and smoke, and many people stopped many porters to ask questions.

There were three massive great locomotives against the buffers. All three were wide awake; one went 'ever-clang-hiss! ever-clang-hiss!', the other sighed 'ah-shoo-shoo! ah-shoo-shoo!', and the third went 'ah-wisher-bang! ah-wisher-bang!' Black smoke drifted from their stacks, and hundreds and hundreds of little puffs of steam pop-pop-popped from their many metal joints. Their red oil lamps seated on their laps had black streaks of oil, and oil and water dripped from under the giant wheels which were joined by a great rod. They had names – Samson, Goliath, and Vulcan – and this made Paddy jump with happiness; he pulled a red notebook and pencil from his pocket and wrote them down.

'I've got Planet, and Hector!' shouted Paddy. 'And I've got Ostrich and Caledonian! They all live here! I know 'em, and they know me, 'cos I'll tell you why . . .' He dropped his voice secret-like, and he brought a medicine bottle out of his other pocket. ''Cos I bless them.'

'Is that real holy water?'

'Aye.'

'Jake?'

'Aye.'

'And you bless the puffer-billies?'

'Aye. I'm going to be a railway engine priest, like St Francis was for cats, dogs and pigeons. Railway engines need a priest, like a missionary to go among 'em.'

'Why?'

'So's they won't bloody crash. There hasn't been a crash since I took up blessing 'em.'

'How many was there before?'

'None. But there'll be even less now.'

Kitty pointed to Goliath. 'I'm watching.'

They walked across to Goliath. Paddy took the cork from the bottle and sprinkled a drop or two of water on the nameplate.

'*Dominus vobiscum*!' he said.

'Piss off!' shouted a voice from above. Way up high in the cab was the engine driver. The man wore his blue jacket, patched like a map with oil, his face was streaked with icicles of coal dust, on his head was a black oilskin peaked cap. Another oil and coal head joined his and looked over his shoulder: this was the fireman.

'What you wetting my engine for? It's bloody wet enough!' said the driver.

'I'm blessing it.'

'Messing it, if y'ask me. Sod off!'

The fireman behind him jumped down from the high iron footplate. He winked at Paddy.

'Would ye know now,' said the fireman, 'that me blooming driver doesn't understand at all what ye're doing, for 'tis blessing the train that ye're doing, am I right?'

'Aye,' said Paddy, ''tis so.'

The man gave him a penny. 'Now 'tis here I'm handing ye a penny o' the king's realm that not many hours ago was circulating in the city o' London town. And I'm awarding ye this London penny, me fine feller, to take to your church and light a candle for Goliath and for Sean O'Riordan, which is me, and for Ivor Thomas, which is me driver: and so that our furnaces will always light with grace and charm, our steam pressures always be perfect as a woman's kiss, and the signals always be in our favour to get us to our destination before the pubs shut. Ye'll do that?'

'I'll do that.'

'Ye're a fine feller. And if ye give me yer hand . . .' The fireman climbed back up into his cab and hoisted Paddy in with him. Then there was a clanging and banging, and everything glowed bright red for the fireman had opened the furnace door to show Paddy. Kitty looked up at the red glow on the fireman's head, and for a second thought of a song of her dad's: '*Seven feet is his height with some inches to spare, and he looks like a king in command.*' Paddy was lowered down again: he blinked and looked dazed as though he had been baptized into a new life. Kitty herself thought how miraculous it was that Goliath and great engines like him should come from London, past the pigs and sheep and cows and trees and through the tunnels all the way to Ancoats.

A lady's crackling voice said places like 'London Euston, Birmingham, Macclesfield, Bristol, Plymouth.'

'We've got to bless Samson next,' said Paddy, and the two of them strolled across to the next platform. Samson was the locomotive which had been saying 'ah-shoo-shoo! ah-shoo-shoo!' as though it was having forty winks. The big wheels were so much higher than Kitty she had to look up to the top of the rim. She began to remember things from Mrs Giyaski: Samson was good, and ten times stronger than any man in a leopardskin who bends iron bars at the wakes, and his wife, who was very beautiful, but sneaky beautiful, cut his hair off while he was asleep, and he became weak as a kitten, and they fell upon him and blinded him.

Things were being done in and around Samson's coaches. Boys, always whistling but whistling snatches of no songs at all, pushed mailbags on two-wheeler trucks like grocers have, and their bags were thrown through a wide-open coach door. A man with a long iron hammer walked down beside the tracks and tapped coach wheels as he passed. He was whistling a real tune, 'Keep Young and Beautiful'. Perhaps he was whistling it to the coaches, but the coaches, especially those without windows, were far from beautiful: they were dirty, and the few windows they had were black with dried smoke, and the bars ran upwards like a prison cell. The carriages with big windows were cleanish, and had one brass bar running sideways across. On the tops, near the rounded roofs, were boards which said 'Birmingham, Bristol, Plymouth'. They were not quite beautiful, but nearly. The lady who cut Samson's hair was beautiful. It must be nice for Samson up in heaven, seated comfortably with his eyesight restored, to look down and see that the London North Eastern Railway had called an engine after him.

'Pooooooop!' The scream from Samson's whistle rattled, screeched and echoed from the million dirty glass panels in the great glass roof dome of the station, and frightened her.

'Did you make it do that?' she asked, rubbing her fingers in her ears to get her ears right again.

'It was saying, "*Et cum spiritum tuum.*"'

'Was it heck! It went poop and made me ears rattle.'

Samson hissed louder, and puffs of steam, like the puffs in comics, like ice-cream cornets, came from all parts. There was also action on Goliath's platform.

A man with a green flag under his arm and a teacher's playground whistle between his lips had been studying a waistcoat pocket watch, fastened to his waistcoat by a chain. Kitty thought this was a puzzle because above the station, near the 'H. Samuels' sign by the roof, was the largest roundest clock in the world, and she wondered why he'd not studied that clock, because the people who were walking fast to get on the train kept looking back and up at it. The man slowly took the green flag from under his arm, never taking his eyes off the pocket watch: it was quite clear he was going to get the train going.

'I'll be back! Stay there!' shouted Paddy. He glugged the bottle of holy water down on the track and ran up the platform to a footbridge, then up the steps two at a time.

Kitty stood alone, a very small nervous girl looking up at a very large confident locomotive.

Samson was the nearest she'd ever been to a god, any kind of god, a living god, for there was no denying that the mighty thing was alive.

'Oh, great Samson,' she thought to herself, inventing a prayer, 'thou hast the wheels and the power to go forth all the way to Israel. Goeth thou therefore this long journey hence in order to intercede for me that I may become a famous actress, for I doth not wisheth to becometh a nun, or owt else.' She opened her eyes and thought how clever she was and what a very good prayer it was, until she went hot with blushes due to another awful thought: that she had blasphemed.

Paddy returned with his bottle, banging the cork down with his fist as hard as he could.

'Where've you been? What've you been up to? What's in't bottle?' she asked.

'Engine smoke from Goliath,' said Paddy proudly. 'Not many have it.'

'I don't reckon many want it. What's it for?'

'I do engine smoke like I do train names, they go together. I've got Planet in me dad's chest liniment bottle that was, and Hector in me mam's cough bottle that was.'

'Aye, but you've chucked away holy water, and God'll get you. He always does.'

'I didn't chuck it away. I blessed the track for a safe journey.'

'About six inches of it. And what about Vulcan standing there on platform three? What's he done to you?'

'I'll nip to St Alban's and get a refill specially for Vulcan.'

'You're not going to be a priest, are you?' she asked Paddy candidly.

''Course I bloody am, but that's when I'm grown up. There's nowt to stop me praying I'll get a train set in me Lewis's parcel when Father Christmas comes, is there?'

She walked back up Store Street with him; the day was drab now they'd left the station. She didn't go with him to St Alban's: she didn't think she was ready for St Alban's.

St Alban's was a tiny church hidden up a back street. Her dad said it was the headquarters of the Foreign Legion because foreigners went there to forget.

On the city side of Ancoats were the Italians with their church of St Michael's, and on the museum, river and railway side were the Irish with their St Anne's. But if either Irish or Italians, or even Saxons, committed sins which they'd rather their own priest did not get to know about, they'd go to Confession at St Alban's in preparation for Holy Communion at their own church. The church had two priests, an Irishman and an Italian, and neither spoke English too well: so the Irish went to the Italian box, and the Italians to the Irish, and it was thought that if a confession was said quickly enough it would go above the heads of the priests and direct to where it was meant. People never admitted they were going to St Alban's. If asked, they said they were going to St Mary's off Albert Square.

Paddy tried to entice her to stay with him by suggesting they spend the London penny on a penn'orth o' sherbert to lick between them, but she reminded him that an entire trainful of people including an engine and an Irish fireman who'd taken him up into the cab, which had never happened to any boy before, were depending upon him lighting a penny candle. She turned right down Ancoats Lane and went home quite happy for she now knew that if she ever had to leave home, there were trains to London Euston, Macclesfield, Birmingham, Bristol and Plymouth.

When she got home, her dad was like a caged Belle Vue lion walking around a ham bone, wary lest it was poisoned. On the table was a large white typewritten envelope.

'D'y'see it?'

'Aye, I do.'

'With yer own two peepers?'

'An' all.'

'What d'y'make of it?'

Her dad walked around the table, eyeing the envelope from all angles. He tapped the side of his forehead in order to liven his brains up. 'It makes ye think,' said he.

'Aye,' said Kitty.

'You and me, and all our born days we've never received a typewritten letter before, not even when yer darling mother – God rest her soul – passed away.' He made the sign of the cross. Then he did a bit of a jig, but his brow was wrinkled as though it pained him to jig. He stood on a chair and looked down the mirror above the mantelpiece, but it would not go from his sight.

'And 'tis addressed to you, me darling.'

That came as a little shock to Kitty. She held her hands behind her back to prove that she wasn't touching it, and she leaned over the table, not touching that either. She read the typewritten name and address.

'So it is, dad.'

'Oh, me love, what have ye been up to?'

'Nowt I ken, dad.'

Kitty knew she'd lied, and she felt the lie. It most likely was a letter from the police about her anonymous letter, and anonymous letters were poison pen letters and were crimes. Her dad didn't help matters, and she wanted to scream at him. She wanted to run out of the house and catch a train, perhaps the unblessed Vulcan.

'Typewritten,' went on her dad.

'That's right – typewritten.'

'On a typewriter.'

'Aye.'

'Poor Timothy Nolan got a typewritten letter, and isn't he now doing three months inside Strangeways Prison? For money he owed, they said 'twas.'

'We could burn it, dad.'

'And a fine bit o' good that'd do. Tim burned six, but they kept coming.'

'Then I best open it.'

'Aye, but keep yer voice down case there's a priest passing the house.' He was always worried about a priest passing the house when they were talking, which Kitty thought was silly because their house was a dead end, and a priest could only be passing the house to jump in the river.

She washed her hands in the slopstone first, for it was a pure white envelope.

'I'm ready now!' said her dad, and he picked up the poker and brandished it as though expecting something to jump out and attack them.

Kitty screamed as she read: she had to rub her eyes with her arms for tears came flooding from her eyes.

'It's the Children's Theatre! They want me to go and see them about acting in their plays!'

There was a knock on the door. Kitty, still blubbering, answered it. It was Mick Dowd.

'I got jam jars for the mat at the bug hut. You coming, tart?'
'Sod off!' she said, and slammed the door in his face.
Her dad was doing a jig with relief.

'Here I am, on a tram,
And don't give a damn if we ram
Another tram-tiddley-am-tam tiddley-am-tam-tam-tram.'

She set off all washed and clean and shining as a new pin: she had only to make the cobbled climb up Ancoats Grove and there on the left stood the museum and Children's Theatre waiting for her. People would know she was going to be a famous actress – somehow they would be able to tell: but nobody bothered looking at her, smelling of soap as she was, so how could they know she was going to be famous?

The Italian barrel-organ at the bottom of Ancoats Grove was a good luck omen for by chance it played her dad's Convent Garden tram song, except it went click-click-click from time to time instead of getting on with the melody.

Some little girls played the bouncing ball game in which the ball had to be bounced under a cocked-up leg. 'One, two, three, alairla: four, five, six, alairla!' A boy kicked the ball as he passed, and it thudded against the closed door of Old Granny Witchie. The girls would get the blame.

A man sprawled on his doorstep, feet wide apart, boots sticking up so that the newspaper patches on the insides of his soles could be seen, the peak of his cap to the back of his head, and he played 'Oh Susannah!' on a Jew's harp.

'Get yer bloody big clod-hoppers out o't way!' shouted his wife, trying to step over his boots. He stopped playing.

'Where'm I going to put 'em?'

'Up yer arse or behind yer ear, so's you shift 'em.' He moved his feet, and carried on with *a banjo on my knee*.

Kitty looked up at four big chimneys: three were smoking, the fourth wasn't. The fourth hadn't smoked for weeks and weeks, and they said the mill was dead. She felt sorry for the dead mill, there must be a world somewhere in which live church buildings looked after dead mill buildings.

A boy held up a jam jar to show his pal the little grey fish. 'See, look at its underneath, it's red, it's a robin redbreast, and it knows its name.'

'What's its name?'

'I just call it any bloody name. It answers.'

'Call it summat then.'

'Not with you watching. It'll do nowt with you watching.'

A dog was being dirty with another dog, and a woman in a shawl, with a finger like a skeleton, pointed at the underneath dog. 'You can take that bloody grin off your face 'cos I'm bloody telling you I'll drown 'em like I did last lot.' She turned to another woman in a shawl. 'Lovely little things they was too. I had to pull lavatory chain twice for one of 'em: he didn't want to go down, little sod.'

A gang of men threw pitch and toss on the cobbles. They all wore caps, they all had white silk scarves tied round their necks. Kitty guessed they were miners from Bradford Road Pit because that was how miners dressed. Maybe they were out of work because the fourth chimney wasn't smoking and the mill was dead.

A woman dipped the head of a clothes peg in a tin of golden syrup and pushed it in her baby's mouth, and the baby gum-sucked with relish. Clothes pegs were soldiers to Kitty. They had split legs but no arms – she imagined their arms tightly by their sides; their heads were round like knobs; they were like miniature peggies. Babies had choked to death when clothes pegs had gone down their throats, but this mother held on to the legs of the peg.

'Bye, Baby Bunting, daddy's gone a-hunting, to get a little rabbit skin to wrap his baby bunting in,' sang the mother.

Paddy Byrne ran up to Kitty. He was breathless and he waved a bit of paper. 'I've just blessed two trains what I've never seen before!' he panted.

'Oh aye, what are they?'

'That's the trouble, I can't say them. I asked a man and he said summat like Felix and San Fairy Ann.'

'Couldn't be Felix not for one of them big locomotives,' said

Kitty, 'for Felix keeps on walking. And San Fairy Ann sounds cissie, too.'

'No, it's not. It's what the French said in the trenches, me dad told me, and it means "I don't give a shit".'

'A locomotive wouldn't dare say that, not and expect passengers to get on it.'

'That's what I thought. Anyway, I've written the names down, and I wondered if you'd ask.'

'Ask who?'

'The Protestants. Well, you know a lot of Protestants, and they're a bit cleverer than us micks.'

'And you going to be a Catholic priest? What's the world coming to?'

'Will y'ask?'

'I'll ask.'

'Don't tell Mick Dowd: he'll pulverize me.'

'Lips buttoned.'

'*Dominus vobiscum!*' He ran off, leaving her with the bit of paper.

Three kids sat nudging on a step, and their mother came out with a plate. 'Right – here's your sugar butties!' she said. They took one each. It was Thursday, the end of the week, and most people had to make do with sugar butties: tomorrow, pay day, they'd get fish and chips.

At the top of Ancoats Grove was the Spread Eagle and a man, perhaps another miner because he wore a white silk scarf, played the spoons with one hand, and the bones with the other, outside the pub. '*Little Dolly Daydream, pride of Idaho,*' he sang, but Blind Andy brought out his fiddle, threw down his collecting cap, leaned against the wall, and began to play 'The Mountains of Mourne'.

'Aw, come on, Paddy, give us a chance,' said the spoon man, 'just to earn a tanner for me wife's cough bottle.'

'Take the long mile,' said Blind Andy.

The pitch-and-toss men stopped their throwing and, hands in pockets, mooched up towards the Spread Eagle for they knew the micks would fight for Blind Andy's fiddle.

'Lerrim earn a couple o' coppers for his wife's medicine,' growled one of the men.

'Sure I'm not stopping him,' said Blind Andy. 'Let him go and do the spoons outside o' the Bunch o' Grapes, and all power to his elbow, and may his wife live for ever.' And he pointed his bow with ship's compass accuracy to the Bunch o' Grapes.

'D'y'know 'The Road to Mandalay'? 'Cos if so, bloody take it!' another man shouted in Blind Andy's ear. Blind Andy immediately changed his tune to 'The Rising of the Moon' and closed doors began to open. There would be a street fight for sure, and Kitty hurried on.

'Hello, chuck!' said the one-armed one-legged attendant. 'We've missed you, love!' Kitty was so delighted with his greeting that she wished there and then he could have his other arm and leg back, and she made a note in her brain to pray for him. He must have lost his limbs fighting the mighty Prussian army in the Great War: he had medal ribbons on his chest which proved it. Yet he was lucky, for he was still in uniform even though a museum uniform, whereas most men who had lost limbs begged for pennies in the market. She must have looked too long at him, for he patted his pinned sleeve and his wooden leg. 'Lost these fighting the Irish,' he smiled. 'Ambushed we was.' Kitty felt a sudden wave of guilt: she now felt she personally owed him his arm and leg.

'Was it outside the Spread Eagle?' she asked, hoping she didn't look Irish.

'Wish it had been, chuck,' he said, 'there'da been more supping than shooting. No, it were at Macroom by Tom Barry's Flying Column – '

'My goodness, the return of the little princess,' interrupted the voice of the Water-Baby lady behind Kitty, and there was the golden lady floating like a fairy godmother. 'We thought you'd gone off with the raggle-taggle gypsies oh!'

The lady put her arm around Kitty's shoulders and escorted her through the marble hallway to the theatre, and opened the door so that the brass handle wouldn't swing back and thump her. She introduced herself as Miss Hindshaw.

Inside the theatre was all the clatter, chatter, shouting and coughing of a rehearsal: it was something about people passing while the lentils boiled, and Kitty stood there for a long time completely ignored. Once more the feeling gradually came over her that she wasn't wanted, and that it might be a good idea to sneak away, for she was one of the people of Ancoats Grove, and would always be one of the people of Ancoats Grove, and would grow up to stick a peg in a baby's mouth.

'That's right – you! Miss Noonan! Kitty Noonan! Wake up!' The voice snapped her out of herself. Mr Davies was pointing at her. 'Step up, Kitty! Step up on the stage!'

She climbed up the wooden steps.

'Recite something for us, something from the top of your head, whatever comes in!' went on the teacher.

The feeling was lovely: it was like lying down flat in the warm galvanized bath before the glowing fire with the door bolted and the curtains closed and the women on the wireless saying, 'Violets! Lovely sweet violets!'

'I dreamt that I dwelt in marble halls,
   With vassals and serfs at my side,
And of all who assembled within those walls
That I was the hope and the pride.'

There were two-finger whistles from the shadows down below, and a voice shouted, 'And now show us your bum!', and she knew whose voice it was. Another lad's voice shouted, 'More!' She loved it, but she couldn't understand how she'd remembered the words, it was the magic of Merlin. 'Come on, more!'

'I dreamt that suitors sought my hand,
   That knights upon bended knee,
And with vows no maiden heart could withstand,
They pledged their faith to me.'

'And this time, for an encore, the genuine – beware of copies – bare bum! Alley Oop!' shouted the voice again.

'Shurrup, Ratbag! Else we'll get your dick out and spit on it!' said another voice.

Mr Davies clapped his hands as he approached her.

'Will I do, sir?' she asked.

'Oh, you'll do, Kitty. You've got natural talent. Thank you very much for coming.'

She felt her eyes and face bursting to cry. She'd believed she wasn't wanted, and when all was said and done she was wanted after all. He gave her a book.

'There's your part, if you can manage it, which I know you can well enough. It was written by George Bernard Shaw – ever heard of him?'

'No, sir.'

'Not much more than seven years ago, so it's a fairly new play and a risky venture for the Ancoats Children's Theatre.' He gave a bit of a smirk to himself. 'And it's about a fairly new saint. I think she was elevated, if that's the right word, about ten years ago, about the time you were born. St Joan – heard of her?'

'Yes, sir.'

'And I'll let you know when rehearsals start, and we'll put the play on after Christmas when the days are drab and the nights are drear.'

'Thank you, sir.' She clutched the book. And then she remembered Paddy's piece of paper. 'Oh, sir, one of me friends who blesses railway trains wants to know what these are.'

He read them. 'Well, they might be your fortune. Do you believe in fortune-telling?'

'I read the stars in the newspapers, but they're papers from the tram bins and everything has usually happened. Sometimes they've been right, 'cos one said "travel" and "lucky" and I remembered it was the day I was sent to the school clinic, which was travel, and they found no lice in me hair, which was lucky.'

'The first is Phoenix, which was a very beautiful bird. It burned to death, then rose from its own ashes. I suppose you might say St Joan did that. And the other is Sans Pareil which is French – and Joan was French – and means "without equal". Could that be you?' he smiled.

'*She climbed aboard each whaler,*' sang the accumulator man, in his bubbling accumulator shop. 'Who's that, tell me?' he asked Kitty, after he'd finished singing.

'Les Allan, Henry Hall's crooner,' she answered. 'And here's another of his.' This time Kitty sang ' *'Twas on a steamer coming over*'. 'Perhaps the one explains the other,' she said. 'He met her on the steamer, told her he loved her, kissed her and that, then skidaddled, leaving her going on whalers asking for him.'

'Ah, but perhaps . . .' He gave her a wink, and cleared his throat. 'This is Billy Bennett. ' *'Twas a dirty night, 'twas a dirty trick, when our ship turned over in the Atlan-tick!*'

'That's it – the ship with them on sinks – '

'Aye, like the Titanic – '

'And they go in different directions in different lifeboats.'

'Aye, like "Row, row, row the boat".'

'But they meet again eventually and live happily ever after.'

'You always say that, kid. You're dead daft for saying that.'

She and the accumulator man had evolved this game. He listened to the wireless all the time, and even claimed he could pick up America when the moon was right. He knew all the latest songs, and he knew the jokes of comedians, and he would try them out on her when she came, and she would fit the songs into a story for him.

He was a Saturday night man if ever there was one, but it was Saturday night on his own, or maybe it was with the fairies, if all the voices that slid through the air and through the walls could be called fairies. To put more salt and vinegar on the Saturday night fish and chips, and listen to voices singing about steamers and jackets of blue, or even hitching old Dobbin to the shay, must be heaven: and no bedtimes. He knew all the news of the world, and he understood what was happening. He treated the wireless as toyfully as a clockwork train or a doll's house; whereas her dad looked upon the wireless as one of God's living creatures who told tales from one to another: once when he'd turned a knob to get the sound louder he'd apologized to the wireless and hoped it didn't hurt.

'It says they'll be topping that murderer after three clear Sundays in Strangeways,' the accumulator man suddenly announced. 'There'll be no happy ending for him three weeks come Monday, eh?'

'Which . . . ?' and Kitty was immediately sorry she'd asked, because she knew.

'Him as slit that little girl's throat up on Barney's Field. Feathers, y'know? Cockadoddledoo!' He flapped his arms like a grotesque human bird. 'Mind you, up on Barney's field, I ask you. No little girl should go there, I bet you wouldn't, would you, chuck?'

'Gorra go!' said Kitty, grabbing the handle of her accumulator. 'Miss me tram else.'

'They said it was lucky, though I don't reckon feller thinks so. An anonymous tip-off from one of his victims, they said, and when bobbies went round just to make enquiries he ran off, and later, when questioned, he confessed.'

'Ta-ra!' said Kitty.

She was grateful that their wireless set wasn't allowed to give the news. Her dad wouldn't listen because he said the English news was all about how blooming clever the English was, and when he'd listened to the Irish news from Athlone it was all about the price of pigs.

The tram guard was the ginger-haired cheeky one who thought he was funny, and Kitty cringed in case he joked about her being on Barney's Field.

'This tram turns round at the university,' he told all the passengers. 'Y'know the university? It's where they've got that ancient mummy pickled and preserved.' He started to do a belly dance. 'An Egyptian tart named Salummy, had a big bulge in her tummy. She said it was put there by King Tut, who stuffed her and made her a mummy.' He then pretended to whip them. 'Come on, ye lazy swabs, ye miserable slaves – get moving them oars! This boat has got to be in New York tomorrer morning! The only tram to cross the Atlantic! Best nip upstairs and see them angels has all got tickets! You gotta watch them angels upstairs, dead shifty! If you got wings, you can bloody fly, but you ain't coming on my tram without a ticket. I'll punch their bloody tickets for 'em, I will.' He ran upstairs, and for a few seconds Kitty could breathe freely: but perhaps he was thinking of a limerick to say about her, like the one of the mummy. Oh no, please God don't let him know who I am! she prayed.

He flew down the spiral stairway by just holding on to the brass rail. 'Here we are, folks!' he began. 'Ancoats, home of the micks, the leprechauns, the little people – begorrah, begorrah, begorrah!' Kitty was compelled to get off the tram at the next stop, for he would be sure to say something about her. 'Ha, Kathleen Mavourneen!' He smiled at her as she stood on the deck. 'There was a young lady of Erin who said, "I've no clothes to be wearin'. I feel quite undressed 'cos I haven't a vest, and people keep stoppin' and starin'!"'

Kitty felt naked and exposed as she jumped off the tram. The guard was dirty, dirty! She ran past the empty haunted church into Palmerston Street. Ancoats was sanctuary, Ancoats was cosy and safe: even the men of Ancoats who went to prison for crimes committed, committed them in the posher districts. She was sure that even the black weeds on the railway embankment felt free and happy But there was something strange about the street. Women were kneeling down on their steps and saying their rosary beads.

'Ach, get down upon yer knees, child, and say a Hail Mary before ye go a step further,' said a woman.

'Why?'

'Is it "why" ye're asking? Whisht now and say yer prayer.'

Kitty knelt. 'Hail, Mary, full of grace: the Lord is with thee: blessed art thou among women . . .' She got to thinking. It had been like that when Mr O'Leary had been shot and killed while blacking his boots before going up to the Men's Confraternity to play in a darts match. He'd been a nice man with a nice wife and five nice children, and it was said he did a lot for the church. But they said he'd once betrayed the IRA back in Ireland, and the IRA caught up with him and blew his brains over the fireplace. There had been praying in the street. And then Mrs O'Leary had swallowed a bottle of washing bleach, and there'd been no praying for she was a suicide, and doors were bolted in the street when the cart came to take her body away. And the children had been taken away in a motor lorry, and had been shouted at for honking the horn while the lorry was being wound up, and frightening the man who was doing the winding.

When she reached the end of the Hail Mary, she asked again who the prayers were for.

'For the little nun Sister St Pius,' said the woman. 'And to be taken so young!'

Oh my goodness, thought Kitty, the poor nun has died from a broken heart because I informed on the murderer instead of praying for him, and it is to be hanging by the neck he will be like they do in the fun house of Belle Vue.

''Twas the pale disease, consumption, poor dear nun. And didn't I say to Brendan the first time I clapped eyes on her that she'd not be long for this world? Still, 'tis consolation to know that with her being a nun and that she'll get a seat near the front in the next.'

Kitty ran home and up to her room. She wanted to pray for the nun, and she made Wendy lie flat on her face to pray too. 'Dear Jesus – '

'*Show me the way to go home . . .*' Her dad's singing as he came down the street spoiled her prayer.

'Good day to ye, Mrs Fearnley!'

'And a good day to you too, Mr Noonan.'

'Ye're a beautiful woman, Mrs Fearnley.'

'Would you tell my husband that, Mr Noonan?'

'*Wherever I may roam . . .*' sang her dad.

''Tis a fine voice you've got, Mr Noonan.'

'Aye, so it is. And there's many other fine qualities I possess, for 'tis said there's many a good tune played on an old fiddle.'

'And 'tis said chance'd be a fine thing.'

'Oh it would, Mrs Fearnley, it would indeed.'

Kitty didn't like the conversation she heard down below. Perhaps her dad didn't expect her to be home: and the one time she needed her dad to talk to! It was all right for Wendy, for Wendy had Kitty, but it couldn't be said that Kitty had Wendy. Wendy listened silently to Kitty, but Wendy couldn't respond. Sister St Pius had listened to her and responded, and now she'd disappeared and died. Perhaps even now, with three clear Sundays to go before they put the rope round his neck, she could write another anonymous letter and say she'd been mistaken, but that'd be no use for he'd confessed to murder but then it wouldn't be so much on her conscience. Sister St Pius should have stayed alive happy ever after so that Kitty could tell her all her cares and woes, bye, bye, blackbird.

She was worried about the condemned man's hens, and hoped they would be fed and have their water changed, and hoped that whoever took them over would not chop their heads off.

And there was her being St Joan. Somebody would have to be told: she couldn't just go right off and be St Joan for the Protestants. Doing the Virgin Mary for her own Catholics had been a different kettle of fish: she had been the priest's choice. Sister St Pius had told her to be the very best at acting, but Sister St Pius hadn't known it was going to be St Joan. There was a lot to ponder upon.

She wished she could be poorly, not really ill poorly, and certainly not dying poorly, but getting better poorly so that everybody would visit her and tell her not to worry, and the small fire would be lit in the bedroom at night and make shadows dance cosy dances on the wallpaper, and light up the brass bedknobs like a friendly all-seeing archangel's eyes.

The nun was to be buried in Scotland, near a castle which had once been her family home. All Kitty knew about Scotland was from a poem about a naughty boy who ran away there to see what he could see, but he found that the ground was as hard, that a cherry was as red as in England: although her dad, who had travelled around a lot as a soldier, said the Guinness in Glasgow was nearly but not quite as good as the Guinness in Dublin.

The children prayed loud and a lot in their classroom the morning of the Requiem. Everybody wept, and Mrs Giyaski wept. Boys had to look away from other boys so as not to be seen crying; there was not a girl without a clean handkerchief, nor was there a handkerchief that was dry.

The school formed lines outside the church door all the way to a waiting motor hearse, the like of which had never been seen in Ancoats before because only a plumed horse was considered right for the poor. The nun's father, who was said to be a lord or something, would not be coming to Ancoats, but had paid for the coffin to be escorted on a train to Scotland. Kitty had told Paddy Byrne to play wag and be at the station to bless the train, which she expected would be the Phoenix because a phoenix bird rose from the dead. Paddy had promised to do a special Requiem. He admitted not knowing the Latin, but he could recite parrot-wise the first verse of 'Adeste Fideles' and if while saying it he thought, 'Deliver the souls of all the faithful departed from the pains of hell and from the deep pit: deliver them from the jaws of the lion,' he felt God would be dead pleased. He was confident he could do two things at the same time because just a few days before he'd made music by playing a paper and comb with his mouth, and banging together two tin pan lids which he'd tied to his knees, although his mother had clouted him for waking the baby which had taken her hours to get to sleep.

The church Requiem seemed to last for ever, and the children outside felt that great secrets were being said in the church. When the nun's coffin was carried out, it was shouldered by four strong men who wore kilts like on the packets of Scott's Porage Oats.

There were women in shawls who passed comment upon how small the coffin was, and others who said what a dainty maid the nun had been, and others who said they couldn't wait because the rent man would be calling.

The children under the direction of Mrs Giyaski sang:

'Farewell Manchester! Noble town farewell!
Here with loyalty every breast can swell:
Here as in a home, whereso'er I roam,
Lancashire, ever here, my heart shall dwell.'

Mrs Giyaski had told them the song had been written by Bonnie Prince Charlie when he'd found how many loyal Catholics there were to support him in Manchester.

Everything was very bright and proud after the hearse and its following motor car with the big-kneed Scotsmen drove away. The light seemed lighter, and people looked cleaner; the classrooms looked smaller; pigeons were shyer. Kitty envied the nun setting forth on a silk-soft voyage of music and love straight to the very Father who art in heaven.

Before the class settled down, it seemed a good time to tell Mrs Giyaski about her being St Joan. She held up her hand, and her voice talked. 'But I'll be a good St Joan,' she bragged at the end of her speech, which she realized down in her stomach had been a confession.

Mrs Giyaski was silent for a long time, and the classroom clock could be heard tick-tocking.

'You will be a good St Joan?' the teacher sneered. 'You will be a good St Joan?' she repeated. 'I am sure St Joan will be very grateful to you. Come out here!'

Kitty crept timidly to the front of the class; her hands could already feel the leather strap.

'Oh no, Miss Kitty Noonan,' said Mrs Giyaski, shaking her head in the negative. 'I'm not going to strap you like I would a normal healthy naughty child. It is your mind which needs punishment, not your body.'

The teacher brought out the large conical dunce's cap, which was rarely seen. Kitty had to put it on. The teacher then chalked 'Do Not Speak To Me' on a slate, and Kitty had to stand on a chair holding the slate and facing the class.

'You will stay there until I pardon you,' said Mrs Giyaski, and she began her lesson about the Eskimos in the land of the midnight sun who hunted seals for clothing and blubber, and caught fish through a hole in the ice, and lived in ice-houses called igloos, and boated in kayaks, and rubbed noses to kiss their parents, and who had never heard of Jesus. A prayer was said for the Eskimos.

When the dinner bell clanged and the class filed out, pulling fat bacon at Kitty, Mrs Giyaski gave her a bitter glance. 'And see you stay there and talk to no one!' she commanded.

Kitty stood alone in the empty classroom. It had a smell of Plasticine which probably came from the infants' classroom, and it had a smell of yellow rulers and yellow desk wood and exercise books. It had once had the green smell of Irish fairy-story books, but now that the class was learning about the countries of the world, and arithmetic, and the history of archbishops arguing with crowned kings, the smells were more brown and dark red.

The clock tick-tocked louder and slower.

Kitty imagined she was an Eskimo girl and she was sewing a patchwork quilt of polar bear skins, but the polar bears didn't mind because she'd knitted them woollen pullovers which kept the cold out: and the polar bears looked quite pretty because the northern lights kept changing the colours of their pullovers. The teacher could not make her stand on a chair because everything was covered in ice, and she would slide off the chair on her bum – zoom-plonk. The thought made her laugh.

Then she imagined she was the man going to be hanged, and the chair was the trap door, and people were putting pennies in the slot to see her hanged. The lever would be pulled, and her toes would tingle, and her neck would snap hot. She would fall into the waiting arms of Jesus, but she knew this couldn't be so: it would have to be the black arms of Satan. She closed her eyes. 'Dear Satan, please take care of the man,' she said. And then she wondered to herself that if everybody in the world prayed for the soul of Satan, then perhaps he would be forgiven and become the Archangel Lucifer and one of God's pals again, and he might start saving people instead of burning them.

And then she imagined she was St Joan standing upon a heap of desk wood, waiting for the archbishop to strike a match. And bold Sir Lancelot, bridle bells ringing, thick jewelled saddle creaking, flashing helmet and helmet feather, blowing his mighty bugle, would ride in to rescue her before the first firework banged.

'Ooh, it's sweet Kitty Clover, it's beautiful Kitty of Coleraine, it's here pretty kitty, kitty, kitty!'

She opened her eyes and looked down. It was Osbert Plunkett.

'It says not to be talked to,' he went on. 'Pity is that. Best not talk to you then. Can you talk to me?'

Kitty squeezed her lips tight.

'Ooh, dead lucky is that. 'Cos if I ask you can I put me hand up your skirt, and pull yer keks down, and have a little feel, y'can't say no, can you? I like tarts what don't object.'

He began to finger-walk from her knee until his hand disappeared up her skirt. And she cracked the slate down hard on his head. He screamed, 'You've cracked me skull open! Me brains'll come out!' He put both hands to his head, and blood streamed from between his fingers. 'Help! Help!' he shouted, and he limped badly out of the classroom as though his foot were crushed. Kitty heard him yelling down the corridor. She was afraid. Suppose he might die? There were so many things to worry about.

She imagined she was the aeroplane man at the wakes, and she was high up on the tower, and there was a tank of blazing water below her, and the crowd chanted for her to jump.

Mrs Giyaski walked in with a book under her arm.

'You may step down, Kitty Noonan!' ordered the teacher, and Kitty stepped down, but she stumbled and fell because she thought she had to go all the way down to the burning tank from the top of the tower. Mrs Giyaski helped her up, and looked a little worried. 'I'm sorry; I was longer than I expected,' she half apologized. 'Sit down!' Kitty sat down.

'Did you talk to anybody?'

'No, miss.'

'Good girl! I'll say this for you, Kitty, you always know when you've done wrong, and you always accept your punishment.'

'Yes, miss.' Kitty was afraid the teacher might ask about the slate, but she didn't.

Mrs Giyaski brandished the book. 'I've been to the library,' she began. 'You see, I haven't eaten either – I've been too concerned over you.'

'I'm sorry, miss.'

'This is *Saint Joan* by George Bernard Shaw. Now I must tell you that Shaw is an atheist. Do you know what an atheist is?'

'A man who tells God he doesn't believe in him, miss.'

'Something like that – yes. But you should read some of the things Shaw has said about our newly created saint, St Joan.' She read. '*The queerest fish among many eccentric worthies, one of the first Protestant martyrs, it is hardly surprising that she was judicially burnt*! At one point in his preface, he even questions whether her martyrdom was suicide.' She slammed the book with a startling bang. 'And George Bernard Shaw is a Socialist! The kind of person who shot Tsar Nicholas and his little children twelve years ago; little children in their nightdresses. And if anybody deserves to be burnt at the stake, George Bernard Shaw does.' She calmed down. 'Now, Kitty, do you want to think his thoughts, and learn his wicked words? Can't you see the Devil at work, Kitty?'

'I wouldn't be thinking his thoughts, miss, 'cos I'd only be acting. And as far as his words is concerned – '

'Are.'

' – are concerned, they don't sound no different to other words what I've read.'

'I want you to promise me that you'll stop all this nonsense,' said Mrs Giyaski, giving the child a warm and encouraging smile.

'I hear voices telling me what to do. They come from God,' said Kitty without thinking.

Mrs Giyaski's forehead heaped up, and she looked like black thunderclouds before a thunderstorm.

'Go back to your desk!' she ordered.

When the class tumbled back from dinner, the lesson was about Peter the Hermit and the start of the Crusades in 1097, and the children might well have been Saracens for Mrs Giyaski waded into them with a vengeance. Most children received the strap for something or another, except Kitty: she was ignored, even when she held her hand up with an answer. She wished Mrs Giyaski would give her the strap.

Home-time should have been relief, but it brought upsetting news. Osbert Plunkett had been taken to Ancoats Hospital to have many stitches in his head, and he limped around very badly. Constable Kennedy had carted Mick Dowd to the police station for causing grievous bodily harm to Osbert by slashing his head with a slate.

'Best get off to't police station and tell 'em truth,' said Kitty.

'Like shit!' said Osbert. 'And bloody confess that a daft tart did it to me? Sod off!'

'Then I'll go and tell 'em.'

'You bloody won't.'

'That a slate fell off roof.'

'I'll do that. I'll say I was blurred.'

'Right then – let's go!'

'Go where?'

'Police station.'

'You coming with me?'

'Aye – make sure you find it.'

'It's in Mill Lane.'

'Aye, I know. But with cotton wool soaking yer brain up, ye might lose track and get more blurred.'

She went with him to the doorway, then waited. After ten minutes he limped out and ignored her. 'Me eyes is going,' he murmured as he passed her.

Almost immediately Mick Dowd rushed out. He ran up to Kitty and thumped her hard on the arm, kneed her between the legs, and slapped her across the face. 'And you'll get a bloody drainpipe shoved up yer arse next time I see you!' he shouted.

'What've I done?'

'What've ye bloody done? Told Twatbag to come to't bobbies and tell truth, that's what you've bloody done. There's me gang thinking I cut him up for not obeying me, and now they'll bloody laugh 'cos a slate fell off the roof. Bloody skirt!'

He ran after Osbert. 'I'll bloody take them bandages off yer head and let yer bloody head fall apart!' he shouted. Osbert started running, without a limp.

It had been a covered-in miserable day, the Requiem hadn't lasted long enough, the soot had dirtied the incense, and all pigeons should have been shot. She walked down Mill Lane, perhaps with the railway station in mind, perhaps with nothing in mind.

'Kitty!' It was Paddy Byrne. His face was black and oily like he was a molly-dancer. 'I did what you asked,' he said, waving his little red notebook.

'That's summat.'

'Only the locomotive weren't that bird what's-its-name.'

'Phoenix.'

'Mind you, it were a bird none the less. Least I think it's a bird. Here it is . . .' He pointed in his book. 'Ostrich.'

Kitty stamped her foot and spat in the gutter. It was the Devil's day.

'To shave his horn on Sunday morn were better that man had ne'er been born.' That's what Mrs Beckett said when Kitty told her she'd do the washing on Sunday afternoon instead of Monday morning, but when Kitty asked her what it meant, Mrs Beckett couldn't tell her. 'Ah well,' sighed Mrs Beckett, 'the better the day, the better the deed.' And with that it was agreed Kitty could do the washing on Sunday evening as long as she didn't put the things out till Monday.

It was important, because this was the third clear Sunday, and tomorrow morning quite early Kitty had asked Dermot Mac-Mahon, the wandering boy, to call for her and get her to Strangeways Prison for eight o'clock in time for the hanging bell. She hoped Dermot wouldn't let her down: he was such a called-for lad and had so much to do.

She had seen him during Mass, and he'd put his finger and thumb in a circle to signify okay. There had been a commotion in Mass that morning, and it was during the commotion he'd been able to make the signal without the Italian priest, who normally patrolled the aisles, seeing him.

On the way to church, Mick's gang had grabbed Osbert Plunkett, mobbed him, and pinned a paper with the word 'Shitehawk' on the back of his coat. They also dabbed some iodine on his head bandages and told him he'd smell injured and have the sympathy of the entire church. He believed them: consequently with palms tight together and fingers pointing to heaven he limped up to the altar rail for Holy Communion. Not only was the sign plainly visible on his back, but his head bandages were smeared brown like a map of nowhere, and there was a dab of iodine on the tip of his nose which Osbert hadn't noticed when it was put there by Vincent Cochrane. The priest was about to place the body of Jesus upon Osbert's tongue when he noticed the boy's funny face looking up at him. The priest replaced the host in the chalice.

'Is this the way you normally enter the house of God?' boomed the priest.

'Yes, father.'

'Stand up and face the congregation!'

Osbert stood up and turned around, thus giving the priest the opportunity to read the label on his back. The priest then shouted some difficult words – difficult because they were foreign and strung together – and demanded that Osbert named the names of those who had perpetrated such an evil trick on him. Osbert was afraid to do so because Mick Dowd had told him they would hack his thing off with a jagged Fray Bentos tin and turn him into a tart if he breathed but a single word.

The girls were given Holy Communion, but the boys, all the boys, had to stay behind. They were told that as they'd been refused Holy Communion they would be dancing a tightrope with hell beneath them until the wicked ones had confessed. There was even more in store, for Father Murphy was sent for, him being apparently an expert on hell and the conduct of Satan: and he lectured the boys on the burning tortures of hell for fifteen minutes. Eventually Mick Dowd admitted he was the leader, and he was ordered to be punished on the platform in the main hall before the entire school on Monday morning. He said, outside church afterwards, that he knew he and his gang were doomed to suffer the tortures of everlasting hellfire, but he didn't want daft cissies like Paddy Byrne going down there with them.

The gang had a heavy day ahead, and this turmoil had thrown them behind: most of them would have to skip the cemetery, which of course would mean further punishments ahead from parents. Kitty was allowed to listen to their plans.

Mick had decided it was now the essential time to turn the Jackie Coogan caps into hard cash because the whole wide world had lost interest in Coogan caps. Accordingly, Dermot MacMahon had earlier in the week been sent off as a Buffalo Bill Indian scout, and he'd come safely back to report that there were a lot of rich kids who wore school caps with owls, bees and circles round them in far Withington. They rode chromium bicycles, and seemed to have money jingling in their trouser pockets; they looked as much in need of Jackie Coogan caps as Hottentots were of the Bible.

Benedict Boyle, who was going to be a schoolteacher because of the long holidays schoolteachers got, and because it was well known to his mother and father that he'd got a brain, said it would be in keeping with holy Irish history. There was a tale, he told them, called 'The Cattle Raid of Cooley' which was in the *Book of Spells*, which had taken a monk two hundred years to write, and which was now closely guarded in the Trinity College of Dublin, the monk himself having died.

'What's it about?' asked Mick.

'Cattle rustling,' summed up Benedict.

'Where'd you learn that?'

'Didn't learn it. It's been handed down.'

'Aye, well best thing to do is keep handing it fast before someone finds out what a load of shit ye're handing 'em.'

'Dead true! God's honour!'

'It's a reason, I suppose,' said Mick, and the gang set off for Withington, arguing, punching, kicking and laughing as they went.

As soon as her dad came home and went up to bed for the afternoon, Kitty lit the scullery boiler fire and filled the copper with water. It would be evening before the water was hot for washing: she would have to keep the fire shovelled.

Next door she could hear Mrs Fearnley treadling her sewing machine and singing 'Oh Charlie, Take it Away!' so she knew somebody else was shaving a horn on the Sabbath.

She brought Wendy down, seated her comfortably, and began rehearsing *Saint Joan*. Kitty felt the scullery was as good a place as any as the castle at Rouen, a name she couldn't pronounce and would have to ask Mr Davies about. In time there would be a glow and flicker from the boiler grate like it said in the book.

'Oh Charlie, take it away! Take it away!' came through the bricks and faded wallpaper. 'Oh Charlie, take it away!'

'*Nay, I am no shepherd lass, though I have helped with the sheep like anyone else,*' she told Wendy as casually as she knew Joan would have said it, just like saying she'd done the washing. '*I will do a lady's work in the house – spin or weave – against any woman in –* '

She must ask Mr Davies how to pronounce the word.

It was a dark day, and a glow came from underneath the fire grate; wisps of steam came from under the wooden boiler lid. Kitty became frightened. The scene was frightening because so much of it could be about the man waiting on his last clear Sunday to be hanged in the morning. There was the chaplain and the executioner. The steam turned the scullery like a flowing dream. Other lines, not the lines of Joan, rushed through her brain.

'*Is the stake ready?*'

'*It is. In the market-place. The English have built it too high for me to get near her and make the death easier. It will be a cruel death.*'

It will be a cruel death, a cruel death, a cruel death! The words banged into her head and swirled with the steam. She was afraid of opening the grate door with her foot to put more coal on: the flames might grab her foot and pull her in the furnace.

'But Lancelot mused a little space:
He said, "She has a lovely face:
God in his mercy lend her grace."'

She felt safe as she recited her poem. 'There's nowt to be afraid of,' she told Wendy, because Wendy looked frightened too. Sir Lancelot was good, he came to the rescue, he brought sunlight to a drab day. They said St George was good, he slew dragons and rescued damsels in distress, but the English claimed St George as their patron saint, and they had killed Irish in the name of St George. The Irish said St Patrick was good, he gave the snakes and toads a twist, he'd suffered all the suffering of becoming an ancient druid in order to become a bishop and a saint, but he wasn't the kind of man who would tell a lass she had a lovely face: he'd the more likely ask her when she'd last been to Confession.

Dermot MacMahon knocked on the door to say he was back and was it still on for the morning, and could she pay him the twopence fee in advance.

The sale of the Coogan caps had been very successful, he told her. They'd surrounded the first kid who was on his own and going to Sunday school. He said he didn't want a Coogan cap, but the gang said he did.

'Look,' said Mick, 'before Mass this morning we dressed a kid up so that he looked like a turd. Would you like to go into Sunday school looking like a turd?'

The kid said he'd only got his Sunday school money on him, and they said it would do nicely.

'What's more,' said Mick, 'y'can keep all the lice what's in it and make pets of 'em. They'll come when called.'

And then they'd made the kid wear it as an example and stand outside the Sunday school door advising his friends to buy Coogan caps with their Bible money: he'd been threatened with a Fray Bentos tin if he refused. The gang then told him to pass it on that they'd be waiting in hiding after Sunday school just to make sure the lads were wearing their newly acquired Coogan caps.

'This was to prevent 'em sending for bobbies,' explained Dermot, 'and as Mick told us, remind the posh kids that the working-class kids was always lying in wait. 'Course we didn't wait, but we found a can and kick-canned it all the way home.'

Dermot was surprised how much money the Withington kids were given for Sunday school.

Kitty and her dad had a boiled egg and several thick slices of bread and jam for tea, because it was an egg which began Bernard Shaw's play: then her dad had to go off to the Ben Brierley.

Kitty got stuck into the job of washing the clothes, but Wendy seemed to want her to rehearse the last scene, the ghost scene, for it was a funny scene and made Kitty laugh loud. It was when Joan appeared from nowhere and made King Charles jump into bed and hide under the sheets, and Joan asked if she could be unburned, and all the bigwigs who had sentenced her came in and apologized if burning her had caused her any inconvenience whatsoever: and there was talk about a statue to her in Winchester Cathedral. Winchester Cathedral was where King Alfred had been crowned either after or before he'd burned the cakes. She shovelled some more coal on the fire. She wondered if a burning body smelt like burning meat, or if Joan's body had smelt of incense. Winchester was a long way off.

Mrs Fearnley looked in for a cup of tea because she said her husband had gone back to sea and she was fed up. Her husband was like the man on the Bovril bottle: he was always at sea. Nobody had ever seen him, he came by night and left by night. Some said he went to prison a lot, others that he'd got a couple of other wives and fancy women hidden away and had to keep them all happy, others that he was a different husband each time he called, the kind of husband who could be readily obtained outside Lewis's arcade.

'You've seen his trousers on the line,' she told Mrs Beckett once when Mrs Beckett had raised the matter.

'Aye, but they're different trousers each time, Mrs Fearnley.'

'That's 'cos he shits himself whenever I mention your name, Mrs Beckett.'

'Then you must talk about me an awful lot, Mrs Fearnley. It's flattered I am.'

'Then 'tis a blessing of God ye've not heard the things that are said, Mrs Beckett.'

After that, Mrs Beckett never broached the subject again.

'Aye, off to the seven seas,' said Mrs Fearnley, saucering her tea and blowing on it as though demonstrating waves.

'Must be nice,' said Kitty.

'Aye, if you're a feller.' Mrs Fearnley looked around the scullery. 'Nice house you got. You keep it clean, I'll say that.'

'Don't see many black beetles,' said Kitty.

'Use Keatings?'

'Aye.'

'Puts 'em on their backs. You still got to belt 'em with your shoes.' Mrs Fearnley sipped her tea with a loud sip. 'Dad gone for his . . . ?' She made a quick drinking movement with her hand.

'Aye.'

'Pity, that!'

'Aye.'

'Need a mam, ye do.'

'I manage.'

'As the old woman said.'

'Aye.' Kitty poured a second cup.

'You singing that song to rile?'

'What song?'

'Jacket o' blue.'

'Didn't know I was singing owt.'

'Just watch it!' For some reason, Mrs Fearnley gave Kitty a wink, and again sipped with a loud noise.

It was the half-aggressive conversation Mrs Fearnley seemed to enjoy. A polite conversation meant she was bored, but a give-more-than-you-get backchat signified she liked the person she was spitting at. Kitty enjoyed the conversation: it took her mind off a burning St Joan.

'Right, chuck – I'll be off, as the knickers said to the thighs. Which pub is it yer dad goes?'

'Ben Brierley.'

'I might look in say how'd'y'do. Don't worry, I'll stand me whack. Ta-ra.'

Kitty dollied by candlelight for there was no gas fitted in the scullery. The room filled with steam which made a halo around the candle flame. Trains ran on Sunday night, and Kitty felt glad they did.

She heard Mrs Fearnley's front door close shortly after chucking-out time, and quite a time after, her dad staggered in. She was relieved they'd not come home together.

Her dad put his arms around the wireless and kissed it. ' *'Tis the last rose of summer left blooming alone: all her lovely companions are faded and gone,*' he sang, and tears rolled down his cheeks. He kissed the wireless once more, and Kitty helped him upstairs to his bedroom. He hadn't noticed the scullery was a heap of steaming clothes, so there was no need for an explanation.

After a time, when her dad had used the enamel po several times and broken wind a lot, the world became quiet, apart from a shunting engine, and Kitty said her rosary for the man who was waiting for the hangman. The night never ended.

She felt ill and old by the time her dad got up for work. She needed him to stretch the clothes-line on the street hooks. He didn't ask why, but just did what she asked. It was a frosty morning, the round cobbles were sugar-coated with sparkling frost, steam rushed from the open door of the house. The stars could be seen bright and twinkling because the chimneys had not yet got the Monday morning smoke going. There was a crescent moon between the two silhouettes of big chimneys as though they were playing diabolo with it. A mist came up from the river, and Kitty imagined the steam from her washing had rushed out to become friendly and enjoy the freedom of the river mist.

Her dad kissed her on the forehead and set off up Angel Meadow, shouting, 'Damn-and-blast and tarnation take it!' when he slipped on some ice on his bottom: although he picked himself up immediately and sang himself to work as though he'd never stopped singing since the night before.

It was a wonder the two didn't pass each other, for almost immediately Dermot MacMahon arrived to take Kitty to Strangeways, many miles away. It had been no trouble for him to keep such an early appointment because he had been working for himself all through the night. He was the unofficial place-keeper at the all-night chemist's. After midnight, the alcoholics and drug-takers were allowed to queue up on a line of chairs inside the chemist's, and at the chemist's discretion, when nobody had come in for urgent night medicines, and the midnight all-night tram had left, he sold them methylated spirits and drugs. It meant a lot of waiting through the black hours of the night, and often one of them would need to leave the shop to pee down the grid, or spew up down an entry, or maybe have another swig of what was left in their bottle. Dermot would sit in for them so they'd not lose their place for a penny.

He had inherited the job from a boy who had been greedy enough to buy a couple of packets of Epsom Salts and sell it privately as a happiness drug. The boy was now in hospital with some very serious injuries because he'd been hammered with half-bricks, and it was said he'd even lost an eye through a piece of slate.

Kitty had to promise she'd tell nobody, not even Mick Dowd, about Dermot's Sunday night job, but then it was tit-for-tat because she didn't want anybody to know about her visit to Strangeways.

Because of Dermot's pharmaceutical connections, she knew he'd be a scientific expert on hanging, which of course he was. He told her that after the body had been cut down, it was dumped in a pit of quicklime inside the prison grounds, where it dissolved into nothing, not a bone nor a button, and no name was placed to mark the spot.

'What happens on the Day of the Resurrection when Gabriel blows his horn?' she asked. 'There'll be no body to step out front. There'll be a complete shortage of executed murderers, and it could upset the archangel's tally.'

'Well, if they can't be found for heaven, they can't be found for hell either,' said Dermot. He was unsure of himself on religious questions, and brought the subject back to the pharmaceutical inclination. 'They dope 'em,' he said, touching his nose to indicate it was privileged information. 'Dope 'em up to the eyebrows. They don't know what day it is or where they are or where they're going to go. I heard as one feller thought he was waiting for the pubs to open, then he stepped inside to order a pint – and yank! You've got to bloody laugh, haven't you?'

They took all the side roads to Strangeways Prison. In one street, a man in shirt-sleeves peeped from an entry. 'It's only a coupla kids,' he said, and a young woman, holding a shawl to her face, sneaked past him and half ran up the street. In another street was a chimney sweep fastening brushes to his bike, with his face as black and sooty as it had been the night before. Down another street two young men had a bicycle. 'It's only kids,' said one, and they lifted the bike over a yard wall where hands were waiting for it. Most streets seemed to have a railwayman, carrying his basket and two flags. There was another chimney sweep in another street, and it upset Kitty. One sweep meant good luck: she feared two sweeps would cancel out like two minus two.

They reached the Jewish district of Cheetham Hill which held Strangeways Prison in its black overcoated arms. There were sewing machines grinding and whirring in some of the cellars, and Kitty guessed that the black-bearded men whom she could look down through the dirty cellar windows at had, like her, worked through the night. There were temples with strange writing which she was sure was Hebrew, and Kitty understood why the hangman had chosen to build his prison among the Jews, for the Jews were Old Testament people who believed in an eye for an eye, a tooth for a tooth.

The great prison was gaunt and black and fat and silent. Its walls were higher than she thought walls possible. There were towers beyond the walls, but they were not the towers of Camelot, they were the towers of Giant Despair. There was a high door with panels of thick wood and bolts and hinges: a dragon would be safe from a million lances on the other side of that door. Around the door a dozen or so people were scattered. A woman stood on a kipper-box platform and shouted how horrible and inhuman it was to kill prisoners, and hanging should be banned by Parliament. It was ten minutes to eight. There was a sweet brewery smell coming from the brewery next to the prison. It would be incense for the condemned man.

Dermot said the man would be just finishing breakfast and saying Grace after Meals because it would have been a good meal. A condemned man can have anything he wants for his last breakfast, and Dermot said to imagine six fried eggs, a dozen slices of bacon, and twenty pieces of fried bread with two bottles of sauce, hot sauce and tomato sauce. He felt hungry, but there were no pie shops near the prison, probably because prisoners wouldn't escape to get pies. Some people had brought sandwiches and flasks of tea because they'd been there most of the night, but they wouldn't sell anything to Dermot even though he showed them his pharmacy money.

An argument began as to whether the trap door would open on the first bong of eight or the eighth bong of eight. A man said he'd been told on the wireless that it was the first bong of Big Ben in London which told the time, and if it worked for Big Ben it'd work for the Manchester town hall clock. Another man said time changed when you crossed the Atlantic.

The town hall clock could be seen in the distance, but the prison had no big clock, and everybody hoped the wind would be in the right direction so they could hear the first bong.

Kitty noticed that workers' trams and buses passed down the main road, but nobody looked out through the windows. Jews pushed rails of clothes on wheels out of shops, but they didn't look across at the prison. A postman just looked down at the letters he had in his hand. And yet a man was going to be killed.

A woman in a shawl knelt down on the frosty croft before the door and began to say her rosary aloud. Kitty was about to do the same – after all, it had been Sister St Pius's wish. A tram ding-dinged at a man on a bicycle, and the man on the bicycle ting-a-linged his bell at the tram. A man stepped forward among the crowd of waiters and watchers. He was dressed like the posh tramp in the tramp cartoon of Nutty and Sam. He wore a squashed top hat, a black bow tie, a long black coat with tails, striped trousers tied up with rope, odd socks, one red, one grey, and old physical training galoshes which seemed to laugh because the rubber soles flapped from the toes. His thin face had the black stubble beginning of a beard. He took off his hat, bowed slowly to the crowd, then held his hat in the begging position as he sang to them.

'After the trial was over,
After the judge's black cap,
They said you are done as a rover
Once you set foot on the trap.
Many last words have been spoken
Seconds before the fall,
Many a neck has been broken
Over the wall.'

The woman preaching against the death penalty raised her voice to compete. Another tram ding-dinged. A factory hooter blew. A man shouted, 'Will ye all bloody shut up!!' There was a sudden silence, and they could hear faint bongs from the town hall clock; they had missed the first bong. They'd all missed it. Kitty felt she had missed New Year. She tried and tried to keep awake on New Year's Eve so that she could hear the ships blowing their sirens down on the docks, but she always missed them, and people asked her, 'Did ye hear the ships?' Suddenly Kitty felt there was something missing from her life: she felt empty and lonely.
'Lend us twopence,' she asked Dermot.
'Shan't! What for!' asked Dermot, getting twopence from his pocket.
'To put in the feller's hat.'
'Bloody why?'
''Cos he turned up. Suppose nobody turned up?'
'Ta, little lady,' said the singer when she dropped the money in. 'Got to be in Liverpool for another in a coupla days. Not much fun follering the hangman.'
'See what I mean?' said Kitty, nudging Dermot. 'He turned up. Suppose you had a funeral and everybody stayed away?'
She shivered and felt very cold. Her feet were like ice. She couldn't stop her teeth chattering.

*

Kitty hated the night of November the Fifth, Guy Fawkes Night, Bonfire Night, for fireworks frightened her. Boys threw bangers at girls. However, it was a necessary annual ritual to spend some time at the nearest fire in order to prove that a girl was nearly as good as a boy. And a girl couldn't lie about a fire: she daren't say she was at the Carruthers Street fire or the Raglan Street fire because there would always be somebody to say she wasn't.

There was always danger, there were always hospital casualties, the Devil had a free hand. Last year some boys had put a Little Demon up Jenny Beswick's skirt, and she'd had to be taken to hospital: and her dad had thrown one of the boys who did it on the fire, and he'd had to be pulled off and taken to hospital: and then the two dads had fought rings round with bread knives until one of them had to be taken to hospital. Rockets and rip-raps were tied to the tails of dogs and cats, and Kitty had seen how the animals had trembled with bulging eyes while they were being held tight for the fireworks to be tied to them. A burning cat was flung over the wall into the river with jokes about what a stink a smouldering cat made.

This year the guy took four men to pull. It was as though the guy was trying to resist being burned, but Kitty knew no mercy would be shown to the guy, for no mercy would be shown to anybody on the Fifth of November. The guy would be burned, to a thousand jokes and a million sparklers. She felt frightened of being Joan of Arc: she wondered if the soldiers who watched Joan burning had sung 'Boiled Beef and Carrots' out of mockery.

The guy was made of large and heavy sacks filled with horse manure and wet horse straw from the railway arches. The face was a skeleton mask, and on it was a policeman's helmet: it was a policeman's helmet in good condition, but nobody asked or whispered about where it came from. It was felt with great pride that no other 'bunny' in any street in Ancoats would be burning a bobby for a guy.

Because of the wet horse manure and straw, it left a damp trail on the flags as it was pulled towards the fire.

'Hey!' shouted Benedict Boyle, 'it's pissing itself like them blessed martyrs did when they was dragged to Tyburn to have their bums scraped out alive.'

'What's bloody Tyburn?' asked a voice.

'This is bloody Tyburn!' shouted Mick Dowd, and within seconds he'd pulled Benedict's tie from his shirt collar and thrown it on the fire. 'There! Watch his tie burn!'

'Let's put Benedict on after it!'

'Aye – let's do that!'

A gang of lads moved towards him. He grabbed a piece of burning chair leg. 'I'll put anybody's bleeding eyes out what touches me!' he screamed.

'Hey – does yer mammy let you play with fire?'

Kitty had seen enough: she was trembling. Benedict was going to be the chosen victim tonight. They would tease him and rough-handle him until eventually he would have to be taken to Ancoats Hospital.

On the other hand, they could just as easily turn on her, and taunt her, and try to light Thunderflashes or Mars Rockets up her clothes.

In the red glow of the street fires it was the south bank of the River 'Lwar', and she was Joan in splendid armour.

I am a soldier. I do not want to be thought of as a woman. I will not dress as a woman. I do not care for the things women care for. They dream of lovers, and of money. I dream of leading a charge, and of placing the big guns. You soldiers do not know how to use the big guns: you think you can win battles with a great noise and smoke. Aye, lad: but you cannot fight stone walls with horses: you must have guns, and much bigger guns too.

A rocket sizzled out in the Medlock over the wall: a tremendous firework made windows rattle on her left. She sneaked into the shadows and then ran home. Her dad would be home because he'd said he wasn't going to the Ben Brierley until the big fires had died down a bit. She could give him her firework money for an extra pint of beer.

He wasn't in the parlour when she got in, but the gaslight was on, and the fire was built up. But she heard him puffing and gasping upstairs in his bedroom, and that was how Mrs Malone said Mr Malone had been taken, 'a-puffing and a-panting like an old grampus for 'twas his poor heart unable to carry the heavy burden of his body.' She ran upstairs two at a time. 'Dad! Dad! Oh, dad!' she yelled, and she burst into his room.

Draped over the bedrail bars were Mrs Fearnley's light pink corsets with the pink silk rose patterns, one strap hanging higher than the other: and Mrs Fearnley's stockings, the Sunday silk ones brought from Zanzibar, again one hanging high, one hanging low: and over one of the brass knobs, Mrs Fearnley's white silk knickers.

'Oooops! Caught red-handed!' said Mrs Fearnley's voice.

'Darling! Me own lovely darling Kitty!' said her dad.

Kitty rushed out and slammed the door, and rushed into her own room and slammed the door. There was silence. Kitty hugged Wendy. Poor Wendy had overheard everything. They both deserved to be hanged like that man was hanged: they were dirty and wicked.

Her dad's door slammed shut, and Kitty heard the high-heeled shoes of Mrs Fearnley going down the stairs and out through the front door. The windows rattled with firework bangs. After a few seconds her dad came into her room.

'Get out! You're not me dad!'

'Oh but I am, me love. A bad un I may be, but 'tis your father I am. And it's sorry I am that such a lovely innocent little soul, white as the driven snow, should have such a dad.'

'You're dirty!'

'Aye, that I am. Me job's dirty, and me soul's dirty, and 'tis hard to know which is the dirtiest.'

'Why don't ye be off to the pub?'

'Maybe I'll do that.'

'Me mam was watching, y'know. She's up there watching.' Kitty pointed up to the ceiling.

'Sure, that's right enough. She doesn't miss a trick, does yer mam.'

He shuffled out, and in a minute the front door closed again.

Kitty cuddled Wendy hard, and her warm tears rolled on to Wendy's face as though Wendy herself were crying.

'Oh mam, I love you and miss you and need you!' sobbed Kitty. 'Why did you have to leave us, mam? You were a good mam, the best mam. Please punish dad for his dirtiness. No, don't punish him, forgive him, but forgive him in such a way that he knows his forgiveness is punishment. And please send Mrs Fearnley a million miles to Afghanistan or Tibet where there are mountains which she can't ever cross and come back, and may she pray to you for forgiveness. Everything is dirty, mam. Please make things clean like they're done with Reckitt's Starch.' She made the sign of the cross, and went downstairs, holding on to the wall for support. She had no need to hold the wall: indeed she felt like marching down bravely to 'Petty Colette is loved by all the college boys' but it seemed right, after praying to her mother, that she should lean against the wall and hold her forehead.

She had barely seated herself down when in walked Mrs Fearnley bold as brass.

'You're a whore!' shouted Kitty. 'A dirty, stinking, filthy whore!'

'Not much chance o' being owt else in Angel Meadow and such like places, chuck!'

'You won't cop me being one.'

'We'll see, chuck.'

Kitty felt that she already was a whore, but only a hanged man and a dead nun, one in hell, one in heaven, knew that.

'Why've you come? To dirty my house?' said Kitty.

'I'll put kettle on,' said Mrs Fearnley, and she took over, swinging the iron kettle on the hob, reaching for the teapot and the tea caddy with Queen Victoria on all sides, and getting the Sunday cups from the cupboard above the gas cupboard.

'I spose yer dad's gone guzzlin'?'

'Aye, well he's safe there, in't he?'

'I wonder.'

'Me mam's seen it all, y'know.' Once more Kitty pointed to the ceiling.

'Needs a bit o' whitewash does that ceiling.'

Mrs Fearnley brewed the tea as soon as the kettle started singing. She reached for the milk jug and the sugar basin with cool, swishing efficiency.

'I wonder what yer mam's been seeing since the day she passed away? Y'know, chuck, me and yer mam got along a treat, like a house on fire.'

'Makes it worse, does that.'

'Listen, lovey, yer mam must have been in hell these years, not heaven. She's had to watch yer dad go boozing every hour when he's not been working. Since she died, he's wallowed in ale like a pig, supped like a fish. Folks laugh at his drunken staggering. He holds on to lamp-posts, does yer dad: that's how he finds his way home. And what does he do Sat'day and Sunday afternoons? Sleeps it off, snoring like a porker, and shits his trousers. Can't you smell him? If you can't there's others can, and they shift away from him. There's talk of getting him barred from Ben Brierley 'cos of his stink.'

Kitty instinctively wanted to stab Mrs Fearnley with the potato-peeling knife, which was sharp enough to sharpen pencils; instead she took hold of the cup of tea which Mrs Fearnley handed to her.

'Sup that!' said Mrs Fearnley, saucering her own at the same time.

'Aye, I'll sup it. But it dun't mean you'll ever be me mam,' Kitty blurted out, not knowing why she'd blurted it.

'Don't talk bloody wet, kid! You, me daughter? I wouldn't have you as me daughter if you was thrown at me or even given away with a quarter o' tea. You're too bloody toffee-nosed and holier-than-thou.'

'You and me dad have sinned.'

'Have we buggery! I'm not married. There, that's let cat out o't bag.'

'Me dad – '

'Aw, shurrup about yer dad. You know nowt about your dad. You've not even noticed he's shaved today, and he shaved day before yesterday, and he's started to comb his hair best he can, and he's changed his mucky shirt a coupla times this week. Never bloody noticed, did you? Why, he's actually listened to the wireless without bloody grovelling to it. Your mam'd thank me.'

Kitty knew she'd have to leave home. Soon as Mrs Fearnley left, she and Wendy would be over the hills and far away. They'd sneak on a train at London Road, perhaps Samson or Goliath was there waiting, and they would take her somewhere like the prophet was taken on a chariot of fire: they'd travel a million miles, and she'd change her name and become a nun, but only if they let Wendy wear nun's clothes and be with her in the convent. Nobody would ever hear of Kitty Noonan again ever, and that would serve everybody right.

But Mrs Fearnley's departure, and consequently her and Wendy's departure, were delayed when Mrs Beckett rushed in. She went immediately to the teapot, felt to see if it was still hot, reached a cup from the cupboard and poured herself out a drink.

'By heck! I needed that, I can tell you!' Her fingers trembled on the cup handle.

'What's up? Seen yer face and don't like the look of it?' said Mrs Fearnley.

'Had to run out on me job, I did. Even Mr Robino the manager's had to run out – '

'Bloody earthquake, was it?'

'Mick Dowd and his gang. Want bloody horse-whipping.' The tea went down the wrong way, and she started coughing and spluttering.

'Choke up, chicken!' said Mrs Fearnley.

And then Mrs Beckett fixed Kitty in the eye. 'You're the one what wants to go into show business, aren't you?'

'Show – ?'

'She means the theatre, chuck. It's her way of expressing since she's been at Palmy.'

Mrs Beckett had recently taken on an evening job as usherette at the Palmerston Picturedrome. There was really no ushering to be done: she took the ticket money, then spent the rest of the evening spraying disinfectant over the heads of the audience. The talkies had just arrived and Mrs Beckett, seeing a film at least ten times a week, had begun to come out with picture talk like 'Sez you' and 'Okay, baby' and 'You big palooka'.

'Theatre – aye,' said Kitty.

'Down't drain, kid. Bloody forget it. They'll kill you in the end. Tell you this for nowt, I daren't show me face at Palmy again: they'll hang me from nearest lamp-post.'

'What happened? Or in your lingo – spill the beans,' said Mrs Fearnley.

'Ink – that's what happened. Ink and Mick Dowd. I saw 'em

snooping. They put ink in me disinfectant spray gun. And of course I go round every half-hour spraying their heads to prevent plague or venereal disease. Stops things becoming contagious because of its strong lavender smell. Well, me and Phil – er, Mr Robino – was in the ticket office taking tickets when Mr and Mrs O'Brien came out with blue spots on their faces. And then Jim Mulligan the street fighter comes out, and he's flecked blue. And we figured out what had happened because the liquid dripping from the spray gun drum was blue. 'Best thing is to piss off,' said Mr Robino, and he put his cycle clips on. He's such a nice man, and wouldn't harm a fly – '

''Cept with a spray gun,' said Mrs Fearnley.

'Nowt to laugh at. Poor projectionist has barricaded his room for when "God Save the King" comes on.'

'Lucky the king weren't in the Palmy when you sprayed 'em.'

'He's not likely to be seen dead in the Palmy.'

'Or even blue.'

It was a long time before the two women left. Mrs Beckett refused to budge until long after the Palmy had let out. Mrs Fearnley advised her not to let on she'd ever been near the place.

'But I was recognized.'

'Who by?'

'I don't know – but a feller clicked his tongue and said, "Drop yer keks, Amy" as I passed down the aisle.'

'Sounds like a wedding, does that. And the feller in question'd be Bert Grimshaw. And d'y'hear talk like that in the Palmy?'

'Worse.'

'Then you're best shut of a place like that, and, if you ask me, they deserved being sprayed with ink, and ink's too good for 'em. Come on, I'll see you to't door.'

Kitty walked sedately up to her room. She didn't feel like clutching the wall with anguish because it was getting late, and it was much too late for going to the railway station, and there were still fireworks banging. She needed to be in her room with the candle out before her dad came home.

She sang to Wendy a song about being lonely and blue, and she wept at the thought of poor Wendy, a helpless doll, being all on her own when she was far away. The fireworks, suffocated by the night, banged tired.

*

'God rest you merry gentlemen
Let Cohen pawn your suits,
He'll give you twopence for your shirt
And twopence for your boots:
And fourpence buys a jar o' meths
To rot you at the roots:
Oh tidings of comfort and joy.'

As always, when the ashes of Bonfire Night had been trampled into houses on boots, came the first street carol for Christmas, and with it the late November fogs.

Kitty liked the fogs. They were private: she could walk around in her own personal grey or brown world, occasionally story-book glow-wormed by glows from lanterns and bull's-eye flashlamps. The men carrying lanterns in front of tramcars and cotton carts laughed and joked with each other, and wiped their dripping noses on their sleeves, when their glows met.

'Ee, tha's a gormless bugger,' a carter told his horse, 'tha's going in't wrong direction. Tha'll never make Grand National in a month o' Sundays.'

'Hey, is this bloody London?'

'No, gaffer, it's bloody Glasgow. Can't ye see me kilt?'

'I can't even see the fingers on me hand to scratch me arse with.'

And a woman's voice said, 'You always gets this when me husband changes his socks.' And another woman's voice said, 'Aye, well, be grateful for small mercies he only does it a coupla times a year.' And another woman's voice added, 'Here lie I, broken-hearted, paid a penny and only farted.'

'While shepherds washed their socks by night,
And dried them by the fire,
A lump of coal came tumbling down
And made the sods retire.'

'Won't cop for much carol-singing tonight. Y'can't see buggers.'

'Happen they're angels: heavenly throng, like.'

'And they'll get bloody bronchitis.'

'So will I. Could do with me chest rubbing.'

'Did I hear you calling for help, missus?' said a man's voice.

A fog signal banged blurred.

Kitty thought of the happy man up there on his beef bottle riding a clean sea.

More than ever she wanted to be on her own. Life wasn't the same with her dad any more: the small house was even smaller. Their conversations were grown-up and mainly about the weather. Her dad shaved a lot, and sang as he shaved; he put boot-blacking on his boots, spat on them, and rubbed them; he put soap on his moustache and hair; somebody – Kitty could only guess who – gave him a bunch of striped ties. He had tipped his money over every Friday as always: she hadn't noticed it but it must have been more money than he used to give, for she no longer had the romance of stealing from market bags, or the excitement of dancing outside the Land O' Cakes. It was gone: the men's faces had gone, and their Saturday tarts, and the smell of beer and port wine and penny cigars, the crackle and splutter of the flares above the market stalls, the smell of hand-wrestled humbugs, the country smell of fruit and vegetables from the greengrocery stalls, the clink of auctioned plates and dishes: they'd gone. She sat in her corner and learnt her lines of Joan of Arc, but she was more imprisoned than Joan, for Joan led soldiers through green fields and over rivers, and Joan was at home in cathedrals.

Fog was good because it hid her sins and the sins of others: maybe heaven was fog. The worst thing about fog was treading in cat shit and carrying it into the house on shoes.

Fog was the beginning of Lewis's Christmas windows. The fog made them light up brown like a dream. The dining-room changed each year. The pictures on the wall were changed; this year there was a humped-back bridge over a stream, and a splendid sailing ship with white sail upon white sail getting smaller as they neared the tops of the masts; the wireless set in the corner was different, it said 'Electric'. As Kitty stared into the window, she knew she had grown up. She did her share of the street-washing, some men looked at her knees instead of her curly hair, she had been hit and hurt by things, she had seen her own father being dirty with her next door. More than ever she wanted to live untouched for ever in a window, to have the dining-room neat and tidy for Christmas dinner, to listen all the time to the wireless, to be waiting for her husband, but not wanting her husband ever to come: to be glassed in with comfort and security.

But good things had happened with her growing up. There was Ancoats Hall, the museum, the theatre and Thursdays: and somehow the marble halls of the museum seemed to promise a connection with the wealth of the rich Christmas windows. Her first rehearsal had been like Alice stepping into Wonderland: Ratbag, Kakikeks, Snottynose and Dogface had become French and English noblemen and archbishops, and exchanging dialogue with them had been like dancing with words.

Miss Hindshaw unlocked the secret room, the Athens room. The boys had been there before and thought nothing of it, but entering it for the first time Kitty knew why it was kept locked, for it was filled with larger-than-life white plaster statues of naked men and women who were Greek gods and goddesses. The gods had large leaves covering their rude parts, but the lady gods had nowt at all, neither knickers nor bust bodices.

'That's Venus,' said Ratbag, giving Kitty a nudge when he saw her looking up at the statue, 'and she's waiting for autumn for the leaves to fall.'

Kitty wondered for a second what kept the leaves where they were without elastic, and then she remembered that Jesus on the cross had a towel girded round his loins without a safety pin: obviously it was a special thing with gods.

The reason for the group occupying the Athens Room was for them to be tested for make-up. This was a luxurious experience for Kitty; she had never been sweet-smelled and fussed over before. Miss Hindshaw smoothed beautiful face cream on her face and under her nose, and then she added touches of colouring with lipsticks, and added face powder, and everything had smells similar to but nicer than any smells from Boots Cash Chemists. Miss Hindshaw referred to her as Joan, and not Kitty.

'We'll need to make you look healthy and robust at first, like a girl who has lived on a farm and had fresh eggs, cream and butter, eh, Joan?'

'Fried eggs,' added Kitty.

'Fried eggs sizzling in the pan with bacon and freshly picked mushrooms. And then later on, Joan, we'll have to make you look pale with worry and responsibility, having seen men die in battle.'

'And the thought of going to me own death.'

'Indeed – and going to your own death.'

'And spending too much time in cathedrals with all that incense and burning candlewax.'

'Very likely. There – what d'y'think?' She held a mirror to Kitty, and Kitty saw a young woman whom she hardly recognized. 'And now,' continued Miss Hindshaw, 'if you'll come along to my office, we'll try you on for your suit of armour. I made it myself.'

'She can change in here, miss: we won't mind,' said Snottynose, who'd been listening. Miss Hindshaw dabbed his nose with a red lipstick as she passed.

The armour was a cotton trouser suit which fitted tightly, and Kitty became aware that her body had a shape. Sewn to it were rows and rows of ridged awning. It was dyed greyish-blue with curved yellow streaks on the edges of the awning: it looked like glistening chain mail such as in history-book pictures of William the Conqueror. Miss Hindshaw handed her a sword, a real sword, not two pieces of wood nailed together.

'Yes, it's real,' assured Miss Hindshaw. 'It was my brother's sword, and it's been in France, so how's that? I thought about making you a wooden one, but after I'd listened to you at rehearsal I felt you deserved a real one. But don't go cutting heads off with it, will you?'

'It's Excalibur!' she gasped, and swished the sword. 'The sword that rose from out the bosom of the lake, and Arthur rowed across and took it – rich with jewels, the blade so bright that men are blinded by it.'

Miss Hindshaw looked at her with pride and amazement: Kitty too was amazed that from somewhere she had remembered the lines. 'I know a lot of Tennyson by heart, miss,' she said, a little apologetically.

'Yes, you certainly do.' Miss Hindshaw was taken aback, as though Kitty had spoken Sanskrit. 'It's not Excalibur though. But it's a sword which once led a charge against the enemies of France, so if you do your part as well as that sword has done its, Mr Davies and I will be very happy, and so, I hope, will the audience.'

Kitty brandished the sword again.

'*I am a daredevil: I am a servant of God. My sword is sacred: I found it behind the altar in the church of St Catherine, where God hid it for me, and I may not strike a blow with it. My heart is full of courage, not of anger. I will lead: and your men will follow!*'

'I think you've just struck a blow! Be careful!' smiled Miss Hindshaw as she bent down to pick up a heap of Roman coins which the swinging sword had knocked to the ground from her table. The coins, found in Manchester, had once been on general exhibition in a glass case, but they'd been stolen and apparently tried out in a cigarette machine. As they didn't fit the coin slot, the machine had been stolen, and the coins had been left on the flags. Miss Hindshaw had been only too glad to get them back, and now they were kept in her office, and were locked in the safe at night, but could be shown to people who asked to see them.

Kitty in her make-up and armour and sword stepped on the stage, and the coloured lights came on. She was at last in the department store window. The ambers were like a summer afternoon when there was no school because it was a saint's day; the reds were like the fire in November when there were stolen chestnuts on a tin lid; the blues were as fresh as the early morning before the chimneys. She could be the living Joan of Arc, maybe in the great cathedrals. Joan only died once, but Kitty would have the tingling excitement of dying before the red lights every night the play was put on: and every night she would live again in the epilogue.

Miss Hindshaw cleaned the make-up from her face with another nice-smelling cream. She looked under the outstretched arm of Apollo and through the window. A shunting train was puffing and shunting, and it brought her back to the drabness of real life: somewhere under the puffing train was Angel Meadow. It would be comforting to think her dad was in the Ben Brierley but she knew he'd be next door at Mrs Fearnley's mending her backyard coalshed, drowning her cat's kittens, fixing the lavatory cistern which wouldn't fill up properly, oiling her sewing machine which was jumping stitches.

She was glad to see Paddy Byrne at the bottom of the museum drive. He asked her if she'd like to go to the seaside with him on a tram, and he'd pay the tram fare.

'It's not exactly the seaside,' he explained. 'It's the Manchester Ship Canal, but you get big ships sailing down the alley big as the *Titanic* is most of them.'

Kitty had never seen a ship or the Ship Canal. She'd seen coal barges on the canal by the Danish Bacon Curers: they always had a dog that barked, and a man so wrapped up he couldn't move, and a splutter which went chug-chug. She knew that every tram had a brightly coloured oval on its back and front driver's glass: the oval showed big ships being unloaded by high cranes in a blue canal under a blue sky, and the ovals said 'Use The Ship Canal'. Paddy explained that trams were good friends with ships, and that was why they asked people to use them. For reasons which he didn't understand, perhaps religious reasons, tramcars never bothered with motor buses or trains, and they never asked people to use them.

His missionary work as a railway priest had been terminated. The stationmaster had told him to 'piss off' and not bother the locomotives again: in any case Samson was a Jew and didn't want a Roman Catholic blessing. Then the stationmaster had felt sorry for his hasty words and given Paddy a Bradshaw's Railway Almanac which he told the boy he could bless like the Good Book, so now Paddy read epistles and liturgies from its pages in his bedroom.

He had taken to going to the Ship Canal to bless the ships, which he told Kitty were more in need of blessing than any other thing which travelled because they were always sinking. Indeed, so many ships were sinking all the time that he'd thought of doing the last rites for them instead of just an ordinary go-about-your-business blessing.

The docks were noisy. The buildings were high. Funny little matchbox-boilered locomotives with tall chimneys pulled wagons up tracks in the middle of the roads, often disappearing with their lines of trucks through archways into some of the buildings. The locomotives made loud squeaks which made Kitty's teeth grind together like eating lemons, and all their wagons squeaked, and the seagulls above them squeaked and squawked: it was impossible to tell which squeaks were which. The roads often became wide like football grounds, and were cobbled with a million cobbles. The locomotives never stopped to rest: neither did the rattling motor lorries filled with bales of cotton, or the traction engines blowing steam and smelling of steam and pulling giant tree trunks, or the horses, often as many as six harnessed in twos, dragging several carts of barrels and packing cases. Men rode bicycles and criss-crossed each other, and perpetually dinged their handlebar bells. Pigeons ate grain: there was grain everywhere, lacing the cobbles golden. She saw a Chinaman with a pigtail, and thought 'Chin-ching Chinaman, vellee vellee sad'. And she saw two brown-skinned men with towels around their heads, and though of Ali Baba and Lawrence of Arabia. And everything still squeaked.

Paddy took her up on the Canal swing bridge, and they looked down on the line of ships, just like it was in the tramcar advertising ovals. The canal water was black and stank like a gas leak, smashed-up orange boxes and patches of coloured oil drifted slowly under the bridge.

'Was a man-eating shark up here last week.'
'Give over.'
'Telling yer. Swam all the way up from the Coral Seas. And a killer whale week before.'
'Pull the other one. Wasn't born yesterday.'
'Bloody thump you if you don't believe me.'
'Thump me then.'
'You wouldn't talk like that if I was grown up and a priest.'
'You wouldn't talk wet if you was a priest. And you wouldn't thump.'
'I could. Priests are allowed to thump. Jesus said. But they rarely do.' He put the flattened palm of his hand to his eyes like on

look-out. 'Oh aye, there's all sorts come up here from the seven seas: submarines, octopuses, slave boats with dozens of slaves being whipped to row.'

'Quinquereme of Ninevah?'

'You get them too. Every second Sunday.'

Whistles were whistled, and voices shouted, and traffic stopped. Kitty and Paddy were waved by a man to get off the bridge.

'Make tracks!' yelled Paddy. 'Bridge is falling.'

They ran as fast as they could to the other side. But the bridge didn't fall: it swung sideways very slowly.

'In God's name then, let us cross the bridge, and fall on them!' shouted Kitty.

'You can't fall on man-eating sharks,' said Paddy.

'I was being Joan of Arc.'

'And she couldn't neither.'

A tubby boat, freshly painted, shiny varnished, and polishy brassed, chugged confidently down the canal. It had a green, white and gold down-striped flag blowing from its aft. Paddy stood to attention and saluted.

'That's the flag of your country! Salute it!' he shouted.

'What country?'

'The Irish Free State.'

Kitty didn't salute it because she wasn't sure of her country. Even though she'd been born in Ireland, she'd been French on stage, and it had worked well, and consequently she felt very happy and English at the moment.

'It's a Guinness's gunboat,' said Paddy. 'Comes right from the River Liffey in Dublin's fair city where they became free at the post office: and it fights sea monsters and pirates flying the deadly skull and crossbones to get here. And there'll be many more of 'em for it's getting near the season to be jolly, and all the inns in Bethlehem was sold out of Guinness when Jesus was born. It's going to dock in Pomona, and there'll be horses waiting.'

The vessel pooped 'Thank you' to the bridge and swirled on its merry way, and the bridge closed slowly again.

This time Paddy stood on the middle of the bridge and trickled his sauce bottle of holy water into the canal, at the same time reading from a piece of paper, 'Eternal rest grant unto them, O Lord, and let purple light shine upon them. May the angels lead thee into Paradise!' He screwed the paper up. 'There!' he said. 'Them ships is laughing now. They can sink in peace.'

'You've blessed man-eating sharks into't bargain.'

'Sharks was in the Garden of Eden with all the rest o' God's creatures,' said Paddy. 'And they was on Noah's Ark. God made sharks to know him and to love him.'

'And they seem to have spent more time out of water than in at the beginning,' teased Kitty.

'That was before God said, "Let there be light", and nobody could see where they were.'

Kitty put her arm around him. 'I'll say this, Paddy, you'll make a good priest – you've an answer for everything.'

There had been a freshness and excitement about visiting the Ship Canal even though the stink of it was still in her lungs: but the return trip on the tramcar sickened her more than any canal stinks. Opposite her and staring at her was the local dog poisoner. When people with diseased or injured dogs wanted them putting to sleep instead of drowning, they sent for him. For a shilling he poured caustic soda down the dog's throat, then immediately, fast as lightning, he coiled a long piece of cord around the dog's long nose and mouth. He also lashed the paws together tight. He told people, particularly children, that dogs didn't like being poisoned, and they would make the howl of the banshees for a couple of minutes unless restrained for their own good. People said he really was a nice man deep down, and very fond of dogs: it was because of his love for them that he couldn't bear to see the suffering. Kitty was repelled by the very sight of him. He did everything on the tram to make himself liked. He 'koochie-koo'd' a baby, and picked the baby's rattle up; he looked in an empty Players cigarette packet on the floor, and found a cigarette card of Don Bradman, which he gave to Paddy, and Paddy said, 'Thank you, master'; he clicked his tongue and said, 'Hello, Bonzo' to a dog on a woman's knee, and he said, 'What a lovely little doggy' to the woman, who smiled at him; he stood up to clang the roof bell for the driver to stop each time a passenger moved to get off. But all the time he had his muzzle cords around his neck like beads.

Two lads argued over swopping comics on the seat in front. One kid was offering two *Wizards* for one *Hotspur*, the reason being that the back page of one of the *Wizards* had been torn off by his mother to wipe the baby's bum, but the kid with the *Hotspur* was concerned that some of the story of Clickey-Ba, the Afghan who used a cricket bat as a weapon, might be missing.

The dog man reached over and offered the kid with the *Hotspur* a ha'penny if he'd make the swop, for he said it was a good thing for boys to read a lot. Girls didn't have to read, but boys did, he said. He winked at Kitty.

Kitty could stand it no longer. Without so much as a nod to Paddy, she ran downstairs and jumped off the moving tram. She fell on the cobbles and hurt her knee, but in doing so she found a blood glassie, and this she saw as a sign of God, maybe telling her to forgive the dog poisoner. St Joan heard voices from St Catherine and St Margaret: Kitty would have preferred to hear voices, instead she found ha'pennies and safety pins in the gutter, but they were signs from heaven nevertheless. The blood glassie was a very definite sign from heaven, for she collected bloodies. She was never any good at playing hit and dob with the glassies. She rarely made a hit, and her glass marble was invariably more than the finger and thumb span which counted as a dob: but she loved the coloured ribbons which spiralled and twisted inside the glass alley, in particular the rare ones with deep red stripes and streaks, the blood alleys. She bought these, very often with the ha'pennies which God had sent her way.

She soon realized that the blood in the glassie which she held tightly with possession signified real blood.

When the safety boundary of her Ancoats should have begun, and when the blind fiddler should have been heard playing, at the corner of Pin Mill Brow and Palmerston Street, there were crowds of people, and ten policemen, and an ambulance.

'What's up?' she asked an old woman.
'What's always up? Big street fight.'
'Aye?'
'Hundreds o' kids. Knives and razors.'
'Aye?'
'Some been hauled off in paddywagon like a cage o' monkeys.

Two on their way to Ancoats Hospital for sewing up. Yellin' and shoutin' were awful. And language – blue!'

'What over?'

'What's it always over? Religion! Catholics said Protestants had kidnapped a Catholic girl and were going to burn her at the stake for being St Joan. Protestants said Catholic girl was only acting, and she'd asked to be St Joan. Catholics said no Catholic girl would ever do that. And that's when first knife came out. Who is this St Joan anyway? She's not an Irish saint.'

Kitty felt that blood was oozing from her glassie, and she dropped it down a grid.

*

'Good King Wenceslas fell out
From his bedroom winder,
For he'd sat without a doubt
On a red hot cinder.'

The morning of Christmas breaking-up was free and funsome. There were no lessons, and teachers came in and out of classrooms with pieces of paper in their hands. The children sang their own carols:

'A poor man staggered through the snow
And fell into the mire mud.
To the workhouse he must go,
Chop his share of firewood.'

There was always speculation as to where the teachers disappeared. Some said they went to the school scullery where the gas stove was, and made coffee instead of tea, and told each other what they were getting for Christmas. Others knew for sure that they sneaked across to the priest's house for a glass of whisky and a Christmas blessing: one brave boy declared on God's honour he'd seen the priest give Mrs Giyaski a picture kiss under the mistletoe, and everybody put their hands to their chests and their tongues out and pretended to be sick.

The children themselves, who didn't believe in Father Christmas, boasted about the magnificent presents Father Christmas would bring them: they could always deny him if they didn't get their fantasy toys, which of course they wouldn't in any case. The boys bragged of brand-new racing bicycles, roller skates, and wooden forts with lead soldiers; the girls talked of dolls' houses which lit up, and dolls' prams with chromium handles, and real dolls' bedding. None of this they would get, but when they went back to school in the New Year Christmas would be forgotten, so it didn't matter how they made-believe on breaking-up day. They were allowed to bring books and toys that morning, and Kitty took Wendy, for Wendy had never seen the school or Mrs Giyaski even though she'd heard such a lot about them.

They would all go into the church later in the morning and file past the crib, which wasn't a very good crib because the lamb was a child's push-lamb and still had its handle and wheels on. And St Joseph had a very broken nose which was all dirty white plaster. One of the boys had said he'd got the broken nose fighting with the angel who'd told him his wife was going to have a baby: the boy said something like that had happened in his street, only the angel had been the lodger, and he'd had his jaw broken. The priest had tried to repair the nose with Plasticine but in the heat from the candles it had softened and elongated, and somebody had said Joseph looked more like Pinocchio. This year, Joseph's nose had been left scarred and unrepaired.

The caretaker in his blue overalls, and carrying his ladders, limped into the classroom. Kitty had long since observed that all caretakers had been crippled in the Great War, and she'd made some comment upon it to her dad.

'Ah well, that's war now,' he'd explained. 'Corpses and caretakers, and I dare say we made a few German caretakers as well: sure what else can a cripple do but take care?'

The children whistled 'Aukiduck' behind his back. One of the girls whispered that he'd got a stone in his boot and was too lazy to take his boot off and get it out. Most of the girls hated the man: he told tales about them to the teachers, like smoking in the lavatories, or drawing boys' things with chalk. At the moment they hated him more than ever, for he had limped in to destroy Christmas.

For two weeks, paper decorations had stretched in all their many concertina colours across the classroom, and the lights had been shaded amber, and history lessons had been about castles, and the children had sung 'See Amid The Winter Snow'. Now the caretaker clumped up his stepladders slowly, lifting his gammy leg from step to step, and he took each paper streamer down, folded it carefully, and placed it on Mrs Giyaski's desk. He folded and positioned the decorations as sanctimoniously as the priest places the chalice and prepared the blessed sacrament. The children knew why. He had barely been whistled out of the classroom to 'Aukiduck, Aukiduck, broke his leg and he can't get up', when Mrs Giyaski came in with the class examination results. The winners would be awarded one of the decorations to take home, and Kitty had been set on winning one: they would cut in two and go from corner to corner of the parlour. She had worked hard for the exams; maybe a beautifully decorated parlour would being her dad back to his love for her again. What's more, she'd saved her patchwork quilt money in a Christmas club at Hugh Fay's the grocer, and it would supply some of the things she'd only ever seen in Lewis's window – a turkey, a real turkey, Christmas puddings, a box of dates, mixed nuts in their shells, a Christmas cake with a little robin on, a box of Christmas crackers with a novelty and a paper hat in each, a small bottle of whisky, a larger bottle of Green Goddess cocktail, and a dozen mince pies. Mrs Fearnley would not be able to compete and a school decoration would put the top hat on it all.

She was read out as top of the class, but Mrs Giyaski awarded her no decoration, although the second, third and fourth girls were given decorations. Tears welled up in Kitty's eyes.

The bell rang for playtime, and after play it would be the church and end of school. Mrs Giyaski called her back as she shuffled out in disgrace.

'Congratulations on coming top,' said the teacher.

'Thank you, miss,' sniffed Kitty, and continued on her way out.

'Just a minute.'

'Yes, miss.'

'This play-acting of Joan of Arc has caused a great deal of violence. There have been street fights among the children, and I hear some of the men have joined in. There has been injury and bloodshed – and all because of your personal pride and ambition.'

'Yes, miss, but I'm going to pack it in. I didn't know it would cause hatred and fighting. Half Ancoats hates the other half 'cos of me.'

'So you see I could hardly have given you a decoration in front of the class.'

'Yes, miss. I'm sorry for coming top, miss. I won't do it again. I have sinned exceedingly in thought, word, and deed, through my most grievous fault.'

'Don't be silly!'

'Sorry, miss.'

'It's a bit late for packing it in, isn't it? I don't agree with you acting the part of a saint and reciting the words and thoughts of an atheist and a Socialist, but you're committed now, aren't you? If you packed in now, do you think they'd be able to put the play on?'

'No, miss.'

'You'd let the entire Children's Theatre down, and it doesn't matter if they're Catholics or Protestants, I wouldn't want one of my girls to do that.'

'No, miss.'

'So you'd better be good when you step on that stage.'

'That's what Sister St Pius said.'

'Yes, I know she did: she told me. I want your acting to be so good that people will ask your name, and then what school you go to.'

'I'll do my best, miss.'

'Think on you do.' Mrs Giyaski gave a slight smile, which was unusual because she never smiled; it was said her face would crack if she tried. 'Or I'll make your life a misery when school begins again. Oh, and . . .' she lifted up her desk lid. 'Do you like holy pictures?'

'Yes, miss, I love them.' This was a downright lie: she'd never had a holy picture in her life. Mrs Giyaski gave her two. The first was of a very colourful and elaborate Madonna and Child. The Madonna looked delicate, consumptive and Italian, but very lovely: the colours were mainly blue and yellow, and the yellow glistened like gold. 'That's all the way from Rome,' said the teacher. The other was of an ornamental baby, wearing clothes and a heavy crown which only a doll could wear without complaining, but it was obviously the Infant Jesus. 'And that's the Infant of Prague, all the way from Prague in Bohemia.' Kitty guessed that Arline, the Bohemian Girl, would have had such a card in her caravan and probably made the sign of the cross to it: it was a treasure. Kitty clutched both cards to her chest; she wanted to clutch Mrs Giyaski and cuddle up to her. 'However, perhaps you may value this the more. This is not from Rome or Prague, but from Marks and Spencer.' She handed Kitty a paper bag with a Christmas decoration inside.

'Oh, thank you, thank you, thank you! I'll always work hard for you, miss, and try never to make you cross.'

'There's one more thing. In a church called the Holy Name in Oxford Road there's a statue to Joan of Arc. You may care to call in there and light a candle to her and ask her permission to let you act her on the stage. And you might care to light another candle and ask St Joan to pray for the black heathen soul of Mr George Bernard Shaw.'

'I'll do that, miss, oh I will, I will!'

Mrs Giyaski returned to her former self, and frowned. It was like the early morning shadow of the great gasometer darkening the playground. 'You understand why I couldn't reward you in front of the class. It would have been condoning all the trouble you've caused. Parents would have come up.'

'But there's still the violence.'

'There'll always be the violence over something in Ancoats. St Joan was just one more excuse, but better a few black eyes over a saint than over money or the breaking of one of God's commandments.'

Mrs Giyaski had neither approved nor disapproved, but in a way had challenged her to merit approval. She took Wendy into church with her in a dancing mood.

Even though the school Christmas was over and done with, Kitty was happy. She lived by signs, and the Bohemian holy card was a sign if ever there was one.

Mick Dowd ran after her and thumped her in the gob as she walked down the street.

'What's that you've got, tart?'

'Nowt,' she said.

'Bloody nowt?' he said. 'Nowt in a paper bag? Let's have a look at this nowt.' He snatched the holy pictures and the paper bag from her.

'Best thing with these pictures is drop 'em down't grid,' he said, and he let the pictures flutter one by one down the gutter grid. She rushed to him. He thumped her in the chest, and it hurt. 'And bloody decorations,' he went on. 'I might get the gang round for a Christmas treat and let 'em watch me shoving the decoration up yer arse like I did wi't pipe. They can sing carols.' He suddenly grabbed Wendy. 'Now this bloody doll. Tell you what I'll paint her black with road pitch and lock her in the gas cupboard with a golliwog. Golliwog'll have time of his life with her.'

'You're bloody evil!' shouted Kitty.

Constable Kennedy, unseen by them, had been striding slowly and confidently down the street. He grabbed hold of Mick's jacket collar.

'Well, ye little sod! What's it ye've been up to this fine morning?'

'Nowt.'

'Ah, there's many a man serving ten years in Strangeways for doing nowt.'

'I was just admiring her doll, and about to give it her back. It's a very lovely doll.'

'D'y'think so now?'

'Oh aye, a very beautiful doll.' He returned it to Kitty.

'And what's that ye have in yer hand?'

'Coloured paper, master.' Mick pulled the decoration out and tore it into shreds. 'Now ye can't arrest me for tearing paper up, can you now? Imagine trying to arrest Machinegun Kelly or Al Capone for tearing paper up, eh?'

Constable Kennedy grabbed hold of Mick by all the clothes in the small of his back, and began carrying him as if he was a carpet bag.

After but a few yards, a chimney sweep pulled up on his bike and asked the policeman the way to some place or another. The constable placed Mick face downward on the flags and put his boot on him, to hold him down while be brought his address book out and looked up the street required. Then he picked Mick up again and strode on his way.

Kitty ran to the grid and looked down. Half of the Infant of Prague was blackened and sinking into the filthy slime: the face looked up at her. She was about to run home, and then she saw all the tiny pieces of decoration blowing in the wind. Mrs Giyaski would see them and think she'd torn the decorations up out of spite. It took her a long time to collect each small piece. As she put the handful down the grid, she made the sign of the cross to the little face looking up.

'Please, God, make it rain,' she whispered. But it didn't rain.

It took Kitty five trips to Hugh Fay's the grocer on Christmas Eve morning to fetch the items paid for from her Christmas club: the turkey was heavy enough to merit one trip on its own. She had enough money left over to buy decorations, but nowhere near enough to run to a tree. Each item was placed on the parlour table until the table looked like a market stall. She pinned up the streamers, including a green paper bell and she waited excited for her dad to come home. He'd given her good warning that he'd be stopping for a drink after work because the dustmen would be sharing out their 'compliments of the season' tips. What a wonderful surprise he'd get.

True to his word, he was home before afternoon chucking-out time; and there was such struggling and blowing and puffing and panting to get through the front door because he was lugging a turkey in one hand, and fighting with a Christmas tree with the other. He put a great half-moon smile on his face as he banged his turkey next to Kitty's.

'Now if them birds was alive we'd be able to start up a turkey farm,' said he.

'Oh dad, why did you? I've been saving me quilt money to surprise you.'

'And ye have at that, me darling, for wouldn't any hard-working man be surprised and calling snap to be seeing double.' He looked up at the decorations. 'Is it a mistake I've made for have I not stepped into the middle o' fairyland instead o' just Angel Meadow? Ah, the festooning and festivity of it all!'

Mrs Fearnley stepped in, and held her hands up when she saw the table.

'I'm going bloody daft,' she said. 'Put me on the next tram to Prestwich.'

'And isn't them me very sentiments too?'

'I'll never get two in me oven.'

'That's all right, Mrs Fearnley, 'cos I'll be doing me and me dad's in our oven.'

'We could have one for the New Year,' said her dad with a splendid compromise which caused him to twirl his moustache. 'Y'see, me darling, we decided to share our Christmas: Mrs Fearnley being on her own and that, d'y'see.'

'And I'd do the turkey and all the things that go with it,' added Mrs Fearnley.

'But I've always cooked for me dad since me mam died.'

'Ah, indeed ye have, me love, and 'tis a splendid cook ye are.'

'But have you ever done a Christmas dinner?' went on Mrs Fearnley. 'And I've done a pudding which is so big it'll have to be boiled in the copper boiler, and it's got brandy in it.'

'D'y'hear that now?' said Kitty's dad, giving her a nudge. 'Brandy, eh?' He licked his lips.

'And I've done a coupla dozen mince pies, and they got rum in 'em.'

'Ah, d'y'hear that, mavourneen? Rum in 'em.' And he licked his lips again.

Kitty was defeated. Throughout her long finger-sore sessions of quilt-making she'd thought of the mince pies and Christmas pudding she'd buy with the club money.

'And what's in yer cake?' she asked Mrs Fearnley with a sarcastic sneer. 'Methylated spirits?'

'Sherry,' said Mrs Fearnley.

'I mighta guessed.'

'Mind you,' said her dad, with another brisk twirl of his moustache, 'any woman can cook a turkey and bake a cake, but we've had to leave the real touch o' Christmas to you, me love, for who the hell's going to decorate that magnificent tree in the manner it deserves to be decorated?'

'Aye, and who's going to dress the cake? I haven't a clue,' said Mrs Fearnley. 'Dead artistic stuff is that, more for someone with stage experience, like you.'

The flattery hit Kitty like a thump in the stomach: her spirit doubled up and yielded.

'Tell you what,' went on Mrs Fearnley. 'I'll give you ten bob what I've saved from me quilt money to buy snowmen and red robins and a frill for the cake, and some o' them coloured glass balls for the tree. Whatever you fancy, eh?'

Kitty was pleased that Mrs Fearnley had also sewn her patchwork quilts towards Christmas.

'And bless me if I won't chuck in five bob for them little candles for the tree and the cake,' said her dad.

She was rushed off her feet for the rest of the afternoon. Every snowman and robin on yule log in Woolworth's was closely examined. Kitty liked to think that the snowman and the robin had both chosen her. She held the green and red stretches of tinsel to the light in order to judge the colour. A long time was spent deciding to buy the red candles instead of the pink ones, but feeling sorry for the colour of pink after rejecting it, she bought a pink cake frill. She didn't like blues and greens, not for Christmas, but she didn't want to spoil Christmas for the blues and greens, so she bought little things with those colours in. The little Father Christmasses for the cakes were all sold out, but somebody had dropped one on the floor and though it was a bit trodden on, she picked it up and put it in her pocket and thanked God for another sign. She examined every glass ball and bauble, pretending to herself that inside each was a ballroom and dancing, with men in old-fashioned clothes, gorgeous silk jackets, knickerbockers with white silk stockings up to the knees, and hair tied at the back in ribbons, who with vows no maiden heart could withstand, pledged their faith to her. If she did not get this feeling as she held a ball, it was returned to the counter tray and another was tried out: the purples seemed to be the most charged with such magic.

And then she spent hours back home arranging them as the decorations themselves would like to be arranged. The candles had to be clipped to the ends of branches with great care, making sure that when lit they would not set fire to the branch above, for the fire engines were out quite a lot on Christmas Day, and sometimes houses were burned down, and often people were rushed to hospital, and once or twice somebody had died because of the Christmas Tree.

In the evening, Mrs Fearnley, deep with lipstick, and smelly with scent, and hair home-permed, brought in slices of cold ham and a jar of pickles and three hot mince pies and a bowl of trifle. They opened the Green Goddess cocktail, and Kitty couldn't be denied a drink because her money had bought it. It was lovely and naughty and seemed to be Christmas, and for a split second it took her right into a Lewis's window. After tea, her dad and Mrs Fearnley had to go out for an hour to the Spread Eagle in order to bring back the beer.

She was glad to be alone. She knew the hour would turn into three hours: she could have a pretend Christmas. She stole another glass of her patchwork Green Goddess, and brought Wendy down and moistened the doll's lips.

There came the sound of carousing from somewhere up the street, and she couldn't resist taking Wendy to see what was going on. Round the corner in Palmerston Street, Bernard and Vincent and Dermot had blackened their faces with soot, and reddened their noses, like they did when they went molly-dancing. They had a card which said 'The Three Kings'. Bernard juggled two tennis balls: it should have been three to be professional, but he couldn't do three. Vincent walked on his hands, and Dermot played 'If I Had a Talking Picture of You' on a mouth organ: it didn't sound very good, but that was the fault of the mouth organ which had a lot of broken notes and just went 'fuff' on occasions.

At the end of their acrobatics, the three sang, 'Silent night, holy night, round yon Virgin mother and child, holy infant so tender and mild.'

They had a captive audience because just a few doors away there was an ambulance, and a large crowd had gathered to gawp. From what Kitty could gather from two women talking, Brenda Grimshaw, who was only fourteen, had been badly beaten by her father who'd found out she was having a baby. He'd taken his belt off to her and laid into her with the brass buckle. The women said the screams were awful. More and more people rushed to the scene, but they obviously didn't want to be seen staring at the ambulance, not at Christmas, so they half watched the three kings.

Brenda was brought out moaning and groaning under a red blanket on a stretcher, and some people said, 'Oooooh!' The three kings switched tactfully from the Virgin carol to marching soldiers, and sang, 'It's a long way to tickle Mary, it's a long way to the po' a song they'd learnt from their dads.

Mr Grimshaw was dragged out, handcuffed to two policemen. 'I'll fucking kill him! I'll fucking kill the pair of 'em!' he yelled.

'Watch yer language at Christmas!' said one of the bobbies, and he belted Mr Grimshaw on the back of his head with his truncheon: he must have belted him very hard for the dull thud seemed to echo, and thereafter Mr Grimshaw remained silent with his head dangling on one side.

'And don't ever bloody come back, ye rotten galoot!' yelled Mrs Grimshaw from the doorway.

'Regular Punch and Judy show,' said one of the women.

'Happen kid'll lose her baby, and just as well,' said the other woman. 'Meself I prefer the jug o' gin method.' They both laughed.

The lads reached their last act, for the show was over anyway. 'We three kings from the Orien – Ta!' they sang, with loud emphasis on the 'Ta' by way of 'thank you' for they got a lot of coppers thrown at them.

Kitty rushed Wendy home because it wasn't the sort of thing she wanted Wendy to know about. She apologized to the doll for Christmas, which often got very dirty.

She longed to light the tree candles and switch the gas out, but she daren't without her dad. However, she had another Green Goddess and switched the wireless on. It was going all over the world, from a lighthouse keeper at Bishop Rock to an apple grower in Canada and a sheep farmer in Australia, and each one said, 'Merry Christmas' and a carol was played. She saw a man's head pass the window, but he'd only come down Angel Meadow to pee against the river wall; a lot of men, and sometimes women, did that.

Her dad and Mrs Fearnley and two other men and two other woman sang their way in through the front door. Their pockets and shopping-bags clanked with bottles of beer. They'd come to play cards, and Kitty knew it was the beginning of the Christmas Eve ritual. They would play cards, break wind and laugh about it, and tell dirty jokes until the morning: often during the night there would be vicious swearing arguments over cheating and pennies. But first there was the lighting of the tree and the giving of the presents.

The tree looked lovely, as though it had become magical and holy and gone into a pleasant tree sleep, dreaming it lived for ever in an enchanted forest where trees loved each other and were always Saturday-night happy. Kitty gave her dad a pair of woollen socks, and he gave her a pair of cotton socks and a handkerchief with a rose in the corner: it was traditional. But he gave Mrs Fearnley a pair of red and black silk garters, and everybody said, 'Hello, hello!' and Mrs Fearnley, with a sideways smile, said, 'I might need some help to put these on later.'

The cards were brought out, and the glasses for the beer, and a large bowl of nuts and nutcrackers, and saucers for ashtrays; and there began a discussion as to whether the game should be Newmarket or Rummy.

'Come and behold Him,
Born the King of Angels,
Oh come ye! Oh come ye!
To Bethlehem.'

There were real carol singers in the street, not kids.

'Must be the Protestants,' said one of the men. 'Catholics stay in church for Midnight Mass and keep warm. Only Protestants and brass monkeys'd risk getting their balls frozen off in the street.'

'St Andrew's,' said Mrs Fearnley.

Kitty always liked the sound of St Andrew: he seemed a merry saint, perhaps it was because of Andrew's Liver Salts which gave people that springing feeling, and gave them the strength to jump over five-barred gates.

The group decided to go out in the street and see the carol singers.

'Sing choir of angels.
Sing in exultation.'

The stars were shining over the rooftops, and the frosted rooftops were silver with the moon.

'Have any of you ever been to the Holy Land?' asked Fred, one of her dad's friends, and probably a muckman.

'No, sir!' said the jolly clergyman. 'But we all wish we had – mmm!'

'You do buggery!' said Fred. 'Last bloody place on earth! I was out there with Allenby, and I've seen Lawrence of Arabia, so I know what I'm talking about. I tell you, them bloody Turks used dum-dum bullets. D'y'know what dum-dums is?'

'No, sir!'

'What? And doing all that bloody singing about Jerusalem and Palestine and that! Well, dum-dums is when they split the point of a bullet so it spreads your guts: splatters yer bloody innards, it does. Makes grown-up fellers scream like tarts while they're snuffing it!'

Terry, the other man, and no doubt a muckman as well, had gone to the river wall, was leaning on it with one elbow, and was spewing up.

'But worser than bloody dum-dums in the Holy Land is the knocking shops: you can get yer end away for a penny and a puff on a fag. "Keep away from them bellydancing whores," said Allenby, "'cos they'll devastate the British Army far faster than Johnny Turk." Bloody crawling with it, they was: all kinds of clap from syph to gon, and crabs that could jump three feet – '

'Merry Christmas to you all, and God bless you!' said the clergyman.

'Here, have some mince pies,' said Mrs Fearnley, and Kitty noticed that she gave one of the singers a box of Hugh Fay's bought mince pies. The singers beat a hasty retreat out of Angel

Meadow. Kitty watched their lanterns bobbing up and down fast, and she was embarrassed to blushing.

'What did ye go and talk dirty like that for?' asked her dad.

'They shouldn't sing about places they've never been to,' said Fred.

'Don't tell me you've been to Laguna?' said Mrs Fearnley.

'Hey, Terry, have ye done spewing yer guts up?' shouted one of the women. 'It were them meat pies,' she explained to everybody in a quiet solicitous voice. 'I bloody tell him, don't touch meat pies in pubs, but soon as he's had a coupla pints – "Have ye any meat pies?" he asked the barman. Wouldn't be bellydancers he'd want in the Holy Land, be meat pies: then he'd be sick as a dog.'

'Long as it wasn't my trifle,' said Mrs Fearnley.

'Come on, we're losing money standing out here. Let's get the cards dealt!'

The cards began, and nobody noticed Kitty take Wendy to bed. She looked through the window at the stars. She was sure that somewhere people were enjoying Christmas. The people on the wireless would be enjoying Christmas. She bet herself that the Canadian apple grower, the Australian sheep farmer, and the man in the lighthouse at Bishop Rock were at this moment holding a hot mince pie in one hand, a glass of steaming punch in the other, and had just finished reading the tearful ending of Charles Dickens' *Christmas Carol*. Christmas in Ancoats was rotten: it began nice, but went stinking rotten.

She awoke in a grey and quiet house. There was a smell of stale beer. Her dad wasn't in his room: she guessed where he was, and she could imagine the red and black silk garters. The house was hers, but it was a house of devastation. Empty bottles lay on their sides, there was at least one scattering of broken glass on the floor, nut shells were everywhere, the saucers were mountains of cigarette ends, more cigarette ends were strewn over the floor, and there was sick in the backyard.

Christmas dinner was to be next door, and her dad's excuse for being there would be that he'd helped with the turkey. She could get stuck into cleaning the place up, and get the house looking like a shop window.

In the distance she could hear the trombones and trumpets of the Salvation Army playing 'The First Noel'. They wouldn't venture into Angel Meadow. There was a knock on the door. Perhaps they had: perhaps a man had come collecting. She reached for a penny.

It was Ratbag. She felt faint with surprise.

'Merry Christmas!' he said.

'Aye, oh aye! I mean Merry Christmas! Aye!'

He handed her a parcel done up in Christmas paper.

'This is from Miss Hindshaw. She said I'd got to find you and give it you before Christmas Eve, and I said I would, but I didn't 'cos I didn't know yer address till last night.'

'Last night?'

'I was with St Andrew's, carol-singing. That feller yer uncle?'

'What feller?'

'Him what was telling us about dum-dums and that?'

'Never seen him before. He was a poor man came in sight gathering winter fuel, so we asked him in for a game o' cards: well, you do on Christmas Eve.'

'He was very interesting.'

'Don't be daft. Hey, come in for a Green Goddess, if there's any left, and a cigarette, if I can find one.'

'Best not. What about your parents, me being a Proddy?'

'You don't look Proddy. You could easily be taken for a Catholic. Sides, I've no mam, only a dad, and he's gone a-courting.'

There was still a drop of Green Goddess left in the bottle, and she found a half-cigarette on the floor, and she lit the tree candles. 'Here, have a funny hat,' she said, and she slapped a pink paper hat on his head, and a green one on her own. Then she became serious. 'I'm sorry about this part of Ancoats,' she said. 'It's dead rough.'

'This part, what? You want to see my part. We had a murder down Cockie Win's entry last night.'

'Cockie Win's? S'where we go sliding when there's ice.'

'Could be another Switzerland but for all them midden tins.'

'Murder?'

'Aye – a woman. I bet you didn't have a murder.'

'We had a nearly.'

'Nearly's don't count. Best be off.'

He left, with his funny hat still on. Kitty couldn't wait to open her present. She bit the string with her teeth, and ripped the paper off. It had a nice card with Miss Hindshaw's best wishes for Christmas. It was a book called *Drury Lane* and she didn't fancy the title until she found it was about a place called the Theatre Royal and underneath the picture it said 'The Greatest Theatre in the World'.

Flicking through it, she saw that the book was about kings and lords and dukes, and it was about posh names, Byron, Browning, Charles Dickens, Douglas Fairbanks, Oliver Goldsmith, and Nell Gwynne, oh yes, Nell Gwynne; and there were names she felt she'd seen in library books, John Dryden, Alexander Pope, Richard Sheridan, and lots of Irish names; and Shakespeare's name was sprinkled like salt from an enamel salt pot over chips. And there was a list of over four hundred plays: *Hamlet, Babes in the Wood, Aladdin, The Beggar's Opera, The Bohemian Girl*, oh *The Bohemian Girl, Caesar and Cleopatra, Rose Marie, The Desert Song, Showboat, Alexander the Great, The Fairy Lake, The Relief of Lucknow, St Patrick's Day, The Garden of Allah, Humpty Dumpty, Uncle Tom's Cabin, Cinderella, The Tempest, Queen Mab, Thief of Baghdad*, and on and on: and each time she glanced she saw new names and new plays. It was like Belle Vue fireworks sparkling before her eyes.

This was a wonderful Christmas! She was hungry for Mrs Fearnley's Christmas dinner.

Opening night was Monday, and Kitty was frightened and restless on the Sunday before. She didn't want to go on the stage, she wished she could be taken ill, she could remember neither her own lines nor the cues: perhaps this was the time to hide away in the guards' van of a train and end up wherever the train went. She remembered the only gift of Mrs Giyaski's which Mick Dowd had been unable to destroy, the Manchester home of St Joan, the Church of the Holy Name, but where that was she didn't know from Adam.

''Course I know where it is, but I haven't been in,' said Dermot MacMahon.

'Will you take me?'

'Aye, but I'm not stepping foot, and it'll cost you twopence.'

'Soon as you get a Rolls Royce, you'll be a taxi driver, won't you?'

'Wouldn't mind,' said Dermot. 'Got to warn you though, it'll be dangerous.'

'Nowt attempted . . .' She knew his dangers would be imaginary. They set off after dinner.

Leaving Ancoats from Pin Mill Brow, he led her down secret backstreets to the Duck Park. 'It used to be a duck park, but the pond's been cemented over, and the only ducks left is cement ducks, and 'tis said they can give you a right bloody smack on the back o' the head when you're not looking,' said Dermot, and Kitty didn't know whether he was kidding or not, but it didn't matter much, she needed somebody to talk to her.

'Now we're going down Shakespeare Street, Chorlton-on-Medlock,' he went on. 'Called after that feller what wrote them plays 'cos he was born here secretly.'

'Even his parents didn't know,' chipped in Kitty.

'Don't talk bloody wet,' said Dermot, and then Kitty knew he was being serious.

They turned right at the end of Shakespeare Street, and Dermot pointed out the first danger: it was a church.

''Tis an harmonium church,' said he. 'And them what goes there is called dancing dervishes, which anybody knows what's read the *Hotspur*, out every Friday, price twopence, and this week they're giving a free gift of a Sexton Blake detective kit. Dervishes wave curved knives and cut people's heads off.'

'Worse than being a back-entry bookie, is that. I'm surprised the police allow it,' laughed Kitty.

The worst was to come. From what was the Armenian Church, Kitty could see a very large church wearing a fat tower like a top hat at the end of a street.

'That's Ackers Street, and you gotta go down it to get there,' said Dermot, 'So stick tight to me.'

'Why?'

''Cos every house puts up theatricals from the Hippodrome, and the Palace, and the Opera House and all them other theatres, and you can sometimes see educated lions and performing seals in the front rooms.'

'By heck, you're as bad as Paddy Byrne with his crocodiles in the Manchester Ship Canal. It's all them comics you read.'

'Suit yourself, but don't come skrike-ing to me if a tiger follows you doing back-flips.'

Kitty was excited: not, of course, at the prospect of meeting circus animals, but it seemed appropriate for her to be going to meet St Joan for the first time by walking down the special street where stage people stayed. It had all been arranged, she was certain of that.

She said 'Ta' to Dermot outside the church.

'I might be a long time. Don't wait.'

'But them dangers?'

'You've pointed 'em out to me, and I'll avoid 'em skilfully, just you see.'

The church was immense, and comfortably heavenly dark and secure. There were many statues against the walls, and all of them were lighted by rows of candles; they looked like tramcars in the fog. Coughs came from many directions, so, although the four Masses of morning had long since ended, there were plenty of people scattered around the church and incense still wafted lost here and there.

She walked around the aisles. And then, half-way up, and on the right-hand side facing the altar, she met her saint. Joan was clad in chain mail, she had a large sword by her side, she could only have been a few inches taller than Kitty. And Kitty suddenly felt shy. She half expected Joan would ask her to sit down, or better still, kneel down. She lit a candle and knelt down, and stared hypnotically into the saint's face.

She told her she was sorry about her being burned at the stake, hoped it hadn't been too painful, and prayed that she had forgotten all about it: in fact she apologized for reminding her. She also apologized for speaking English. The only French she knew was 'san fairy ann' which her dad had taught her, but she guessed there would be enough English spoken in heaven, and no doubt Joan would have picked it up over the past five hundred years. Kitty imagined her dad whispering in her ear that no Englishman would have gone to heaven in all those years, and she wanted to giggle: she felt sure that Joan would enjoy the joke, but she closed her eyes in case the statue's lips moved into a smile, because that might have frightened her. Perhaps nobody had ever joked with Joan, except Mr George Bernard Shaw: he had her saying funny things at times, particularly in the epilogue, which of course brought her on to the subject of acting. She hoped Joan wouldn't mind her acting her part, and she hoped some of Joan's neighbour saints wouldn't laugh at Joan for getting herself acted. She didn't believe Mr George Bernard Shaw was an atheist because no true atheist would go to the trouble of bringing a saint alive on the stage. She promised Joan she would do her very best. And on and on went Kitty.

She told Joan everything: she told her about the clay pipes, the dancing in front of the Land O' Cakes, the Monday washdays, the stealing of Wendy, but the loving of Wendy, the patchwork quilts, the dirty thing on Barney's Field, the execution in the glass case of Belle Vue and behind the stone walls of Strangeways Prison, the bubbling shop of the accumulator man, Mrs Fearnley's garters, the little girls who were dirtied by men, Mrs Giyaski's strap, but Mrs Giyaski's smile, Miss Hindshaw's Water-Baby loveliness, the wonderful manor house of Ancoats Hall where she hoped Joan would join her on Monday night. She asked Joan to pass on her best wishes to Sister St Pius, which would give the nun a pleasant surprise when the saint asked her to guess who she'd been listening to. She whispered away as the stained glass windows grew darker, and the candles burned brighter. Eventually from the high tower the Angelus bells played the Lourdes hymn, and Kitty had to excuse herself because it would be dark outside and she wasn't too sure of the way home.

The way home in fact was dead easy, for just to the right, waiting like Cinderella's coach, was the Ancoats tram, and the guard was the ginger-haired man.

'Here's my little girl with the lovely curl,' he said, helping her up the step. 'Where have you been, little girl, said he. I've been to the universee-tee. And why did you go to Owen's College? I went for to get a lot of knowledge.' He bowed. 'How's that for poetry?' He then got down on one knee and with his hands to his heart did

Al Jolson: '*Climb upon my knee, sonny boy*'. Then he switched to a knee-stepping strut up the tram aisle, shaking his tram guard's cap at the back of his head for '*My ma-mee*'.

'I tell you, I'm too good for the number fifty-two tram,' he finished.

'Aye, you should be on the number one,' said Kitty, and she was delighted she had the confidence to answer him back.

Four hundred kids clapped and cheered till the rafters rang. And four hundred kids had made the same noisy applause for the past ten nights. Four thousand kids, Catholics and Protestants, had cheered their heads off. For Kitty was good.

The Ancoats schools were issued with free tickets, but after the first couple of nights the tickets were up for barter. Comics, cigarette card sets of English kings and queens, skipping ropes with painted handles, jars of glass alleys with many bloodies, Great War bullets and army cap badges, accurate catapults, holy medals and holy pictures, broken lead soldiers for a fort, broken lead animals for a farm, and one set of brass knuckledusters became coinage for a ticket.

No grown-ups were allowed, no parents, no teachers, no priests: the only adults were Miss Hindshaw, the one-legged attendant, and Mr Davies. Actors and audience and those who worked behind the scenes were children from ten to twelve. They spoke their lines, switched their switches, clapped their hands without encouragement from anybody. Kitty was very good, and they all responded to her.

And the boys were good. To Kitty they were no longer snotty-nosed Proddies, but English and French noblemen who feared and hated Joan, and connived to degrade her, to lower and humiliate her: they were sharp in their sarcasm, cunning in their hatred. She answered them as best she could. She was led out to a red lamp in a square biscuit tin, but it was the glow and flicker of the execution fire. Ah, but there was the epilogue in which the big shots cringed and back-pedalled, and many of the kids in the audience laughed to see the funny side of it.

She said her lines plainly and simply: she answered lords and lord chamberlains, chaplains and captains, bishops and archbishops, and even the King of France with the honesty and dignity of a young country girl, like the daughter of the woman in the Ovaltine advertisement. She was brave and afraid, she strode into the light, she wanted to skulk in the shadows, she played every word like a note of music, painted every emotion like a colour, moved every move like a ballet dancer.

She half closed her eyes when her make-up was being put on, and could see the outstretched arm of Apollo above her, and she felt it was right that the statue of a god should put on the make-up of a girl who was going to bring the statue of a saint to life.

She'd peeped through a tiny hole in the curtain and watched the audience shuffling in each night. Different schools and different churches, they seemed predictably the same. They were the children of rickets, consumption, meningitis, smallpox, malnutrition: the hobbling little girl with irons on her leg, the slithering boy with the club foot, the little girl with one leg hopping on a crutch, the boy with a permanent patch on his eye, the boy with the twisted wrist, the girl who looked up all the time, the boy whose face twitched all the time, the girl with half her face purple, the girl with no teeth, the girl with no hair, the boy who coughed, the girl who coughed, the boy with no arm, and more leg irons, and more patches. They wanted the hall lights off, and the stage lights on.

On the last night, when all the lights went on, she heard Mick Dowd's voice – 'That's my bloody tart, that is!' And behind her Ratbag whispered, 'That's what he bloody thinks!'

My goodness, she, Kitty Noonan, stood in marble halls, the hope and the pride of all those assembled, and knights were pledging their faith to her.

The presentation of *Saint Joan* by a young schoolmaster with young children in the worst slum of Europe had made history. A lot of newspaper photographers flashed their cameras, and a group of journalists hemmed Kitty in.

'What's your name?' asked one.
'What school do you go to?'
'What is your ambition?'